By D. E. Paulson

Sugar, Spice, and Spellcraft

Published by Dreamspinner Press
www.dreamspinnerpress.com

SUGAR SPICE AND SPELLCRAFT

D.E. PAULSON

Published by
DREAMSPINNER PRESS

5032 Capital Circle SW, Suite 2, PMB# 279, Tallahassee, FL 32305-7886 USA
www.dreamspinnerpress.com

Sugar, Spice, and Spellcraft
© 2023 D. E. Paulson

Cover Art
© 2023 Kris Norris
http://www.krisnorris.com
coverrequest@krisnorris.com
Cover content is for illustrative purposes only and any person depicted on the cover is a model.

Trade Paperback ISBN: 978-1-64108-511-3
Digital ISBN: 978-1-64108-510-6
Trade Paperback published January 2023
v. 1.0

Printed in the United States of America
∞
This paper meets the requirements of
ANSI/NISO Z39.48-1992 (Permanence of Paper).

To Bug, my constant companion in the writing of this work. You are missed.

ACKNOWLEDGMENTS

IT IS rightly quoted that nobody writes alone. *Sugar, Spice, a`nd Spellcraft* received a lot of help from many different hands throughout its drafts to become the book you are about to read. While not a complete list, the following are some of the many people who helped my story along its way, and I owe them all (and you my readers) more than is easily put into words—Kit Haggard and Jules Hucke, who helped edit this book, gave me feedback I needed to hear, and made sure I told a story worth reading; Tyson J, who was an early beta reader and helped shape some key elements of my story; Audrey B, who sat with me through many rounds of cider as I worked on my solo edits; the staff of Waldschänke ciders, who wanted to know just what sort of romance I was writing; Annie S and Laura S, who encouraged me to submit the story to publishers over delicious Afghani food in Cambridge; everyone at Dreamspinner who helped *Sugar, Spice, and Spellcraft* reach publication; and lastly, Leo, for putting up with hearing Saint-Saëns' *Danse Macabre* and Rachmaninoff's *Isle of the Dead* at all hours of the morning while I worked. Thank you all for helping this book become what it is.

CHAPTER 1

"YOU'RE GOING out? What's the occasion? Purim's in March, right?" Rashid asked.

"I do go out, Rash," I said.

"The only time I got you out of the apartment when we lived together was when you were apprenticed at Schwa. What's going on, Kuratowski?" Rashid asked. Despite a time zone and some four hundred miles, it was all too easy to picture the look on my former roommate's face.

"I got a house," I gushed.

"You got a house?" The stud in Rashid's eyebrow would have been sky high if I were looking at it.

"I got a house," I confirmed.

"Fucking hell, Jakob! That's a great reason to celebrate. Is Cara giving you the day off tomorrow?"

"You know I set my own schedule."

"Shit. You're telling me this now, Kuratowski? Why didn't you bother… no, wait. Fuck it, I'll start driving and—"

"Don't worry, Ibrahim. You can come out after I finish all the renovations."

"Kuratowski, that'll take you years."

"All right, you can come after I've at least got hot water consistently."

"Sounds like a plan. Go out and make bad choices," Rashid said. He hung up before I had the chance to say anything else or object, and I rolled my eyes. Rashid knew I was the sort of guy who would, at most, have a single beer during the course of a night—sipped slowly, savored, and enjoyed at leisure. For once, as I tapped my foot waiting for the Lyft, I would listen to my former roommate.

I would go out and get whiteboy wasted.

This would turn out to be a Poor Life Choice.

As the rideshare pulled up to a relatively nondescript brick façade with pride flags (LGBTQ, leather, and bear) hanging from the windows, the muggy May air washed over me, promising all sorts of things. It was easy to imagine the waters of Lake Erie, the faintest hint of a breeze, and a late night under the stars. Not that I would get that lucky, but it was nice to imagine it anyway.

I was celebrating my "first real adult endeavor." After over four years of saving, I wasn't renting anymore. I had a house—a place that would become a home of my own. My parents had been over the moon when I called them with the news, and my father's family in Pittsburgh was already threatening to visit. I wasn't engaged (as Rashid was), nor was I a parent (as my elder sister had been at twenty-eight), but being a homeowner at twenty-eight was something I could be proud of. As I strode across the floor to sit at the bar and stare at shelf upon shelf of bottles against the lavender wall, I made my second Poor Life Choice of the night.

I ordered a shot of well tequila.

It was cheap, it went down like water, and when the bartender asked me if there was an occasion for the shot, I told him, and he gave me three more shots on the house. This led me to order yet two more shots, and by the time I finished the sixth shot, I was really feeling the liquor. I was intoxicated, in an unfamiliar space, and I didn't have any talismans, charms, or even a packet of salt. My grandmother would have been ashamed of me. I was a witch unprepared and thus a dead witch.

After that sixth shot, my sense of time blurred. At some point the bar pumped the Village People's classic anthem and I decided to dance. While this was not a Poor Life Choice in and of itself, it was certainly not advisable. I remember heading to the dance floor and flailing through the motions. Instead of retreating to the bar as I should have when the song ended, I stayed out and continued to dance.

Rashid, the last person who saw my attempt at dance, was kind when he said I looked like someone suffering a seizure. I likely wouldn't attract anyone based on the alleged correlation between skills on the dance floor and those in the bedroom, but I followed the old expression and danced as if no one were watching. And who would want to watch me? I was intoxicated, and I allowed the music and alcohol to take me where they needed. When a broad palm ghosted over my rail-thin chest and then moved down to my hips, I was more than willing to go along for the ride.

My partner didn't share my obvious lack of rhythm, and I was happy to let him lead. I knew he was male without looking over my shoulder.

The unsubtle semi-erection digging into my back was more than clue enough. There was also the rich scent of cedarwood, bay rum, leather, and the faintest hint of tobacco. I was far from knowledgeable about perfumes, but I couldn't see many women choosing such a combination for themselves. Finally, chin stubble dragged along my throat, then came to rest against my jaw as teeth worked over my earlobe. My knees almost went out from under me, and it wasn't the tequila.

He kept me upright, pulled me closer, and held me possessively. We moved sensuously, following his silent direction. I looped an arm up and ran fingers through his hair. Alcohol can work wonders with inhibitions, and it had been too long since I had been touched like this—too long since I had felt lust, yearning, and the rich bourbon of desire. I was drunk on all of it, not just the bottom-shelf tequila.

How long we remained on the dance floor, I'm not certain. One song bled into the next, and he kept me on my feet, his muscular forearm wrapped tentacle-like around my waist—as though I would have been anywhere else, even with all of my grandmother's warnings. All that mattered was being held like that, being *his*, even if only for those songs.

"Do you want to get out of here?" His voice was deep, low, unmistakably rich and full—next to a growl. It took me a moment to gather myself. Tequila, sweat, the booming bassline, the sea of dancers around me… it was all too much. I was surprised I could hear him at all, but I inhaled and nodded, still not having seen his face. I felt his lips twist into a grin against my ear before he leaned down and pressed a lingering kiss to a pulse point on my neck. Groaning, I tilted my head back. It was then that I saw him for the first time, though not clearly through the darkness of the club. I made out a jaw that could cut glass, cheekbones any sculptor would have been proud to mold, and a predator's smile.

"Good," he said and he pulled from me and turned. The world shifted on its axis for the moment when I was not in contact with him. Then his hand found mine and I stumbled after him. It felt like half the patrons watched us as he led me from the dance floor. Above the streetlamps and the neon glow of the club's sign, the moon hung full and strong. Had I not been overwhelmed by lust and liquor, I might have put two and two together. The heat of his body, the quirk of his lips when he smiled, and most of all, the brilliant moon, would have told me the truth if I had been sober. But I wasn't sober, and I was content to follow him, my hand still in his, as he turned down one street and then another. Before long we were at his well-maintained F-150. Normally I would have joked that his truck must be compensating for something, but I knew there was no truth to it, not with how he had held me, how he had ground against me.

"Where are we going?" I asked as some sense of self-preservation raised its head from a slumber caused by tequila and desire.

"Don't worry, I won't bite. Not at first and not unless you ask," he said, his voice filled with silken sinful promise.

"I don't even know your name."

"Erik Lindstrom. What's yours?"

"Jakob Kuratowski," I said before I could wonder why he had given me his full name and I had responded in kind.

"It's a pleasure to meet you, Jakob," he said. There was the faint drag of stubble over my knuckles before the feather light pressure of his lips. Anticipation and want ran down my spine. As he raised his head, I saw lust sparking in his eyes. Had I been a prepared witch in that moment… but I wasn't. I *needed*, and I let that overpower what common sense I had left.

Once I was in the cab of his truck, he drove us in silence. I lost track of time and the route we took when he placed one palm on my thigh and traced idle circles with his thumb through the fabric of my jeans. Eventually we reached a two-story redbrick Georgian-style home. I couldn't make out many details through the darkness, lust, and remaining fog of tequila rampaging in me, but I do remember Erik opening the door for me, unclasping my seat belt, and pulling me into a bridal carry. I nuzzled into his neck and inhaled his cologne and the raw scent of him.

We were across the threshold and up the stairs in seconds. The little I saw showed an inclination toward simple but well-made decorations, with wood furniture predominating. I noticed a fireplace and almost wanted to ask him to stop so he could take me there on what seemed to be a deerskin rug.

Before I could form the words, he carried me up the stairs to his bedroom and laid me on the king-size mattress of a sleigh bed with an intricately carved headboard. He removed my glasses and put them on a bedside table made of a darker wood. Although still fully dressed, I couldn't imagine being more exposed than I was in that moment. There was this mountain of a man looking down at me, his face impossible to read. I wondered if he regretted taking me to his house, if the fog of lust from the club had evaporated, and he now regretted his choice.

"Please tell me you're sober enough to consent," he said. I was slightly shocked, but I nodded, not trusting my tongue. My heart echoed in the cage of my chest, and I both felt and heard the rushing of blood in my ears.

"I need to hear you say it," he half commanded.

"Say what?" I asked, barely above a whisper. I still didn't trust myself, didn't know if I would be strong enough to say what was needed. He chuckled and brushed a kiss against my jaw, then my ear. Overwhelmed by him as I was, I didn't catch my legs as they wound around his hips. Our erections dragged against each other through the fabric of our pants, and I rolled. I needed to feel more, to take whatever he would give me.

"Say, 'Erik, I want you to fuck me.'" His voice was even, contained, measured.

"Erik, I need you to take me," I replied.

"Close enough," he said, and then he claimed my mouth in a searing, demanding, masterful kiss. I groaned into his mouth, snaked my hand around his neck, and pulled him as close as I could. Our tongues slid against each other, and I allowed him to take control as I writhed against him to reduce the distance between us.

Our bodies were flush against one another. Every inch of his frame was strong, firm, and radiated raw power and heat. If I had been paying attention, I would have known what was up. If I had been thinking with the larger of my two heads, I might have avoided what happened next. Instead, I was awed by the care with which he undressed me and then himself. His cock pulsed against mine—full, flush, and heavy with promise. Our kiss broke and he nibbled at my neck. Then his tongue teased my nipple and soon after, my navel. Eventually he took the tip of my weeping erection between his lips and worked over the slit, his tongue swirling and darting, a calloused palm holding me in place.

My knowledge of the power, the weight of words means that I am given to swearing as little as possible. He was able to draw every invective I knew in English, Spanish, Polish, Yiddish, and Hebrew. None of my words had any real force or power behind them—they wouldn't become anything truly dangerous—so I swore to make a sailor proud.

I was dangerously close to spilling down his throat when he lifted his head. His tongue, that devil's tool, danced over his lips as he placed both of his hands right above the joints of my knees and pressed my legs to my chest. I was exposed to him.

I generally don't enjoy rimming, even if I have freshly showered and groomed down there. But when his tongue played over my entrance— swiping, circling, and tracing patterns I had never seen in any of the grimoires I've studied—I lost myself for a second. I even lost my words. My hands fisted in the sheets, knuckles white.

When Erik's tongue had finished its wicked work, his fingers came into play. I expected, half hoped, that he would be rough, rushed, and demanding, and leave me sore and aching. Instead, he was coy and playful, fingers as coarse as they were dexterous. He worked my body with maddening precision, finding my prostate easily and crooking his digit just so. It was a minor miracle I didn't lash out in raw pleasure. In the throes of passion, witches have been known to be incredibly destructive. I should have given in, allowed my magic to do something, anything, to ward him off through a show of power. But the only things that came out of me were precum and my pleas for more. I can't say which I did more—beg or leak. When he pressed a second finger into me, I saw stars.

Two fingers became three, and I was all but screaming for him to stop with all the foreplay and to get down to the business of fucking me. I heard as well as felt his chuckle echo through both of us. He pulled all three fingers out, flipped me over, and put a pillow beneath my hips in fluid motions. I shivered when more lube was applied. Then I heard the distinct crinkle of a condom packet being ripped open and changed the angle of my neck to watch him pull the latex down his impressive cock. I had begun second-guessing myself when he leaned forward and pressed a soft kiss to my shoulder.

"Don't worry, Jakob, I'll make this as good for you as it is for me," he promised. Then the head of his prick was against my hole and he pushed forward. I pushed back. When the tip breached me, my eyes rolled back in my head, and I savored the burn that ran through my body. He sank slowly, pausing when he could. It was a struggle, but I managed to resist the impulse to slam myself against him. When he was fully sheathed inside me, he leaned down and kissed my ear.

"So beautiful," he said. Instinctively, I clenched around him, trying to hold him closer, needing more of him, more of this. I needed motion, friction, a spark with the possibility of becoming inferno. He half growled and complied. Unlike when he had been preparing me, he was all drive and determination—all raw, primal hunger. The time for gentleness had apparently passed. He was ready to rut, to claim, to master, and *Hashem* forgive me, I wanted it. Was desperate for it. He pulled almost all the way out and then slammed in. I pressed back, trying to take what he could give, trying to show him I wasn't made of crystal. He kissed me fiercely as he crashed into me again, beginning to fuck as a man possessed. Erik proved to be the merciless lover I had been craving, needing, dreaming of. He set a punishing pace, driving into me, taking me to the edge within moments. He held me there, slamming against me with all the power and force of his body. I was lost to pleasure, offering silent thanks to whatever might be listening, and I was too busy pursuing what I knew would be a mind-melting orgasm to think about what really mattered.

His breath was hot along my neck, and he whispered dark and sinful words into my ear, praising how tight I was, how eager I was, how good I felt around him, and how I had been made for him. Like rimming, dirty talk normally wasn't my cup of tea, but in that moment, it was the hottest thing I had ever experienced. I was leaking over his bed sheets, both my hands captured above my head by one of his. "I'll take you there," he promised as he rested fully inside of me and then rolled his hips—a short, shallow jab, a contrast to the jackhammering I had been subjected to for heaven only knew how long. Time was elusive that night. It might have been seconds or hours. I moaned and he shifted again, hitting a spot inside me that made stars burst behind my eyes.

"Please... please," I said, not sure if there was anything else I should say.

"Almost there," he said, his pace a blur again. While I wasn't a virgin, this was something new. I had never been handled like this, never had a lover who was so possessive. I could feel it building inside of him as his already high body temperature spiked. I drank his pleasure in, taking what was freely given, allowing it to ride through me, to mingle with my own. My eyes were closed, and I was lost in the sensory world beyond sight. I smelled our sex, heard the fevered sounds of his hips rutting into mine, and tasted him as he brought his lips to mine for a brief but passionate kiss.

Then he stopped.

"Är du min?" he asked. Only the head of his member was in my body, and I shivered, my release less than a thrust away. I had never heard the words, the language before. The meaning was clear enough, though—clearer than the rays of moonlight pouring through the window. It could only mean something possessive. He wanted me to belong to him in that moment. It was the question that damned me. My need was too great and, like the idiot I was, I said, "Yes." With that he slammed home and brought his mouth to my shoulder.

Obsidian-sharp pain lanced through my shoulder and ran down my spine even as Erik rocked himself directly over my prostate. I screamed and came simultaneously. The scream continued as he came inside the condom. Pain and pleasure met somewhere in my navel, and I reacted as any witch would. Our pleasure from moments ago, my seed on my belly and the sheet, the blood pouring from the open wound, and my rage— these were fuel, and my skin erupted in emerald fire. Erik emitted a harsh yip and pulled out and back. I drew on the ache from the emptiness, the soreness of my body, and it added it to my power. Energy like this was potent but temporary. I spun in the sheets, wrapping them around my body as best I could. But I wouldn't be covered for long. The witch's fire was already eating through the sheets, using my blood and seed as its fuel.

I looked at Erik, saw blood dripping from his lips and twin voids where his eyes had been. He opened his mouth, and instead of human incisors, I saw lupine fangs. I flung my left hand up, fingers twisted into an offensive casting gesture that my grandmother had drilled into me but that I had never used before. A whip of emerald illuminated the room in eldritch light, and he danced back, a snarl coming from his elongated mouth. In the flare, I saw both the main door to the bedroom and a second door, closer to the foot of the bed. I moved toward it as I pulled the witch's fire back to me. I groped blindly for the handle, not daring to take my eyes off Erik, who raised a hand with long, ebony-colored nails extending from each digit. He wiped his mouth with the back of his hand, his gaze locked with mine, unblinking.

I narrowed my eyes and made the same gesture again. The blood lingering on his teeth and lips smoked and sizzled, getting another yip from him. I had managed to find the handle to the door at this point and stepped backward onto cool stone—a bathroom, I guessed. I pulled myself fully into it and slammed the door shut. Placing a finger to the nearly cauterized wound, I found a little blood that was still wet. I placed it to the lock, drew a crude sigil, and felt the barrier spring into place. Blood magic was as powerful as it was old and crude. I didn't have time for fancy workings; I needed something that would hold. I saw the knob twist and heard a "Fucking hell" follow as it heated red-hot under his touch. This was his home, but I had created a barrier that was uniquely mine, and it would hold until I broke the sigil.

"What—" I said, my body shaking from pain and magical exhaustion. I hadn't used this much magic in a night... ever. While his bite had been sealed by the witch's fire, the pain was still present, gnawing and eager. It rushed along my nerves and through my veins.

"You're a wizard," Erik said, his voice even lower and deeper than when he whispered those dirty nothings to me while we were making love.

"Witch, actually," I corrected automatically.

"A male witch. How interesting," he said, a faint hint of amusement in his words. I rolled my eyes and rooted around the bathroom, looking for something I could use. I had burned all my other resources. As strong as the barrier was, I didn't want to live the rest of my life in a stranger's bathroom. "I thought that male witches preferred to be called wizards."

"A common misconception," I said. "You're not unlife. You're too hot for that." The bathroom was incredibly modern compared to the almost rustic feel of the rest of the house. There was cool gray tile offset by accents of white. A razor hung neatly next to a brush on the right-hand side of the sink. To the left was a toothbrush in its caddy along with neatly capped toothpaste. Even as I searched for something, anything, I might be able to draw power from, I was impressed by how fastidious the toiletries were.

"Unwhat?" he asked. I didn't bother trying to explain. If he had been unliving, I indeed would have been a dead witch.

I could feel him leaning against the door as I opened the cabinet beneath the sink. There was soap, two types of body wash, a face wash, beard oil, all-natural cologne.... He had a range of products, but none of them were ideal fuel to help me escape.

"You're a shifter of some sort," I said as I continued rummaging.

"I'm a werewolf, to be more specific, and the alpha of my pack."

"Hashem dammit," I spat out.

"Hashem?" He managed that name of G-d fairly well, but it was clear to me it was the first time he had used it.

"Ha*shem*," I couldn't help but correct, putting the emphasis on the right syllable. "Also, not the point." I ran one hand through my hair as I pulled at the mirror with the other, disappointed that there was nothing behind it. Would it have killed him to have a medicine drawer somewhere, if only for the pretext of normalcy? "I was bit while a werewolf was… having sex with me." I prevented myself from swearing again. I didn't need to add any more bad energy to the night.

"Something you consented to."

"At what point—" I stopped and remembered the fatal question, the one that should have made me realize what the hell was going on. I let out a choice expression or two in Yiddish, resorting to my grandmother's favored tongue. "Är du min?" I repeated. "That means 'you're mine' or 'are you mine?' or something like that, doesn't it? You asked if I was yours and I said yes."

"Clever mate, very clever."

"And if I had said no—"

"But you didn't, did you?"

"I was drunk," I argued, trying to find some loophole out of my situation.

"I also asked if you were sober enough to consent to—"

"I was only consenting to sex, a one-night stand. I didn't want a life-bond with some *fonferer* werewolf!"

"A what?"

"You—you *shmuck* of a beast! You had no right—"

"You felt it. I know you did. You had to know there was more than just dirty talk."

"I would have said anything to cum!"

There was a low chuckle on the other side of the door, and despite everything that had happened in my night, despite the fact I was naked in a stranger's bathroom, searching for whatever I could weaponize in an escape attempt, I liked the sound of it. I bit my lip and used the pain to draw me back to the task at hand. Now was so not the time.

"I smelled both of them on you, and the lust was far stronger than the tequila," Erik said, his voice lazy and sure. "You were telling the truth when you said you needed me."

I stammered as I searched for words and tried to decide if he would know a lie from behind a warded door. I didn't want to find out, at least not right then. "As an alpha, wouldn't you need to claim me in front of your pack or something?" I asked, getting back to digging through whatever I could find, trying to keep him distracted from my nonresponse.

"You've read too much shitty fiction." He chuckled again. "Although, would that get you off? Being claimed in front of my pack? I know more than a few members of my pack are voyeurs and would love to watch me claim you."

That made me stop for a second. Kinky werewolves... something I hadn't read about in my family's grimoire. Not that any of my ancestors who had been magic-touched would have written about something so explicit. I doubted I would add that specific piece of info, but I might.

"Is that why you picked me up on the dance floor?" I was stalling for time as I spun in the bathroom and searched for something—*anything*— that would be usable and potent.

Silence answered me. I closed my eyes and listened for him. Hearing nothing, I debated whether I would be able to exit through the window over the tub. Even with my slender frame and slightly below-average height, it was still too small for me.

"You are a most troublesome mate, you know that?"

"Stop using that word," I yelled, Yiddish tinting my voice slightly. Even in the moment of my anger, I tried to stream my energy into the sigil, into the invisible wall. Blood and emotion—it was not the strongest of protections, but it was enough. But the sooner I got back to my house and got to sleep, the happier I would be. I saw it then, out of the corner of my eye. It was in the back of the cabinet below the sink—a bottle of expired, over-the-counter painkillers. I didn't bother questioning why a lycanthrope had such drugs, I just grabbed them and crushed them into my palm with my thumb, my eyes closed.

"It's what you are now. The bite sealed you to me, and when we make love again, you'll be able to feel what I feel, know what I know," he said.

"That sounds less like a boyfriend and more like a stalker," I shot back. I hoped the active ingredients would still have enough efficacy for a working. But needs must when the devil drives, and right then I felt as if Satan was donning his chauffer's cap.

He laughed again, deep and echoing on the opposite side of the door. "What I sensed in the club… I wish I could describe it better. You wouldn't smell the same to any other werewolf, you know? At least, not as intensely as you do to me. When you're not using magic, you smell like everything I might want. You smell of pine, cedar, freshly fallen snow, and just a hint of juniper. You also smell of springtime turning into summer. When you danced, it was like you didn't care what the world would think of you. That sort of confidence? That's sexy."

I continued to grind my thumb over the pills in my palm. When I had a coarse powder, I chanted, Hebrew words flowing fast and freely. Again, I was working from theory rather than practice, but it was all I could do. Erik didn't need to know I was improvising. With one hand, I chipped the sigil, and then I opened the door. I flung powder in the air and shouted.

Erik stood opposite me, and I closed my eyes to not see him. I didn't want to see him, not the way his body was bathed in moonlight, not at the way his dick, already hard again, jumped at the sight of me, not at the cocky smile on his lips. I made a swift sign in the air, hoping I could both deafen and blind him, but I would have taken either at that moment. His eyes were closed, but he turned his head, clearly following my footsteps.

"Of all the senses you could have crippled, you chose the most human. I can still hear you, smell you. I know exactly where you are," he said as he took a step toward me.

"If you take another step, I'll have you deaf and vomiting," I threatened, silently praying there was enough of the reagents left for that kind of magic. I had burned most of the powder and I didn't know how strong the drugs were. I was improvising, and thinking on the fly had never been my strong suit. He took a half-step back. I opened my eyes, found my underwear and pants, and pulled them on as best I could with my left hand still balled into a fist.

"I don't know why you're fighting this. Aren't you supposed to be—"

"Aware of the future? Not a Seer. No one in my family has been one for generations. If you were looking to add a personal fortune-teller to your pack, you're all out of luck," I interrupted.

"Not what I was going to say," he countered.

"Really?"

"I was going to say cognizant of the energies around you. You're not the first witch I've known, Jakob, just the first male witch." The way he said my name, despite the circumstances, was enough to send a shiver running down my spine. It was more than fear or revulsion.

"If I'm not the first witch you've known, then you should know better than to be where I don't want you." I pulled on my shirt. I had to work fast. Blindness wouldn't hamper him long—at least not if I remembered correctly what my ancestors had written about werewolves. But translating from eighteenth-century Lithuanian wasn't my strong suit.

"You must be feeling something. After all, witches pull on and manipulate energies, don't you?" he asked. He was persistent, I would give him that. He also wasn't far from the truth.

"I was too drunk to know what you were," I said as I toed my feet into my shoes and left the socks strewn on the floor for the moment. Putting those on correctly required more manual dexterity than I was currently capable of. "I didn't sense anything. Also, being direct here, it's late, and I'm going to have the worst luck getting an Uber."

"You could stay, talk, sort this all out with me." He stepped forward again. I offered a silent prayer as I uttered a choice invective, my hand clenching hard on the remnants of the powder in my palm. His hand flew to his eyes again and I resisted the urge to curse myself. I would have to revisit that section of the grimoire, make sure I actually knew what I was doing if I should find myself in this sort of situation again. I didn't want to end up a dead witch by being unprepared.

"You're going to keep fighting this, aren't you? You'll do everything you can to deny this." There was something in his voice that might have been respect or awe, possibly amazement at my chutzpah. I moved toward the main door out of the bedroom, and he tilted his head to follow my movement. It wasn't deafness or vomiting, but he seemed to at least respect the fact I had blinded him twice over.

"Do you know what a witch is?" I asked.

"A witch can draw on the power of the world around them and through their will, create change. That's what my pack's witch told me when I was a cub," he answered.

That stopped me for a second. His pack's witch had given him a very thorough answer. "Your pack's witch might have gotten along with my grandmother," I admitted.

"Well, if they could have been friends, I can't see why we shouldn't be more," he said, a leer on his face. But he stayed where he was, clearly wary of anything I might try. He might have guessed I was out of ammo, in a manner of speaking, but he didn't want to take a risk. He learned quickly, and I respected that, even with everything else that was going down.

"A witch is one who looks at fate, destiny, whatever you might want to call it and laughs. We see patterns and lines laid out and rewrite what might become. I didn't know what you were when you picked me up, and I refuse to be what you made me when you bit me. If your senses are as keen as you allege they are, then you'll know I would have said or done anything for an orgasm," I said. Then I turned and ran down his stairs and out the front door. I continued running through the darkness of the night pierced by moonlight. I didn't stop to summon a rideshare for at least three blocks.

CHAPTER 2

THE THING before me was a hybrid between Dali and Bosch, perhaps dreamed up after an absinthe binge with Lovecraft. In a second, my heart knew it for what it was—unlife. Seven limbs sprouted from a twisted stump of a torso, and I didn't see a head, but I knew there would be at least one mouth, filled with razor-sharp teeth. One of the arms flailed, searching for me, for my beating heart. The thing, whatever it might be, growled to shame any trash compactor or pit bull. It had but one purpose, one drive—to eat, to consume totally. A tongue, or perhaps a tentacle, serrated and obsidian, rocketed from the top of the thing, highlighted in a halo of moonlight. I opened my mouth to scream, but no sound came. As the tongue twisted and surged toward me, I—

A sharp, slightly computerized trill pulled me from the nightmare, and I sat bolt upright in bed, my heart thundering. I looked down, The sheets were pooled from my flailing, and at the foot of the bed, far from where I had been writhing, a pair of jade-green eyes glowed in the dark. I forced myself to regulate my breathing as my phone trilled again. My phone read a little after midnight, and I didn't bother to scan the number. "Hello?" I asked, my voice thick with panic and sleep. It was an unusual combination, but since meeting Erik a month ago, very little of my life felt usual.

"Eres el brujo?" A smokey voice—deep, but unmistakably feminine—was on the other end of the call. It took me longer than I wanted to remember any Spanish.

"El brujo?" I asked. Had I heard her right?

"Sí, the witch Erik has claimed." She switched effortlessly to English, lightly accented, but still silken and full of smoke.

I focused on my breathing to stop my heart from galloping out of my chest.

"I don't know—"

"Mentiroso," she admonished. "Don't lie to me. You are the witch, Jakob Kuratowski."

"If," I said, "you know so much, then why the question?"

"Mostly to see how you'd react. I can hear your heart over the phone. You're not used to being called what you are, are you?"

I let the silence sit between us. "How did you get my number?" I asked. She laughed.

"I have my ways, brujo," she said. I gave up any attempt at trying to control my heart, and I knew I wouldn't have a chance to get back to sleep. Whatever this woman was calling about, it couldn't be a good thing, especially if she knew Erik.

"What…why are you calling?" I asked as I swung my legs out of bed and set my bare feet on the cool wood floor. Grounded and feeling the house around me, I wasn't any calmer or less worried, but I did feel the barest hint of control, of surety.

"My alpha needs your help," she said.

"Why do you think I'd help him?"

"Because you're his mate."

Anger flared, both within me and along my skin. Viridian flame roared from my left forearm and pooled in my palm as I stood. Witch's fire had never come so easily before. I would have been afraid or astounded if I hadn't let my anger keep the driver's seat.

"Don't say that word."

"Why, it's what you—"

"Ikh bin nischt zeyn," I spat, the Yiddish falling easily.

"Que idioma era ese?" she asked. I swallowed some of the rage, and the green flames died slightly. I didn't need an inferno on my hands.

"I'm not his," I repeated, this time in English, each word punched out with deliberation. "Why would I help him?"

"It's not him. It's not me. It's Nick," she said.

"Nick who?" I asked.

"Nick, he's a cub—a kid under thirteen—he's going through his first transformation. He became a wolf easily enough but… even Erik's voice and presence can't call him back."

I inhaled sharply. My grandmother's words about *gemilut hasadim*, how it was our duty to help those we could in whatever ways we could, echoed loudly. I released a slow, deep exhale.

"What will happen if he can't turn back?" I heard myself ask. I was only half aware of the stairs as I got into my kitchen and reached immediately for a container of Morton's Kosher Salt. No matter what else I'd need, I would need salt.

"It won't be good. Sometimes a cub needs three or four days, but sometimes they never find their way back," she said. I wanted badly to curse. That wouldn't help anything.

"Where are you?" My question was half sighed.

"In the Cuyahoga Valley National Park," she said, and then she proceeded to give me a set of directions. "Got that, brujo?"

"No, text them to me." I rummaged through my spice rack—dried lavender, a dried basil leaf, and paprika. I grabbed a bundle of dried sage for good measure and threw my supplies into a reusable shopping bag. As I left the kitchen, I heard the sound of the cat drinking greedily and deeply from its water bowl. It had apparently forgiven me for disturbing its slumber and had decided to do something productive now that it was awake. As I exited the house, a wave of muggy, dense air washed over me, and a mosquito buzzed in my ear. My phone vibrated in my hand. The directions.

"This isn't going to be free," I warned her.

"You'll have to take that up with Erik," she said.

"By the way, you know who I am. Who are you?"

She laughed again, and it drowned out the complaints of my sedan's door as I swung it open. "Alicia. I'm Erik's second-in-command. His beta, if you will," she introduced.

"I can't say it's been a pleasure," I groaned as I inserted the key and pressed my foot to the brake.

"See you soon, brujo." And with that she signed off. It took me two more attempts before the engine finally revved. As I peeled out of the driveway and onto my street, I swear I saw the cat sitting in my bay window for a quarter of a second, feline judgment fully back in place.

I had no time to worry about what the cat might think.

Miles and minutes passed as I moved from city streets to the highway. While I drove, I turned on the car radio. There were more than a few stations of static, some playing music or ads. The one news station I was able to find had only the standard sort of news—a local sheriff had been caught illegally gambling, and a group was challenging materials at the Cleveland Public Library. Nothing to mirror the images of nightmare. Nothing that whispered of rot, decay, and the cracking of bones.

Nothing that told me anything I had dreamed was more than stress and too many late nights going over my family's grimoire.

Pulling off to a little-used access road, I saw the wheel marks from a car and followed them to a small space in the national park. The night air clung to me as I got out of the car.

"You took your time." Her voice was behind me. I spun and almost dropped my bag.

"You're—are you—" I stumbled, shifting my head up to lock eyes with her. She tilted her head, first one way and then another. Was this how rabbits felt when wolves found them?

"Alicia," she eventually introduced, and extended a palm. I gave it a quick shake and managed not to wince when she squeezed as hard as she could. Apparently enhanced strength was a thing all werewolves had. Then she turned and I followed her. She moved quickly, bounding over barely visible tree roots and breaks in the terrain. I had to run to keep pace, and she didn't even look back. I lost track of her at several points, and it was only by sheer luck I didn't face-plant or end up in a ditch. Around me leaves rustled and there was movement between the trees. Shapes larger than dogs blended into the darkness around me.

I was among wolves.

I felt them moving around me, heard their bodies brush against the leaves and bend the branches. Magic was here and closer to the surface than I had felt since we worked in my *babcia*'s kitchen. I pulled at the threads of power and dragged some of them into myself. They were reluctant to cooperate, straining against my will, sticking and adhering to the earth, to the wolves themselves. "*Elohai....*" I began a familiar prayer, and it pulled threads of energy. For the first time since I woke up, I felt closer to human. By the time Alicia yelled, "Where the hell are you, brujo?" I was able to walk easily into a small clearing where a campfire had been assembled. I extended a hand and a spark of flame leaped into my palm. My babcia had made sure I knew how to call the flame, how to take it into myself, how to use its power to augment my own.

Whispers and barks echoed around me. I felt the weight of human and lupine eyes, but I adjusted my glasses and resisted the urge to look down. The last thing I needed was to show any trace of fear. I didn't want to be their prey. I saw a few human bodies, all naked, and I blinked, hard. Men and women of all ages stood around in the summer night without a stitch of clothing on. It made sense that werewolves would be nudists.

They wouldn't want to ruin their clothing. Still, outside of porn, I hadn't ever seen so many naked bodies in one place. It didn't take long for me to see Erik, standing tall, moving confidently, his lips in something between a grin and a smile. He was as handsome as I remembered, and it took all of my self-control not to have my eyes dart southward to see if all my memories of our time together were correct.

"You came," he said, his voice a deep rumble that sent a shiver up my spine.

"I came," I said.

"This means a lot to me, Jakob—"

"I didn't come for you," I said.

"Really? I remember that differently."

Chuckles and howls of laughter, both human and wolf, filled the night air. I stepped forward and called silently to the flame again. It answered, and my forearms were awash in glowing jade light. Tongues of fire danced and twisted along my palms, my fingertips, and in my eyes. I couldn't see them, but I felt them, hot and pulsing. The laughter, human or animal, faded, and even Erik took a step back. My fire died, but in the remaining light, I saw the broad smile on Erik's lips. "I'm never going to get tired of seeing you do that," he said.

"This is the last time you'll have a chance to see it," I spat.

"I doubt that, Jakob."

"Where's the cub?" I hadn't meant to use their word for Nick, but in this moment, it was the right thing to say. I knew that in my bones.

Whatever amusement had been on Erik's face vanished, and he was a deeply concerned leader. There was something almost paternal, and my heart fluttered. He walked and I followed his footsteps. If I focused on his superlative ass, it was only so I knew where to step.

I swear.

It didn't take us long to find a smaller wolf, predominantly dark gray I guessed with the limited light I had available, but I could tell the right foreleg and muzzle were lighter shades. He looked at me with rich amber eyes, and I saw the fur along the back of his neck rising on end as he bared sharp, alabaster fangs. A young man standing near the wolf raised his head and took in his alpha and me. Dressed in a pair of black basketball shorts and an old T-shirt from the Rock and Roll Hall of Fame, I must have seemed out of place. But the young man spoke quickly. "Relax, Nick, he's here to help." His voice was soothing, his words sure. Near the young man was a young woman, around his age, maybe a little older.

"Can he help us, Alpha?" she asked.

"Zoe—" Erik said.

"He is right here, and he has a name. I'm Jakob, and I'll be the one trying to help your… brother?" I guessed as I stepped past Erik and toward the wolf cub. He still hadn't relaxed, but he wasn't challenging me or aggressive.

"My brother, witch," the young man answered.

"And you are?"

"Micah," he introduced himself. I nodded and dug into the reusable grocery bag to pull out the salt.

"Micah and Zoe, you two can stay inside the circle please," I instructed as I poured salt on the ground. I tried to make it as even as I could, but the topography only allowed so much. "Erik, take a step back please."

"Won't you need me?" Genuine curiosity filled his voice.

"I might, but not in the immediate circle. Even if you are his alpha, I'm guessing Micah and his girlfriend—"

"We're to be mates," Zoe cut in. "We're just waiting for the right time to consummate it with the bite."

I made a mental note to myself. It would be something I would add to the grimoire when I got home. If I survived.

"Fine, but I'm guessing Nick spends a lot more time with both of you in your human forms than he spends with your alpha," I explained. From the corner of my eye, I saw all three nodding as I finished the circle of salt. Instantly the air stilled inside the circle. The sounds of the night were slightly muted, as if coming from farther away than mere footsteps. I looked up in time to see gooseflesh forming on Micah's and Zoe's forearms. Nick went statue still for a second, and then his ears and nose twitched. On the other side of my salt line, I saw Erik's face shift just a little. It was nice to know all of the lessons, all of the time I had spent learning from my babcia, had gone to good use.

"Micah, can you put a hand on Nick without Nick biting you?" I asked.

His face twisted. I could see an insult beginning to form at the tip of his tongue, but he bit it back and nodded. He knelt down and rested a palm along Nick's side. The cub turned his head and pressed his muzzle to his brother's neck, tongue flicking out and over it.

"Zoe, do likewise please." My voice was as even as I could make it. She nodded and moved to Nick's other side and petted him slowly, moving her fingers along his pelt. Nick's tail wagged and his tongue lolled out. I remembered Sitka, the malamute that had belonged to my next-door neighbors when I was all of seven or eight years old, a lifetime ago, but I didn't dwell on the memory.

I dug in the bag, pulled out the paprika, and poured it into my palm. I spat on it and made a slurry of a paste. Then I walked over to Micah and Zoe. Nick's tail stopped wagging, but he didn't growl at me as I drew quick designs on their foreheads. I stepped back and pulled out the basil, quickly crushed it between my fingers, and then dropped the fragments onto the top of Nick's head. Even as he twisted his head and tried to catch a flying flake on his tongue, I gave a command in biblical Hebrew. The single word hung in the air and his body twitched. No, it was more than a twitch. It was a spasm. I saw the expressions on Micah's and Zoe's faces, but with a single look I silenced any comments they might make. It wasn't the evil eye—my babcia had taught me better than to throw that around—but it was as fierce a look as my exhaustion and adrenaline could summon.

It was apparently enough. They kept their hands where they were and their mouths slammed shut as I took out the sage bundle and sprinkled it with lavender. While I did so, I chanted. No one would ever accuse me of being a cantor, but my voice was strong and sure in my working, and in the space of the circle, my words carried. The sage bundle began to smoke, its rich, earthy scent infused slightly with the floral notes from the lavender. I walked a tighter circle around the three bodies, two human and one lupine, and the smoke curled and twisted, lingering in the air. It didn't disperse as it would have under normal circumstances.

My chant built in volume, even as I kept the pace of my words even. I reminded Nick of Micah, of his human brother touching him. Micah's eyes flicked toward me when he heard his name in the string of Hebrew. Zoe did likewise when I mentioned her mate-to-be to his brother. While the chant would be found nowhere in the Tanakh, the words seemed to work. I saw Nick's eyes beginning to lose their lupine shape, the distinct rich amber of a predator's gaze beginning to fade away and become a warm chocolate color, more human than animal.

I said another command in Hebrew and kept repeating it. I picked up the pace each time I said it but kept my voice barely above a whisper. Each repetition rippled through the body of the wolf before me. Micah's and Zoe's gazes darted between me and Nick. Their hands remained in place, keeping the cub as still as possible. After the twelfth iteration of my command, Nick's tail shrank and become less and less noticeable. His snout faded, and the sharp fangs were replaced by more human teeth.

The process wasn't a smooth one, and different parts of his body went back and forth, sometimes becoming more wolf and at other moments resting near human. I repeated the command and lost track of how often the words fell from my lips. Eventually a young boy was on the ground before me, looking up at me with deep brown eyes, an expression of awe and wonder on his face. Mutely, I stepped back to the salt line and smudged it with the left toe of my well-worn running shoes, and the smoke that had been hanging in the air drifted outward and dispersed into the night. The cacophony of nightbirds, crickets, and voices—wolf and human—rushed back to us. I collapsed onto my knees, hands fisting the earth as I tried to regain my balance.

An honest-to-heaven working. I hadn't done one in more time than I would have cared to admit.

A strong arm looped around my back and pulled me to my feet. I was guided to a space in front of the fire, where I tried to regulate my breathing, tried to get my heart back to normal.

"Thank you, Jakob," Erik said. I nodded, said nothing, and stared at the small fire in front of me. It bowed toward me and danced, flickering, as it extended itself from the stone circle. Erik remained at my side unafraid.

"This… doesn't… come free," I eventually managed to cough out.

"I didn't expect it would," he said. His thumb moved in small circles against the nape of my neck and I remembered how skilled his fingers had been as he opened me up, made me beg for him. My Judas of a body pressed against his, and I blamed fatigue for my inability to fight back. "I could drive you home if—"

"Not going to happen. It's bad enough you found out my number somehow," I said.

"The internet is a wonderful thing, brujo." Alicia came into my field of vision from the left and assumed an easy crouch. If my cat had feline judgment, her look had the werewolf equivalent. All the while, Erik continued to massage my neck, and I didn't remove his hand. "Tienes poder, brujo. Nuestro alpha—"

"Él no es mi alpha," I interrupted. Erik's hand flew from the back of my neck as I continued on, "puta."

The only sound for a quarter of a second was the crackling of the flame. Then Alicia opened her mouth and let out a bark of laughter. Next to me I felt Erik's body release tension. Had he been ready to step in, to fight for me? Why would he do that with his beta? Even if he thought I was his mate, we had only had sex once. There was no way he'd be willing to fight for me, to injure someone he knew better, with whom he had a closer relationship. I couldn't be that valuable to him.

"This one, Erik... I might get to like him. Speaks his mind. Powerful too, even if his accent is that of a *gringo*," Alicia said, nodding her head.

"Well, I think he's worth keeping around, at any rate," Erik said. I didn't need to turn my head to know he had winked.

"He—" I rested both of my hands on my thighs and pulled air deeply into my lungs. "—is right here and is getting very sick of everyone talking about him in the third person, so if you would kindly stop that?"

"Sorry, Jakob." Erik put a finger under my chin and turned my head in his direction. I locked eyes with him, and despite the warm night air, I swore my glasses steamed a little, the heat of his gaze was that direct and intense. "I promise not to do it again."

"What about promising not to touch me?" I asked. Erik lifted his hand slowly, his fingertip ghosting on my stubble.

"You're my mate. One of the advantages of that is I get to touch you whenever I want."

"I'm not your—we're not having this conversation. Not here, not now. I want my fee and I want to be safely escorted out of here. Also, none of your pack is to follow me home," I said. Babcia would have been proud—I had been direct and specific about what I wanted. Such things generally went a long way in the reasoning nonhuman community. Unlife was the exception. Unlife could never be reasoned with.

"We'll have that conversation sometime, Jakob. You can't put me off forever," Erik said. Then he leaned in and reminded me of nothing so much as a giant third-grader playing the "not touching you" game. I closed my eyes and called silently to the flame, which sparked, fizzled, and grew brighter. Even behind my eyelids, I felt the world tilt emerald for a fraction of a second. I heard footsteps and paws on the dirt, and I tried not to notice the rich, heady, and purely masculine scent of Erik Lindstrom.

I opened my eyes but kept them narrow. "$1,000."

"$250," he countered. We haggled for the next fifteen minutes. All through our negotiations, Alicia sat nearby, her gaze flicking between us as if she were watching a tennis match.

"Alpha, just give the brujo $600 already. You've been at this too long," she eventually cut in. Erik huffed a sigh but nodded. I exhaled a breath I hadn't known I'd been holding. Erik retrieved the money from a backpack, and before I could ask why he'd have that amount of cash lying around, he extended his hand. As I went to take the bills from him, his free hand engulfed my own. Warmth that had nothing to do with the fire surged from my palm to my heart and our eyes met. "I know you felt that," he whispered as he let go.

"Well, you won't be feeling it again, dog." I spun on my heel and marched out.

It would have been a more dramatic exit if four steps later I hadn't managed to catch my foot on a root and go flying. He was there to catch me before I fully realized what had happened. His breath ghosted over my bare neck, and I remembered how it was to be held by him like this. I was hard, I knew it, he knew it. Likely all the wolves around us knew it too.

"I know you'll be back, mate. You'll find your way back to me."

"There's no way that'll happen."

CHAPTER 3

A SHRILL, sharp beeping from my phone pulled me awake. Blindly, I moved my hand to the bedside table while I offered a silent prayer that the caller would hang up. Sadly, it wasn't answered, and my phone continued to assault my ears. I bit my tongue to prevent a curse from escaping my lips as I fumbled, eyes still cemented shut. It was *him*. There was no one else it could be. It was early October and I still wasn't free of *him*.

"This had better be a freaking emergency," I said as I brought the phone to my ear. Although I had given up hope of the caller coming to his senses, I was still hopeful that this could be resolved easily, and I would be able to get back to sleep before I needed to get to work. I didn't want to know just how few hours of night I had left.

"Actually, Jakob," his rich, deep voice countered, "it is quite literally a fucking emergency." I resisted the urge to shatter my phone with a flick of my wrist. I gave up the illusion that I'd be able to stay in bed and finally opened my eyes. Then I tilted my head and, more fully awake than I wanted to be, grabbed my glasses. At the end of my bed, the cat sat up and lifted its head. There was a moment of silence between us, and the cat did what all cats do best—licked one of its paws and put its head back down. I was out of the bedroom and down the stairs when I asked, "What happened?"

"Do you remember Micah and Zoe?"

"Only vaguely," I replied as I entered my kitchen. This, more than any other spot in my home, was truly mine. I enjoyed the warm mix of spices still in the air. Closing my eyes, I inhaled and grounded myself with a moment of peace and silence that I knew would be the only such moment for the rest of the night. Then I put the phone on speaker, set it down, and moved to the spice cabinet, where I grabbed salt, sage, and rosemary. I didn't know what this call was about yet, but no matter what I would be dealing with, they were always good things to have on hand.

"They finally decided to consummate their bond and—"

"Please, please, tell me it's only that he knotted with her and it won't go down," I said, pressing my palm to my forehead. That would be easy to deal with. I might not even need to leave my home to deal with it, but I thought it unlikely. He wouldn't have called for something that easy to fix.

"Swing and a miss," Erik said.

"Erik, do we really have time for this guessing game?" I asked, imitating his snarl.

"It was the bite; Micah went too deep. While Zoe's not bleeding, she's also not healing, and she isn't responding to my voice." He was somber, serious, and direct. This tone was what I had been partially dreading ever since the ringing refused to stop.

"Oy gotenu," I spat, careful as always with my words. Even the simplest of curses could have dire consequences. I moved to my refrigerator and pulled out cloves of garlic and some fresh ginger. Then I turned to the small closet attached to the kitchen and grabbed my reusable Kroger bag. It took less than ten seconds for me to get everything placed as I wanted it. It was only October, but it would still be chilly, and I knew I didn't have the time to go upstairs and dress in something resembling actual clothes. I would have to make do with old gray sweatpants and a faded Carnegie Mellon T-shirt gifted to me one Chanukah by my youngest sister. I picked up the phone and sprinted toward my hallway. Shoes went on, an old jacket was flung over my shoulders, and I grabbed my wallet and keys.

"You swear in the most interesting way." There was a hint of amusement in Erik's voice again. I bit my lips to prevent a grin. This wasn't funny. Fully awake, I remained focused. Anything I said or did now would have weight and intention behind it. I didn't need to add anything else to the pyre.

"Are you in the usual place?" I asked as I locked the door. I looked into the living room window, where the cat had taken residence on top of the secondhand brown suede couch and was too busy grooming itself to take any notice of me. It took me less than two seconds to cross my small lawn and open the door of the ancient sedan. The night nipped at my hands, face, and any other exposed skin I offered. If possible, my Nissan's interior was worse, the cold concentrated, condensed, and almost stagnant.

"You know where I am," he said simply. "You should be able to—"

"That thought? Stop it right there Erik," I spat out. "Tell me where I need to get off the interstate." I struggled to turn over the engine of the Nissan as Erik told me where to head.

Even as Google Maps configured the route, I pulled onto the quiet suburban street and turned on the fog lamps. The darkness was near total, and the streetlamps cast ghoulish shadows. When I reached the stop sign at the turn out of the cul-de-sac, I briefly flicked my eyes heavenward, searching for stars, the moon, even the faint glow of Cleveland herself. For a brief moment, the clouds parted and the moon hung in the sky, pristine and ivory, either a day past or a day until full. I couldn't say which one.

"I'll be there in about a half hour, depending on how many cops are out tonight," I said. I pulled forward. I knew where I was heading, and Siri's Australian accent only confirmed the turns I knew to take.

"Of all the mates I could have, you are both the most useful and the most irritating. See you when you arrive."

"Erik, now isn't the time to talk about—never mind. I'll be there when I get there," I half hissed. Making my turn, I took some small comfort in the quiet of my phone. I passed the golf course and managed not to slam my foot on the accelerator. It was a notorious speed trap, and the last thing I needed was a confrontation with Cleveland's finest. How could I justify myself to them? What would they think if I told them I was dealing with the consequences of a one-night stand with an alpha werewolf? I knew at the very least, a breathalyzer would be involved and involuntary committal was a distinct possibility.

Eventually I merged onto the interstate and finally pressed down on the accelerator with some real weight. As I sped down nearly deserted highways, I turned on the radio, but I only half listened to the late night/early morning news cast—until I caught the tail end of a story about a grave robbery in Louisville. Likely someone high on meth, I reasoned... hoped.

Finally I arrived at a little-used road for one of the lesser-visited parts of the Cuyahoga Valley National Park. While not calm, I was no longer as angry as I had been. I saw a Hyundai parked and half-buried in the brush. Pulling in next to it, I had barely turned off the engine when I saw leaves rustling in front of me. Outside the car, crisp air teased the tips of my ears and tingled my fingers. The leaves gave me a sense of childhood and the desire to rush outdoors and play. I shifted the bag in my hand, and a woman with midnight hair, bronze skin, and wicked eyes emerged from the trees. She dwarfed my five-foot-seven by at least three to four inches. I looked up and locked my eyes with hers, ignoring her nudity. "You're later than you should be," she greeted, her voice a blend of honey and smoke and just a hint of her first seven years in Honduras.

"Nice seeing you too, Alicia," I responded. She cocked her head and turned, and the wave of black hair cascaded down past her shoulders to the center of her spine. It was hard work traversing the trails in my slippers, and unlike the wolf in front of me, I was unused to walking barefoot. More than once I caught myself as I tripped over a root or pitfall in the path. Alicia kept her steady, sure-footed pace. I didn't ask her to slow down, but the temptation was there. I knew what she would say if I did. It was easy to remember the ways her eyes rolled and the slight "tsk" that would come from barely parted lips.

"Keep up, brujo," she said, turning from a more used trail to one that was nearly invisible, at least to me.

"Remember, human here, puta," I said. There was some small satisfaction in getting away with what many would consider a curse. For her, it was merely a descriptor, and thus, weightless and shapeless. I hadn't given it the intent to hurt, to maim, but she turned to me then, and there was the faintest hint of the predator's grin on her lips. Instinct took over, and my hand fell to the Morton's coarse kosher salt in my bag. It and the silver *mezuzah* around my neck were really the only protections I carried. None of the other supplies were what I needed for combative magic. I had been foolish. The first lesson my babcia had taught me and among the last things she whispered on her deathbed—an unprepared witch is a dead witch.

"That's the thing, brujo, you're not human," she said. My eyes didn't leave her mouth as I searched for the telltale sign of fangs in the dim light.

"I'm closer to human than you are," I said, my index finger touching the top of the salt container. A faint thrum of power traveled through my body. While she might be fast, I only needed one syllable. Surprisingly, she let out a laugh and turned. I made a mental note that if I were called for Erik's group again, I would come fully armed. Even with Erik's open invitation and apparent desire, I still felt like I was *persona non grata*. I moved forward and followed Alicia, not allowing myself to dwell on my status, or lack thereof, in a werewolf pack. We were farther into dense trees, far from where any camper or night hiker might think to look. Deeper still and we came to a small clearing. There was a stone ring around a crackling fire. Half a dozen sets of eyes turned, and I could see the ethereal glow of wolf's light in each of them.

The salt container pinged again, and I stepped forward, exhaled, and dispelled that fragment of power as my hand moved from the bag. Palm outward, I extended it toward the flame. There were whispers, yips, and even a faint growl. Flame leaped to my palm, a familiar fire dancing for me. With my other hand, I grabbed one of the sage leaves and held it until the tip glowed. I kissed the glowing leaf and then blew it into the night, where the leaf transformed into sparkling moths and flew into the night air.

"I never get tired of seeing you do that." Erik's spine-tingling voice ran straight to my groin. I knew he'd be less than three steps behind me. Instead, I focused on the smoke combined with the fragments of sage leaf. As I wove my power into the flame, it danced, shifted, and wrapped itself around me for a second. I had an anchor in this place, a force older than my kind or his. The hisses and murmurs continued from wolves I couldn't name, and I knew my eyes were glowing with the captured power. I turned and tilted my head as I did so. Even barefoot, Erik was easily at least six-foot-five, and he was as much of an Adonis as I remembered. I stood my ground, acknowledging nothing about him—not the way the fire played with his golden stubble, not his wicked mouth, not his arctic blue eyes. I had been taken in by them once before.

Looking beyond him, I silently called to the flame and heard its increased crackling. It sparkled and flared into the night sky. Filled with heat and power, eyes glowing eldritch green, I asked simply, "Where are they?"

"Can't you—" Erik began, a feral grin on his model-handsome face. He was leaning toward me, and there was less than a handsbreadth between his nose and mine.

"Continue your sentence, *dog*—" The flame hissed and spouted, responding to my desire. "—and you'll see how willing I am to help your pack in the future." There were more howls, yips, and barks of fear from the assembled wolves. If I needed, I could pull on those emotions, as distant and fleeting as they were. Granted, they wouldn't provide much power, but every little scrap might help.

"They're your—"

"Not the time for it, Erik," I spat. "Now, if you want me to be useful to the young couple, lead me to them." Generally speaking, I tried not to make trouble for myself—something adopted from another of my grandmother's numerous lessons. *Don't call the wolf from the forest.* Personally, I favored the original Polish—Nie wywołuj wilka z lasu. I knew further sleep wouldn't be possible, but I still had a chance to at least grab a shower and a cup of coffee before running to work. Erik nodded. When push came to shove, he was at least responsible for the members of his pack. He turned and I followed him to a smaller, more secluded second clearing. Here too was a stone circle, but the fire here had died to embers. A young man—no, a boy, perhaps just twenty years old—was rocking back and forth, tear tracks obvious on his cheeks. Micah. That meant—

I swallowed and turned. There was a girl sprawled on the ground. I guessed her to be a few years his senior, but how many, I couldn't say. There was a ragged wound along her neck, and dried blood clung to the lacerated flesh.

Shivering as I knelt, I extended a hand and opened one of her eyes. I tasted blood, not aware I had bit my lip at the sight of milk white and no sign of iris or pupil. Erik was all business. He was a leader, *their* leader, and he was doing everything he could to help those under his protection. "Get him out of here. I'm going to need space and privacy while I work," I said. "Did any of your pack bring water?"

"You don't have a bottle?" Erik asked as he guided the young man from the nearly dead fire. I would deal with that in a moment. The boy, I reminded myself, showed some of the muscular frame for which werewolves are rightly famous, but he was far from Erik. Whatever else I might say about Erik, he was very easy on the eyes.

"Didn't remember to grab one. Goes to show what I get for choosing to answer your call," I almost spat. Erik nodded and wandered off. I exhaled and fire danced forth from the embers. With better light, I searched the ground for even a hint of a footstep but found nothing. I hated myself for what I did next, but I leaned forward and plucked a hair from the crown of her head. It was base, but the most basic things could be and often were the strongest. I wrapped the maple-syrup-colored strand around another leaf of sage. There was a pulse, short, faint, but present. Finally, a good sign.

When I heard a rustling behind me, I spun. I did not recognize the human face of the werewolf who came with a small bottle of water. He was young—a boy indeed—younger even than Micah. Milk-chocolate skin, close-cut hair, the bravado of a teenager trying to be a man, and dark eyes filled with something I didn't want to identify. I just nodded my thanks and mutely took the water from him.

Alone at last with Zoe, I laid out a circle. I turned to face east, using dead reckoning. The salt continued as I moved clockwise; the line was uneven, but it would serve. Even if it wasn't as pristine as I would have liked, an invisible barrier sprang into place, and the rest of the world went mute. I repeated the motion with the sage leaf wrapped in Zoe's hair before I went to her body. As soon as the leaf touched her head, it smoldered. Another good sign.

Next I dropped the sage, took one clove of garlic, and crushed it crudely with my thumb. I smeared the rough paste over her wound, and the flesh sizzled in response. Without pausing, I brought the knot of ginger to her nose and snapped it. Her body twisted. It wasn't much compared to the corpse-like stillness of a moment ago, but it was something. I uncapped the water and poured a little over her wound and then some over her eyes and the space between her breasts. I had begun chanting, "*Ana El Na*," my voice in Hebrew closer to a baritone than my natural tenor. Strands of skin seemed to stretch forth, eager to find their opposite on the other side of the gash. Her body was willing, and the spirit would be bound in place by the circle. I was off to a solid start.

I removed the rosemary next and replaced the formal liturgy with a simple request, again delivered in Hebrew. I pressed the sprig first to her lips, then mine, then laid it across her forehead. There was greater distance now, even with the circle in place, and although I was aware of my voice as it continued chanting, the request repeating, my awareness was not of my body anymore. The colors of the small fire bled away, fading into grays and darker reds—a wolf's view of the world—and my neck burned, aching, sharp fangs pressing too deep, too close to my jugular vein. The pleasure blooming around my perineum vanished and became ice as I struggled for breath.

This is what Zoe had known, what her world had been before she retreated into herself. The cold, the darkness—it was how the world still was for her, even as the wound knit itself together. Fear nearly blotted out everything, and I had to pull my consciousness to myself again so as to not stammer, to not let myself become overwhelmed by her reality. Being in a mind not your own was never an easy thing. Gradually I poured some of myself back into her, maintaining a fragile silver strand of thought, a bridge between us.

How long it took for me to reestablish a connection with her, I couldn't say. In a working, time truly is subjective. Through Zoe's senses I was aware of the monotone chanting of a voice—my voice. Still, there was a rhythm to my recitation, a heartbeat at a human's pace. Through her eyes, colors bled back into the world. It seemed like an eternity before I saw the otherworldly green glow that suffused the eyes of my own body. With the return of green, I pulled some of my consciousness back into myself. She was seeing the world as a human, an important step. An animal of impulse and instinct, the wolf was afraid, but the human could see past fear, past pain, and perhaps even see its way to forgiveness and understanding.

Then there was a first spasm that began at her toes, a convulsion that rocked her and traveled quickly through her body. My voice climbed, the pace of the chant increasing, and I pulled at the pain— pain that had been hers but was now ours. The ache that I had mirrored when I first linked with Zoe now blossomed into a cactus flower of agony. I knew I was crying, but my voice remained steady, sure of itself. My grandmother had been very thorough in my training. Another spasm rocked through Zoe's body, and our breaths synchronized as we gasped together. Shared breath, even across this distance—there was power in such things. I rooted myself as best I could and prepared for the final part of the ritual.

I whispered in Yiddish now of human things, of things that the wolf couldn't know or appreciate. As I did this, the last part of my link with her faded and the gossamer thread of power dissolved into nothingness. Her eyes blinked rapidly, and she managed to turn over before vomiting whatever she might have eaten. I uttered a few last syllables, and the sounds of the pack, of the larger fire, came cascading down to both of us. I pulled myself to my feet and, on pins and needles, made my way to the salt line and slashed my foot across it. The barrier tumbled down, and I fell to the earth, the power gathered in the circle no longer able to support my body. As I went through my own convulsions, power leaving me, Zoe got to her feet. I was aware of rustling, someone rushing toward her, her name called out in a man's soft voice.

It was followed by the sounds of bodies crashing against each other, of lips meeting, and a rush of words I couldn't pay attention to. I was focused on getting my breath back in order, on pulling myself together. By the time I was able to sit up, Micah and Zoe must have left; I didn't see them or hear them. I was on my own in a natural clearing in a national park, less than twenty feet from where a werewolf pack waited.

With what little semblance of strength I had back in my limbs, I pushed myself upright and dumped all my supplies back into my bag in a haphazard manner. I didn't have the energy for the meticulous care I had used to pack them earlier in the night. A last extension of power, and the small flame died. When I turned, I was shocked to see an older woman, again someone whose human face I didn't know. I squinted behind my glasses, not sure if I saw actual strands of white in her hair or if it was a trick of the light.

"You brought my grand-pup back," she said, a direct Midwesterner. Raised in the heartland, I thought. She was sure of herself, as only a werewolf matriarch could be. I knew that if she wished me harm, I wouldn't be able to defend myself, but her smile was genuine. "Thank you. My family owes you, and Alpha Erik was guided well in finding you."

I nodded but didn't attempt to use my voice. I knew better than to refuse thanks.

Reentering the main site, I paused in front of the bigger fire and instinct guided my hand. I reached my fingers toward it and drew some of the blaze to myself. I savored its heat, its glowing heart. The remnants of fear, of raging ice, melted, and I was more fully human. I took my time, careful not to drink too deeply or quickly.

"You know, they're looking at you," Erik said. I knew his mouth was only inches from my ear.

"Let them look," I said as I stepped closer to the fire and rolled my shoulders back. A tongue of flame slithered out and over my fingers. I drew my hand back as the fire serpent rushed along my palm. I kept it away from the sleeve of the ancient shirt, not trusting my control that far yet. The last thing I needed was to be shirtless in front of werewolves. My attention was fully on the flame as it quivered, sputtered, and shifted to become the green witch's fire. I turned to face Erik and brought my palm to my mouth as I did so. The spark jumped into my mouth and raced over my tongue and down my throat in an instant. It was more of a show than I needed, but *I* was wearing the predator's smile at this point. Erik kept statue still and only quirked his left brow at my display.

"It's not prudent to keep them afraid, Jakob. After all…."

"Erik, let's not right now."

"Then when?"

"How about after I find a way to undo what was forced on me?"

"You can't put this—us—off forever."

"Watch me try."

"Damn your stubborn pride."

"Funny, I was thinking the same thing about you. Now, let's talk my fee. $850."

"$375," he countered, and then we haggled in earnest. It was a game of inches, not yards. Living in Ohio, eventually you used football metaphors. Without the flame I had just literally consumed, I would have tired before I got to a figure I was comfortable with. When we settled on $600 and a recipe for a tres leches cake, I was beginning to fade. We shook, and I watched as his hand engulfed mine. My eyes closed and I remembered how that hand had felt on me as it had moved from my neck, over my shoulders, and down my spine. I pulled my hand back and almost stumbled away.

"You're remembering too, aren't you?" he asked as he stepped toward me. His arousal was quite evident.

"Stop it," I stated firmly, my eyes narrowing. I drew on the last of my reserves and willed his mouth closed. Erik struggled briefly, but nodded and made a sweeping gesture with his hand. I knew he hadn't struggled as hard as he might have, but I would take whatever small victories whenever possible. I headed back down the path I had used to come to the clearing, or thought I had. When I felt a hand on my shoulder, I hated myself for giving in to spite and burning my little bit of energy the way I had. Alicia stepped in front of me and made a motion with her head. "This way," she said, and I mutely followed. I tried to stay three steps behind her, and she moved slower this time. It was easier, as I had some vague memory, and she stopped when I stumbled on the path.

"You know, brujo," she said as we rejoined the main trail, not looking over her shoulder as she continued to lead me, "there are times when I almost like you." My foot caught on a root and I went sprawling, my reusable bag and the components for my working flying all over the ground. I managed to twist and avoid a face-plant, but I knew I'd have a bruise for the next couple of days. "Especially when you go and do something like that." Her voice was warmer now, and I looked up. She was grinning down at me, holding my glasses in her hand. I checked to make sure neither the frames nor lenses were broken before I slid them back on my nose.

"You almost like me?" I parroted as I pulled myself up.

"It shouldn't be that surprising," Alicia continued as she stooped and dug around for some of my spilled supplies. "You keep Erik on his toes. Makes my job as his second much easier. It helps stop him from getting too cocky. You also drive a hard bargain. It's not every day I have to give up one of my *abuelita*'s recipes. I respect that."

"Sorry," I said as I grabbed what I thought was sage and shoved it back into my bag. "I'm still getting used to the fact that you almost like me."

"I didn't say that, witch boy. I said there are times when I almost like you. There are other times when you're too much like Erik. Both of you have more pride than common sense, and it's exhausting."

"That's still something of a seismic shift," I said, finding the container of salt, the last of the spilled items. I didn't bother dusting myself off. I needed to both do a load of laundry and take a shower anyway.

"Out of all the mates," she said and raised a hand, silencing my objection before it could escape, "Erik could have been made for, we were lucky with you."

"You should know how I feel about that, Alicia."

"You've never told me why it is, though. What is it you have against us anyway? Are we too animalistic for you? Too far from human?"

"Nothing like that. I've just never liked feeling like a puppet. I'm my own person, not fate's tool," I said. Silence hung between us for a long moment before she turned and continued down the main trail. I followed again, and when we reached the parking area, she stopped. As I stepped toward my sedan, I ignored the distinct sounds of bones snapping, reshaping themselves, and pants of breath that became less human with each passing second. If I didn't see the transformation, I reasoned to myself, there would be less of a pull on me. As it was, feeling the faint flow of magic was nearly intoxicating. I kept my eyes on the ignition as I inserted the key and spurred my ancient sedan to life. More than anything, I needed a hot shower and an even hotter cup of coffee.

CHAPTER 4

AFTER A shower that oscillated between daggers of ice and rivers of liquid magma, I had enough time to grab coffee from my favorite drive-thru and get to Siren's Sweets. It wasn't that I didn't trust Cara to have coffee, but the stuff that bubbled in the small pot in the back of the bakery could only be considered coffee in the most lenient of all terms. I opened the steel door at the top of the three brick stairs. The small entryway at the back of the shop was dark, but ahead of me and to the right, I saw light coming from Cara's office.

Cara's head was bent over, fiery hair pulled into a tight braid, and she was jotting something in her particular chicken scratch as I finished tying my apron. Her handwriting was indecipherable, but her sketches could be hung in any art museum. It was a puzzling contradiction and very much part of Cara's character. Although shorter than most, she had a presence that dominated any room she walked into and a voice that carried no matter the circumstances.

I lifted my glasses from my nose and squinted at her hieroglyphics.

"You know, if you invested in a pair of bifocals…," she said. I knew she still hadn't looked up from her sketch pad.

"I wouldn't need them if you used more than a square inch when you wrote," I fired back. She shrugged, her gaze still on the piece of paper before her.

"Would you mind handling the Lims when they come in? I'm debating whether we should take this order." Cara lifted her head and made a motion to her sketch.

"I don't mind. What was the request?"

"A five-tier hanging chandelier cake with a white-chocolate ganache and edible gold."

I hissed as I went to the tablet I kept near my work station in the industrial kitchen and pulled up the emails related to the Lim account. "Is it just me or does that scream bridezilla?" I asked.

"I've trained you well," Cara said. This was followed by the distinct sound of her teeth worrying the end of her pencil. It was better not to disturb her. She would be lost to her thoughts until she made a decision. The emails for the Lim wedding were relatively uncomplicated. They had asked for wedding cupcakes and indicated that the groom-to-be had a nut allergy. An easier couple to deal with, barring any in-law drama. As soon as the tablet was down, I weighed, portioned, and occasionally sampled the ingredients for the different cupcake batters we offered. It didn't take long, and once they were in the oven, I made the cookie doughs for the day, starting with double chocolate chip, cinnamon sugar, and ginger—traditional favorites. Then came the lemon bars, and I took out the shortbread crusts I had prepared after the front of house had closed the evening before.

As I removed the cupcakes from the oven and put them in the refrigerator, Cara's distinctive staccato cursing echoed through the kitchen. She was just getting started and I washed my hands as quickly as I dared. I headed into her office to find sheets of paper littering the floor and Cara pacing, pantherlike. She swore, turning on her heel, and begin a new litany of swearing. She gesticulated as she turned and her profanity reached a new high. I didn't think I had ever heard some of the combinations she used.

"Which client?" I asked when it seemed the swearing reached a nadir.

"The Michaelson account," she spat.

"I thought they had settled on a traditional white cake, vanilla fondant, and edible orchids?"

"They had, but—"

"But what?" I winced in preparation.

"Now they want to change to a pink-champagne cake with Tahitian vanilla fondant. *Tahitian* vanilla. Someone has been watching too fucking much Food Network. Like they would be able to taste the difference in a goddamn fondant." Cara's voice was arctic. The fine lines around her mouth and eyes were highly visible, and she looked every inch the predator. That was never a good sign, and I knew better than to do anything to add to the coming tempest, so I stood back and let her rant. Sometimes it was the only sane thing to do.

She swore, creatively and fluently, for at least two more minutes. Eventually she stopped, inhaled deeply, and looked at me. My face was impassive. "This," she made a gesture with her hand, "is why I promoted you."

"You've reminded me of that at least once a day since you made that decision, Cara," I replied.

"Well, that and you've always pronounced my name correctly. You've never tried to rhyme Cara with carrot."

"Thanks. Still, are they worth getting upset about?"

Cara made a dismissive gesture with her hand as she turned toward her desk and sat at her laptop. Her fingers were a blur as she went through invoices and receipts. When I started at Siren's Sweets, Cara did everything by longhand. I had helped talk her out of the dark ages and into investing in paperless technologies. She still used paper and pencil for her initial work, but digital records saved her time and space, as much as she was loath to admit it. She swore under her breath as she pulled up the Michaelson emails.

"Is it within the time limit to request a change on that scale?" I asked.

"It is, but I've already ordered all the supplies for a white cake," she replied. "If I had my way—" She cut herself off, growling, and I saw murder in her eyes.

"Cara, if you had it your way, clients would be signing in their blood at midnight at a crossroads," I said. She looked up, and I was thankful to have developed an immunity to her particularly blistering gazes. I tapped my index and middle fingers on my hips, and my face remained calm.

"You say that like there's something wrong with the old ways of doing business," she said. I couldn't tell if she was joking or not, but her anger seemed less intense. I'd take my win. The worst had passed.

"You'd lose more customers that way, Cara. If we want to continue getting the great reviews and be nominated for city's best for a third year in a row…." I trailed off. She grumbled and pulled out a pad of paper and a much-gnawed-upon pencil. She was jotting figures, and I turned to leave the office.

"Write them," Cara said, and I turned again to see her, pencil still flying over the pad, "and the Johnsons too."

"Were they the chandelier cake?" I asked.

"Yes," Cara answered.

"Your decision?"

"We'll take it," she said. I nodded and closed the door to the office. I might have been hired for my baking skills, but I was more often a diplomat, at least with some of the customers. I found my tablet again and modified the form emails I had saved, and then I was back in the kitchen, focused on the world of cakes.

When we opened to the general public at 11:00 a.m., we had our first sets of brownies, cookies, cupcakes, and cake slices arranged neatly in the window. There wasn't a line beating down the door, but for the first two hours, there was a steady stream of customers. I manned the counter, as I hadn't yet talked Cara into hiring a dedicated front-of-house employee. For Cara, the soul of Siren's Sweets would always be the custom orders and wedding cakes, but we had expanded beyond that, and I was a little proud of everything I had poured into the business.

The Lims arrived for their tasting promptly at 1:15 p.m., and when they did, we were already out of lemon bars. I had learned to recognize brides-to-be, and the woman definitely had that aura. She was around my height, and her hair was piled into a loose bun. She wore khaki slacks, a black peacoat, and a nude lipstick that didn't quite match her skin tone, though she pulled it off with an easy confidence. The man—well, I hated the fact that he was straight. He was taller than his fiancée by at least three inches, had closely cropped jet-black hair, and his lips were turned up in a smile that could have let him get away with murder.

I tried to remain professional and offered a business smile as I greeted them. "Welcome to Siren's Sweets. You must be Nicole Kim and Victor Lim." I extended my hand. Nicole laughed, and it reminded me of bells and tinkling glass. Of course she would have an excellent laugh, I thought to myself. She had an excellent laugh, a sense of style that would put her on the cover of any fashion magazine, and a gorgeous fiancé. The universe was just that stacked in her favor.

"I am Nicole Kim," she said, smiling broadly as she shook my hand, "but this isn't Victor."

"I'm Nathan." He extended his own hand, his voice low but nowhere near as commanding or deep as Erik's. I shook Nathan's hand and my confusion must have been evident. "I'm her brother," he continued, "and official cake co-taster while Victor is in Melbourne for a conference on international trade law."

I felt my business smile shift to something more genuine and I let my eyes dart down to the fingers of his left hand for a split second. I didn't see anything, but I knew better than to make assumptions.

"Sorry," I apologized and guided them to a table.

"We'll see if you need to make an apology after we've tried some of your cupcakes," Nicole said. She turned and I saw the distinct Louboutin sole, a contrast to the eggshell-and-azure checkered tile. By the tone of her voice, I could instantly tell it wasn't a threat. I let out an audible sigh of relief, and Nathan groaned.

"If you keep giving her reactions like that, she'll be impossible to live with. Don't encourage her," he said.

"You're just jealous that he likes me more than you," she said as she turned her head toward her brother and stuck out her tongue.

"What are you, seven years old?" Nathan asked.

"Takes a seven-year-old to know a seven-year-old," Nicole fired back.

I laughed at their easy back-and-forth and wondered if they had fought like this all their lives. Then they stopped bickering with each other and focused on me. I raised my hands in surrender. "Don't drag me into this," I objected. Outside the window of the bakery, a hearse passed by. Not the first time I had seen such an ominous omen, but Nathan and Nicole hadn't seen it, and I wasn't going to bring it up to them.

"Too late," Nicole said. I had the feeling that arguing with her would be like arguing with Cara—futile at best and an exercise in madness at the worst. I retreated into the kitchen to get their cupcakes from the fridge. Cara was feverishly working on something, swearing under her breath. Knowing we had customers kept her quiet—at least it did most of the time. When I returned to their table, Nathan and Nicole were speaking to each other in a language I couldn't identify. They were jumping over each other verbally, interjecting frequently. It was obvious this was something they had done before, would continue doing long after they left.

"Here"—I motioned to the row of cupcakes—"are the flavors you mentioned you were interested in. You said you wanted two different cupcake flavors, right?" She nodded and I continued. "Have you thought about what frosting or frostings you might like?"

"We're going to wait on the frosting until we know what cupcakes we want. As Victor would say, 'You need a solid foundation before you think about a roof,'" Nicole said, her voice dropping three octaves as she quoted her fiancé. My eyebrows shot up, and she laughed her high, seraphic laugh again on seeing my facial expression.

"If you think that's good, you should hear her imitate our auntie Irene," Nathan said.

"I'm here to eat cakes, not be your entertainment," Nicole responded, her accent pure Long Island. I laughed and she smiled widely. Then she got to the business at hand—she took a cupcake and ripped it down the middle. Crumbs spilled everywhere and Nathan rolled his eyes. Having three myself, I knew what it was to be frustrated by a sister.

"Hush up, you," Nicole said as she passed him the smaller half of the cupcake.

"Did I say anything?" Nathan asked.

"No, but I can feel you thinking it, and the last thing I need right now is Mom in the room. You already know how she feels about this," Nicole replied. Her tone was slightly sour, and for the first time since she walked in, her expression bordered on something hostile, something bitter, and I felt the weight of words unsaid. I didn't pry. I wasn't paid to be a family therapist, and I admired Cara's policy on dealing with controlling parents. Unless the parents were the ones paying her, Cara wouldn't answer to them. Even if they were paying, Cara would demonstrate rare diplomatic skills and try to get the parents and children to compromise. Of course, she'd swear a blue streak once everyone but me was out of earshot.

"She'll get used to it eventually," Nathan consoled. He reached out and wrapped his sister's hand in his. I wondered how that would feel, despite having his hand around mine earlier. They tasted in silence for a while, but as they came to the black velvet cupcake, both Nicole and Nathan closed their eyes.

"This is one of the house specialties. I would give you the recipe, but I would have to kill you," I informed them in an attempt to bring back the easier humor.

"What if I sold you my brother? He's a good bitch, and his kidneys are probably worth a small fortune on the black market," Nicole offered, a smile back on her lips.

"I might just sell myself for that recipe," Nathan countered, and I relaxed.

"Sorry, we don't accept humans as payment," I said, keeping a straight face. It was Nathan's turn to laugh. Like his sister's, his laugh had an infectious quality, but it wasn't bell clear.

"Mom will likely hate this, but we have to go with these," Nicole said. She had whipped out her phone and was snapping photos, doubtless sending them to Victor.

"If you would like to reschedule so your fiancé and your mother could come—" I said.

"I know Victor will love this, but it's just that—" She bit her lip. "Mom is a very conservative born-again Christian. Anything that isn't all white at a wedding is bad luck," Nicole said, "and as I'm marrying a third-generation Chinese American instead of a nice Korean boy...."

"Please." I raised my hands. "You've said enough."

"I don't know if she has," Nathan interjected. "Our mother isn't the worst of our relatives, though, just the most vocal. For worst, I think that has to be our uncle Kevin."

"Uncle Kevin just loves to complain for the sport of complaining. The real worst is Uncle Doug," Nicole countered. The two went through different relatives—at least I guessed they were relatives—and I leaned back and let them discuss in peace. There was one moment when I caught Nathan's eyes, and he smiled at me. I blushed and averted my gaze. I was not going to be accused of unprofessionalism if I could help it.

"Sorry about that," Nathan said.

"No need. Family can be intense," I said.

"Do you also come from a family where it's not a holiday until there are at least two all-out fights before the table's set?" he asked, leaning forward, a smile on his lips.

"Cool your jets, Nathan, you can flirt with him later. We need to decide which of the white-colored cakes I'm going with," Nicole interjected. My own blush returned in force, and I saw the faintest hint on Nathan's cheeks.

"You're seriously adorable, but where would you point me in terms of cake?" Nicole's focus was on me now. I stumbled for a second and then inhaled deeply and gave her options, including my favorite (white chocolate), something I thought her mother would approve of (vanilla), and something that might be a compromise (champagne). She turned to Nathan and asked a question in the same language they had been using earlier. He replied at length, and she nodded. She turned back to me and asked, "Of those three, which will be the best complement for black velvet?"

"Either the champagne or white chocolate. Black velvet is a denser cake, so you're going to need something lighter but with a hint of a kick or a flavor that will be able to stand up to it, match it, and go blow for blow," I said. I knew I was blushing, and I hadn't meant it to sound like it had. Nathan was also blushing, and Nicole laughed again. It echoed in the otherwise-empty front of house.

"You," Nicole said, looking directly at me, "have a wicked mind. I'm in favor of something that's going to be able to take those blows." I felt my blush deepen, and I silently offered a prayer that she wouldn't tease me anymore. Hashem wouldn't be that merciful with me. "Let's talk frosting." Nicole was willing to change the subject, and I went with it. For the next ten minutes, we discussed flavor and designs. She agreed to come back in about three weeks—with Victor this time—to make her final decisions for frostings as well as to make the first deposit. As she and Nathan stood to get going, a thought rushed through my mind.

Despite the numerous hours I had spent reading over my family's grimoire, I had found no way to break my bond with Erik. Perhaps if there were someone else in my life, if Erik saw me trying with another person, he would understand that we weren't meant for anything. He might drop the whole "mate" talk. Our one-night stand should have remained just that—one night, nothing more than a mistake fueled by lust.

"I don't suppose you'd be up to grab a drink sometime?" I asked Nathan, feeling my cheeks go even deeper crimson.

"How about a full dinner?" Nathan pulled a business card from his pocket and passed it to me with a wink.

"Christ, Nathan," Nicole said, "take it easy with the baker."

"Something tells me Jakob doesn't like it easy," Nathan said, wiggling his eyebrows. I didn't know how deep my blush had gotten, but it felt liked it reached my bones. They exited Siren's Sweets, chatting with each other, and I wiped at the table, half humming an old Polish folk song. I felt ice run up my spine and I spun with one hand on the mezuzah that hung from a silver chain around my neck. I had forgotten to grab it last night when I went to help Micah and Zoe, but that had been an exception. Across the street, I saw the stern face of one of Erik's wolves—the teenage boy who had brought me the bottle of water.

If looks could kill, I would be a dead man four times over.

CHAPTER 5

"PLEASE DON'T say anything about this," I begged for what had to be the third or fourth time.

"Alpha Erik will kill him for this," Terence (his name, apparently) spat at me over a pumpkin spice latte. I was more surprised that I had convinced him to talk to me than by his choice of drink. I sipped a pumpkin spice chai as the teenaged werewolf continued to rant. We were at a coffee shop three blocks down from Siren's. It was a corporate chain—a few tables, some chairs that didn't match the ultramodern décor to give an illusion of authenticity, and a stripped-down soundtrack I had heard in almost every coffee shop like it.

"How much has your alpha told you?" I brought my chai to my lips.

"The pack knows you're marked as his mate. You are his," Terence answered. Venom filled his voice. There was hurt in it. I didn't need magic to know that Terence was crushing on Erik, badly.

"Just how old are you?" I asked.

"You should know as—" Terence stopped when he saw me rolling my eyes. I saw his nostrils flare in anger, and I put down my mug.

"The number of things I don't know about your group outweighs the things I do, by a lot," I said.

"Alpha Erik—"

"Terence," I interjected, "what's around us? What do you smell? What do you see?"

He looked puzzled but answered, "Humans, everywhere."

"Right. We're on their turf, so let's use language that won't make us stand out too much."

"Why do you bother?" the kid asked, clearly puzzled.

"I'm closer to this than not," I answered, "and what are you doing in the middle of downtown Cleveland on a Thursday?"

The teen sipped his drink and took his time, and when he finally put it down, he crossed his arms over his chest. He looked even younger in such a pose. The faintest hint of a mustache shadow on his upper lip only added to his youthful appearance, as did the buzzcut. I prayed the staff of the coffee shop wasn't paying too much attention. While we weren't the only patrons, it was a near thing. Three tables over, there was a young woman, headphones over her ears, her focus on her tablet, and at a booth in the corner, there was an elderly couple, both past the age of retirement, holding each other's hands and nursing nearly empty mugs. The teen didn't seem interested in answering my question, and I silently asked G-d for patience.

"I don't know what, if anything, Erik has told you," I said.

"I already said what's he's told us. He's said you're his." He caught himself, inhaled, and said, "Just that you're his. I don't see why he's proud of it. You turn your nose up at us."

Apparently my prayers were not going to be answered. Was there anything I could say to make him understand? He was young and angry that an outsider had come into his pack, and he wanted Erik. He wanted to be Erik's. I would try to be patient, to be kind.

"I don't hate you. I try not to hate. I've lived most of my life with some sort of hatred over my shoulder," I explained.

The kid turned his head slightly and I took the mezuzah from beneath my shirt and showed it on the thin chain. He continued to look puzzled and his eyes asked a silent question. "Some hate me because I'm Jewish, some because I'm Polish, others because I'm gay. Take your pick, it's easy to hate me," I said.

"Is that why you want so little to do with us? Because you think we'll hate you?" he asked.

"The night Erik and I met—" I said, searching for the right words. "—he thought I felt things. I didn't... *know* what was happening. When we were together, I should have picked up on the clues, should have known what was going on. No one's ever going to accuse me of brilliance," I said and smiled, "and then Erik, well, he made me a part of your group without me really understanding what that meant. I joined without knowing what that would entail, and I should have known, should have some *real* choice." I sipped my chai again.

"I don't understand why he chose you." There was pain in those words, honest and true. That was pain I could relate to.

"He said he liked the way I smelled and that I wouldn't smell the same to another member of your group. More than that, you'd have to ask him." I raised a single shoulder.

"You've tried telling him that you should have known more before he—" Terence stalled.

"Many times. I get the feeling that Erik only hears what he wants to hear, at least most of the time. You'd know better than I would."

Terence sank back in his chair and worried his bottom lip.

"Terence, you never answered me when I asked how old you were," I reminded him.

"I'm—I'm above the age of consent," he sputtered, blushing deeply.

"Seventeen?" I guessed, noticing the facial hair that really hadn't come in yet, and two zits on his left cheek, and his telling choice of words. Apparently, the legendary healing of lycanthropes didn't cover teenage skin care. That would be going in the family grimoire.

"How did you—are you—" He was stumbling again, searching for words. I allowed myself a small laugh, and the blush on his cheeks deepened.

"It's nothing like what you think. I was seventeen once too, and I remember my first crush. Erik is a far better choice," I said.

"It's not a crush." He pouted and looked younger than the age he had claimed. "I've had those, and what I have for Erik... it's real."

"Did I say a crush couldn't be real or serious?"

He looked at me for a long second, looking puzzled. I brought my chai to my lips again and breathed on it, to heat it rather than cool it. A small magic, one that required no great effort. I looked up and really saw Terence—his resentment of what I was, his hurt, and his confusion. I saw what he wouldn't let himself say out loud, a question everyone who gets their heart broken asks at least once—*Why wasn't I enough?*

"Ki—Terence," I caught myself. "I *know* what you're feeling is real and it's probably all you're thinking about," I said. I saw the beginning of an objection, and I raised a single hand. He paused, and I was shocked for a split second that he had actually followed a direction given by someone who had no real authority. "All emotions are real, and crushes or infatuation—they can be realer than most. I don't know exactly what you feel for Erik because I'm not you. Whatever it is, as much as I might dislike him for what he did to me, I've seen the way Erik is with your group. He's a good leader, he's handsome—" Terence blushed again. The kid really was a teenager. "—so I get it, at least on some level.

"I'm many things, Terence, but I'm not a liar. Someone like me, others who do what I do, we can't afford lies," I continued. He looked puzzled and I knew then that I was the first witch Terence had met, but I didn't have time to explain the many aspects of being a witch to him. "I get being attracted to Erik. In addition to everything else, he's got an easy confidence most only aspire to. Your crush on him is better than my crush on Devendra Joti."

"Devendra…." Terence struggled with the name and then finished his latte.

"The captain of my high school soccer team. Willing to kiss a boy behind the bleachers if he thought no one would hear about it, but if I so much as looked at him wrong in public…." I trailed off. High school had been four years I would rather not repeat, but for Terence, I was willing to relive a small part of it.

"At least he kissed you," Terence whined.

"Erik has a good reason why he won't kiss you," I said.

"Why?"

"You already told me," I said, my words weighed down by life experience.

"I did?"

"You're seventeen. Erik is a little over twice your age. That's a huge difference, especially considering you haven't finished your senior year of high school," I said. Terence sputtered again.

"You're not really part of my group. You don't know anything about how we live," he countered.

"In your group, are eighteen-year age gaps common?" I asked. Terence balled his fists and scuffed a sneaker on the café's parquet flooring.

"They're not unheard of," he said eventually.

"Nor are they among broader society," I offered, "but eighteen years is a lot of knowledge and experience, especially now. My great-grandfather, *alav hashalom,* was a father at your age and holding a full-time job. Granted, that was over a hundred years ago, and before he came to America."

"What did you just say?"

"My great-grandfather was an immigrant?"

"No, those words, they weren't—" His brows knit as he hunted for what he wanted to say. "What language were they?"

"Hebrew. Loosely translated it's 'may he rest in peace,'" I said.

He nodded and I touched the small mezuzah around my neck, my lips moving in silent prayer. The silence between us now was no longer hostile. Some of what I said was apparently settling in. In the window facing the street, leaves fell from a nearby tree—dark brown and pale gold.

"You're still not right for him," Terence said.

"I agree."

"He's too good for you," he tried again. How far would this kid go in trying to get a rise out of me?

"That's subjective. If we both agree I'm not right for him, then why shouldn't I be allowed to flirt with who I want?" I arched a brow.

"If you are—why do you...?" He was hunting for words again, and I let him take his time. Cara would be continuing to design and today was a short day for front of house anyway.

"What are you trying to ask, Terence?"

"Why you're not more interested. You said he was a good leader and—" His blush returned. Seeing something of myself in him, I decided to spare the kid.

"Besides, the night when... well, besides that night and the emergencies I've been called to assist with, he's made no attempt to know me. He doesn't know anything about me and seems happy with it. He's content to trust everything to 'fate'"—I made big air quotes—"and people like me, we can fight that. Right now, you know more about me than he does."

"I do?"

"You know the name of my first kiss and that my great-grandfather came over from the Old World," I said.

Terence sank back in his chair again, and I took him in. Someday, he'd be a very handsome man. He still had a lot of growing to do and much still to learn about being a man... and a wolf, I guessed.

"You also know I like pumpkin spice chai, and you've seen where I work. Erik knows I'm a baker, but he still hasn't asked the name of my shop," I said. "Speaking of, how did you find Siren's?"

"I wasn't looking for you, if that's what you're thinking."

"Not what I asked."

Terence sighed, all teenage melodrama for a second. "I didn't feel like staying for Civics," he said, cheeks rosy. "You're not going to tell Erik that I skipped?"

"I won't say anything about you playing hooky, just don't go telling Erik about Nathan the first chance you get?" I offered and extended my right hand. Terence thought for a while, then his palm shot out. We shook quickly. A small amount of progress. He pulled back and continued his story.

"I mean, how is anything from Civics going to be useful for what I want to do?" he asked. I remembered that there were certain high school classes I hadn't thought I'd need, like calculus. I used algebra and geometry on a daily basis, but I couldn't think of the last time I had taken a derivative or used the chain rule. I found myself agreeing with Terence. Depending on what he wanted to do, he might never need Civics.

"I snuck out and decided to find a place to grab a bite. Siren's has good reviews and was an easy run. I figured I'd get back for woodshop. I didn't expect...." He looked at the table between us.

"You like woodshop?" I asked.

"It's something real, something solid. I want to be a carpenter like—" Again his dark eyes flicked down.

"Is Erik the only reason you like woodworking?"

"No," Terence objected. The young woman finally looked up from her tablet and glared at us. Terence squirmed in his seat a little.

"I don't doubt you, Terence," I said, my voice lower, carefully neutral. "Just curious."

"I really do want to be a carpenter, though. Our group has a well-known shop. It's good money, and it's something people can reach out and touch. When I finish working, I want to be able to touch what I've been working on all day," Terence said.

"I get it," I said, smiling. "Pastries and cakes might not be as enduring as woodwork, but they're still tangible. Lots of people take pictures of the things I make, and if heaven wills, they'll remember those cakes for decades to come."

"I hadn't thought about it like that." He grinned briefly. There was an almost-companionable silence between the two of us, something I doubted was possible when I rushed to meet him outside of Siren's. He had been all anger and accusation then, with the faintest hint of jealousy, but I had managed to talk him down. The overpriced drinks might have helped, but I would take the win.

When I stood, so did Terence.

"Come on, I'll drive you back to your school," I offered. Despite being twelve years younger, he had a comfortable two or three inches of height on me. He turned his head so we could lock eyes.

"I can get back on my own."

"I know you can, Terence," I said.

"T. My friends call me T," he said. I stumbled over a crack in the sidewalk. I caught myself but knew I looked far from graceful.

"I'm going to try to get you back so you can attend your shop class at least, T," I said with a shrug. Terence smiled, and I led the way to my Nissan. I wondered, if I were to become more a part of Terrence's pack, would this be my role? Talking to wolves too nervous or otherwise unable to talk to their alpha? I stopped that thought as I turned the key in the ignition. I didn't need to invite those thoughts in—not now.

CHAPTER 6

My FINGERS connected with the mezuzah on my doorjamb. I felt the rush of home roll through me, and I closed my eyes and relaxed for a moment. I opened the door, and the cat rushed toward me, wound itself around my legs, let out a plaintive meow, and then ran back inside. I followed it to its preferred seat on the old couch and scratched quickly behind its ears. My duty to the cat finished, I stepped out of my shoes and headed to the tall bookshelf that dominated the combined living and dining room.

As I had every night since my encounter with Erik, I went directly to the place of honor where my family's grimoire lay. As I touched it, I recited the prayer my babcia taught me. Like my grandmother before me, I hid the grimoire in plain sight. Even if someone found it and tried to read it, it was written in six different non-English languages and would need a cryptographer to decipher what it really was. I opened it and inhaled, bringing in the smell of old paper and countless hands across the generations.

The first time I held my family's grimoire, I was four. My grandmother's hands, as delicate as some of the paper in the book, guided my fingers over lines of crabbed writing. The letters sang beneath my fingertips and heat rushed up my arm. She had tested each of her children and grandchildren this way. I was the only one who felt it—the power flowing from the text—and a thread of light dangled from my finger as she pulled my hand from the book. That day was the first time I heard my grandmother swear, and it was one of the few times I could remember her doing so.

Even though she had left Poland with her parents when she was still young and her English only had the faintest hint of an accent, she always spoke either Polish or Yiddish at home. She didn't want those parts of herself to die.

"What do—" I had begun, my voice high and my Polish nowhere near as flawless as hers. My father had tried to expose us to as much of his mother's tongue as possible, but he preferred English. He said we weren't in the Old World, that he hadn't been born there. Later, in high school, he would push me toward Spanish or Mandarin. He even suggested Russian at one point. I remembered the look in my grandmother's eyes when he said that.

"Those are bad words. Cursed words. Do you know what cursed means?" she asked, her voice tempered with smoke and age.

"Cursed, like in the stories about witches?" I asked. I couldn't remember a night when my grandmother hadn't told me some bedtime story or other in Polish, normally ones that were so fantastic and dark they would have shamed the Brothers Grimm, not that I knew who they were at four. Each story she told me... it felt like a secret between the two of us, something no one else would know.

"Like in the stories I tell you," my babcia confirmed. Outside of the kitchen, I heard my uncle Noah and aunt Charlotte arguing with my father. I knew from the tone that it wasn't a serious argument. They'd all be smiling by its end.

I scrunched up my face and thought as hard as a four- or five-year-old could. My grandmother was fond of asking me something to make sure I really understood what she had said. If my dad saw her doing it, he'd roll his eyes and say, "*Mamo*, don't treat Jake like you treated us." But my father wasn't in the kitchen, so he couldn't object. I was on my babcia's lap—that was all that mattered. I was safe, warm, loved, and protected on her lap.

"Cursed," I said, "is being touched by bad magic?"

"Are you asking or telling me?"

"Telling."

"Then tell, don't ask."

"Cursed is having bad magic touch you, like when the prince was turned to a frog."

"My clever boy. Yes, that's a curse, and it's why you must be careful what you say."

"Why, Babcia?"

"Words have weight and power. If you say something and really mean it, then it changes things. Like how someone feels, or more," she said. I nodded, thinking I understood her; she didn't ask this time. It had been among the first lessons I got on the effects of magic, and would soon be followed by "an unprepared witch is a dead witch." Good lessons to learn young.

My family's grimoire had traveled across generations and countries. My grandmother had inherited the book from her maternal uncle, and he had received it from his maternal grandmother. The earliest author I found was from the 1620s, but they—I still wasn't sure who they were—had been a descendant of Judah Loew ben Bezalel, the rabbi of Prague who had awakened the Golem. There were instructions on how to do it, but as far as I knew, no one since Rabbi Judah had made the attempt.

There was no organization to the book. One page might have nineteenth-century Polish and the next would be written in seventeenth-century Aramaic. Most of my experience with the grimoire had been devoted to creating an index for it. It was an ongoing work, and I often lost track of where and when magical formulas occurred. Since Erik bit me, I had stopped and focused instead on how to unpartner myself from an alpha werewolf. Between my great-uncle's Polish and the Lithuanian of his grandmother, I had learned any number of protections and wards, but nothing about breaking ties. Of course, the fact that the book was written to prevent it from being easily understood didn't help.

When I was seven, I asked my grandmother why our ancestors hadn't been plainer in their writings. She sighed and said, "We are already hated for being Jews. If the book fell into the wrong hands and real magic was discovered, what would happen to us?" While she had been spared the horrors of the camps, not all of our family had been so lucky. I understood her fear.

"Doesn't the Torah say that witches are bad? That magic is bad?" I asked. It was a question I had been wrestling with for a little while. Hebrew school was teaching me that much, and it would later be my d'var Torah at my Bar Mitzvah.

"You always know how to ask hard questions, my clever boy," my grandmother said. I couldn't tell if she was complaining or praising me.

"I don't understand, Babcia," I said.

"I will tell you what my uncle told me. Magic is something we do. It is not what we are. I use magic to help others, for the community. Our tradition is one of wonder workers and sages. Is a prayer not a type of a spell?" she asked. I wrinkled my forehead, trying to think of an answer.

"A prayer asks, a spell does. That's not the same," I said.

"But if a prayer is answered, is that not magic?" She reached out to ruffle my hair and looked down at me, a smile on her lips. "In the book of Kings, when Hashem wouldn't answer Saul, what did Saul do?" my grandmother asked. I closed my eyes, remembering the illustrations in a book I had gotten for my birthday the year before. It was filled with stories from the Tanakh.

"He met a witch," I answered.

"He met a witch, and she helped him. She prepared for what was to come. Later, Jonah was found by the casting of lots. Is that not magic? Did Moses not pray and was Miriam not healed? The scripture guides us, but we have to understand the authors of the scripture."

"What are you saying, Babcia?"

"The hands that wrote our scripture were human. Yes, they felt and knew G-d, but theirs were human hands. Even in trying to understand the Divine, man is flawed." She had turned from me, and I knew this part of our conversation had ended. When my grandmother decided she was done with something, no one could change her mind. My father and his siblings remembered this from their childhoods and had learned to live with it.

Like my grandmother before me, I walked the tightrope between faith and the rich magicks that were part of our stories and traditions.

I turned to a page on which I saw Hebrew characters written to follow the rules of Polish grammar. I put my fingers to the text and let heat and light flow between myself and the book. The characters were uniformly warm and nothing sang. Magic was not guiding me to an answer, at least not directly. These pages had been written by my grandmother and were a reflection of the many trials our family had faced. Like me, she had done some indexing, but in over sixty years as the keeper of the grimoire, she hadn't finished.

I turned to one of the oldest pages. Writing in cramped Aramaic, the first author had been the most paranoid, and all their ciphers were nearly impossible to crack. Perhaps it was why no one in the family had tried to make a golem. We were all afraid that the first author had left something out or deliberately obscured some vital piece of information. Granted, writing about magic in seventeenth-century Prague was a risky undertaking, so the paranoia of the first author was understandable. What little I had been able to intuit from the first author was about the strength necessary to perform a "great working."

When I was thirteen, my grandmother had mentioned "great workings" and said that every witch had only one. They always knew the working when it was done and they felt it deeper than blood or bone. It was something a witch remembered, no matter what. I asked about hers. She sighed and put down the cleaver in her left hand.

"When I am ready to tell you, you will write mine in our book," she told me as she pushed the diced mushrooms to one side and reworked the dough of her pierogi.

"When will that be?" As soon as the question was out of my mouth, my hand moved to cover it, as if I could grab it back. My grandmother glared at me over her shoulder and I retreated, just a little.

"When I am ready to die, you will write for me," she said. I knew she would say no more. I had moved from my spot on the wall and begun mincing the sauerkraut so she could focus on the dough. We worked in silence next to each other, and my grandmother's presence gradually shifted from arctic to its more usual sunshine. I hadn't been aware of the door swinging open and my mother's measured footsteps.

"What's the occasion, Chava?" my mother asked.

"Dinner. That is occasion enough," my grandmother answered. I didn't need to look up to know my mother was rolling her eyes.

"Did Babcia put you up to this?" my mother asked me. The kitchen would always be my grandmother's. No matter how old she became, she ruled the kitchen. My mom had said once that she was uncomfortable with how much time my grandmother spent in the kitchen and that there was no need for an elaborate meal every night. My grandmother shrugged at that. The next night, there were mountains of *gołąbki* waiting when my mother returned from her shift as a nurse.

"No, Mom," I answered, only knowing I had used Polish when I looked up to see my grandmother's smile and my mother's exasperation.

"You two are impossible," my mother said as she marched out of the kitchen so she could change out of her scrubs and get ready for dinner. I had gone back to work on the pierogi, my grandmother and I moving in companionable silence. I didn't need to say anything; I knew where she would be, what she would need. It wasn't magic, but it was close. I felt my grandmother's right hand tremble as she pinched off the top of a pierogi. I covered her hand with mine to help steady her fingers.

A bright strobe flash made both my grandmother and me look up. My grandmother said, "Misiek, you took my picture without warning me?" My babcia had an unexplained aversion to being photographed. My father just crossed the kitchen and pressed a kiss to her forehead.

"That gets you out of nothing," she said, but it was clear some of the fight had left her voice.

"I know, but Jakob looked so handsome, and I had to take the photo." Even then, I was used to being my father's scapegoat and hearing his lies. I would never win best dressed or most handsome in the yearbook. I was shorter than most, rail thin, and wore thick glasses. I wasn't going to grace the cover of any romance novel, even if I hit the gym on a daily basis.

I trailed my fingers down the page of the grimoire and touched the photo my dad had taken. While not a photo album, my family's spell book held a few photos and illustrations. I felt the love of three generations in that photo. This love was power too—a magic all its own.

I put the spell book back on the shelf. Although I hadn't found a way to free myself from Erik, the picture had reminded me of family, of magic that required no words and no gift to access. I went to my freezer and took out pierogi, made by hand. While they would have been better fresh, these would keep my family with me, no matter that my parents were now living in Florida and my grandmother was buried in the Shaare Torah cemetery, over one hundred twenty miles from where I lived in Cleveland.

I thought of my family and of Nathan and Nicole. There were worse things to have in common than complicated families, I supposed.

CHAPTER 7

"I NORMALLY don't have to wait for two weeks before someone gives me a call, especially after I've suggested dinner," Nathan said as I arrived at the table and sat opposite him. The restaurant was set to emulate a Parisian café—dark red walls with racks supporting bottles of wine against the back, dim light with something vaguely classical piped in through the sound system, and a fireplace in one corner with real burning logs. This was the sort of place that was perfect for a first date, and I wondered how many first dates Nathan had taken there.

"Sorry, your sister isn't our only bride-to-be." I smiled.

"I didn't think you'd be that busy in November."

"Nicole's doing it right. She's tasting early and getting everything set up for May. But there are lots of couples who use the winter holidays as dates to get married. Even without weddings, we have panettones, fruitcakes, and gingerbread treats to take care of."

"People still order fruitcakes?" The grin on his face was wide and showed brilliant white teeth. It had been fifteen days since I met him, and in that time, my life had been free of werewolf-related drama. I thanked heaven for small miracles. I had debated warding Siren's itself—as I wouldn't always be able to catch a wolf near the bakery, like I had caught Terence—but how would I explain that to Cara? I doubted she'd like me putting up *mezuzot* everywhere.

"Cara's bringing them back. We've been voted best fruitcake in several online polls. Even if I knew all the steps to baking them, I wouldn't tell you, because if I did—"

"You'd have to kill me. Do you have designs on my life?" Nathan offered another winning smile.

"You don't need to worry—yet."

"You and your boss are both fond of your secrets."

"Cara's not my boss anymore—I'm her partner. Besides, if our recipes got out, we'd lose to the competition. We have to protect what's ours," I said. Even as I joked with him, I wasn't fully in the moment. On the drive over, I had heard on the radio that there had been another grave desecration—at Augudas Achim outside of Columbus. I hoped it was just an anti-Semitic incident and not the unliving damned hunting, feasting, growing in power.

"I get that. I remember when some of the senior partners at the law firm left without warning. I got my first gray hair that day." He grinned. I leaned closer as if to inspect for the offending follicle and Nathan laughed. A waiter approached, and before I had a chance to open my menu, Nathan had ordered us a bottle of wine from the Loire Valley. I wasn't a big fan of wine, and I hadn't drunk anything more than wine on the Sabbath since Erik bit me. I looked at Nathan.

"I thought we had agreed to go dutch?" I asked.

"The wine's my treat." He winked smoothly.

The waiter returned with our wine, and Nathan made a show of inspecting the bouquet and swishing it in his glass. He sipped it and then motioned to the waiter to fill my glass. A little heavy-handed, but still suave as anything.

"Do you have any dietary restrictions I should know about?" Nathan asked when the waiter left.

"When eating out, I keep vegetarian," I said, my eyes finally traveling over the menu and not seeing as many options as I would have liked.

"When I suggested—you should have said something." It almost sounded like an accusation. I managed to not roll my eyes and I was tempted to swat at him, but didn't want this date to be over so quickly. Long-term goals—the most important thing was that this might be a first meaningful step away from Erik, away from the world of magic I did my best to avoid.

"I'll manage, and I'm not going to stop you from ordering whatever you want," I said, trying to soothe him.

"Are you vegetarian, vegan, what?" Nathan asked. I wondered if he was going to ask how my food choices affected my work as a baker, but he didn't.

"I keep kosher—or try to. I fail from time to time, but eating vegetarian makes keeping kosher much easier," I said. Nathan looked puzzled for a moment, but then asked about the different rules of kosher and if all my family practiced. I explained what I could and how my babcia had two different refrigerators for most of her life, two sets of dishes, and two sets of silverware. Nathan had finished his first glass of wine and I still hadn't taken a sip of mine when I felt my phone vibrating. My smile vanished, as I *knew* who was calling me.

"Did I say something?" Nathan asked, and the puzzled look returned to his face.

"I'm... I... I have to take a call," I tried to explain as I stood and my phone continued to vibrate in my jacket pocket.

"Is it a baking emergency?" He might have been joking, but there was again the faintest hint of accusation in his voice.

I didn't answer and instead rushed out into the brisk evening. My lungs burned as I drew in that first deep breath of November air. Down the street I could see one of the other restaurants along the block putting Christmas lights on their awning.

As I pulled out my phone, my free hand traveled to a packet of iodized salt in my other pocket. I was prepared and thus wasn't a dead witch, at least today, but I grounded myself, my lips moving in silent invocation as I accepted the call.

"One of my pups tells me you have a human suitor." Erik's voice was clipped. I shivered and it was not due to the breeze.

"T?" I asked and winced. I should have used his full name. Why hadn't I used his full name?

"He asked you to use his nickname?" Erik's surprise warmed me.

"Not the—what did you do to the kid?" Why on earth was I protective of a werewolf who had opened by threatening me?

"Nothing."

"I'm surprised he kept his mouth shut as long as he did," I volunteered.

"Are you speaking ill of him?" Erik growled. Across unknown miles, I heard alpha authority in his voice and it was not a pleasant thing. I breathed deeply, taking in the smell of exhaust and late autumn, and then I pushed into the hasty grounding I had done, pulling on the earth and the salt in my pocket. The mezuzah on my neck burned and the silver chain sang silently. I had prepared well, but I would have killed in that second to be back in my kitchen at home, where I had layers of protections. Murphy's Law was a real thing, and it wanted to bite my flat Polish behind.

"No... I'm trying to say you may have used your authority in an inappropriate manner," I countered.

"If you knew anything about our ways, our culture, you'd know better than to lecture me on what is and is not appropriate for an alpha to do."

"If you knew or respected anything about me, you'd know how little I want anything to do with this," I all but yelled. A passing pedestrian shot me the evil eye, but it was mixed with morbid curiosity. Apparently I was his entertainment for the night.

"Mate," Erik said.

"For the love of heaven, how many times must I remind you what I am not? When will you listen and hear me?" I realized I had switched to Polish only after all the words were out of my mouth. I still thought in Polish from time to time, and I would speak it with my father and his siblings, but I hadn't needed to honestly rage in Polish in over half a decade—if you excused occasions on the interstate, which I did.

"You'll need to translate that, Jakob," he said. There was something new in his tone, but I couldn't quite identify it. I inhaled, tried to ground myself, exhaled, and grit my teeth.

"Not now, Erik. Not now," I half hissed.

"Why? Were you whispering sweet nothings? Or is it because you're around humans? Because you're afraid for them to know what you are?" Erik asked. "I know you, Jakob, I know you're probably touching salt in your pocket right now, trying to ground yourself. The charm around your neck is probably burning like a sun. And you'll have a third charm or protection on yourself. What is it? A piece of paper wrapped around a bay leaf? An iron nail? Three coins in your breast pocket?" His voice was even and measured. I was stunned. He had identified everything, all of my protections, all of the magicks I was currently using, down to the three coins near my heart.

"Are you actively spying on me?" I asked, and a passing pedestrian gave me what he thought was the evil eye. I wondered if he thought I was crazy. I certainly felt crazy.

"I know you, Jakob," he interrupted, "and I want to know more about you. I can share more with you, if you'll let me." It sent a shiver down my spine. My mind briefly flashed back to Nathan, waiting for me in the restaurant. The date was likely ruined, and I wouldn't blame him if he left while I was on the phone.

I sighed deeply again and watched the vapor of my breath curl and flit into the night. Winter was right around the corner, and the weather was an easy reminder. I shivered and clutched the salt tighter, willing its feeble heat to my heart and then through the rest of my body.

"Erik," I managed to say without my teeth chattering too much, "why would you think I want the life you'd have me living?" There was a heartbeat of silence, followed by another. I had stumped him, at least for the moment.

"Don't you want an open life, a life with fewer secrets?" he asked.

"If I was what you wanted, I'd be burdened in ways I'm not ready for. Instead of my own issues, I'd have an entire community's worth to deal with," I said.

"You can't keep yourself locked away. Not forever."

"I can manage a long time, Erik, you'd be surprised," I said.

"I don't doubt how resourceful or cunning you are, Jakob." His voice picked up a velvet quality and it slid through me. I had forgotten how he could do that with his voice.

"All right, Erik, you claim to know me. How do I take my tea? Where's my favorite running trail? Where did I go to culinary school? When did my grandmother, *aleha hashalom*, die?" I asked, the Hebrew blessing flowing easily. "What's my middle name?"

"You have a middle name?" he asked, and there was surprise in his voice, like there had been the first time he saw me casting.

"I do, and for all your supposed knowledge about me, you don't know what it might be," I said, my lips curling into a smile. I was centered and I had regained my equilibrium.

"Would you tell me any of that?" he asked.

"If you had made any attempts at acting like a normal person, I might have," I answered.

"That's one of the issues, Jakob—neither of us is human," he said.

"You're actively missing so many points here," I objected. "You accused me of reading really bad fiction—"

"I said 'shitty fiction,' Jakob. Please do try to remember." He was teasing.

"Not the point," I all but yelled, getting even more side eyes from passing walkers, bundled in coats, pulling their hats down, doing everything they could to avoid me. If I didn't hurry this up, there was a good chance that Cleveland's finest were going to come and arrest me for disturbing the peace. If my date with Nathan wasn't already in the gutter, being escorted away in handcuffs wouldn't do me any favors. I exhaled and mouthed "*Elohai neshama*," traditionally a blessing for the morning, but the pure soul of the prayer was what I needed. I didn't need any anger.

"When your parents met, was it love at first sight?" I asked, my tone as cool as the breeze that had picked up. I had used a more human expression and Erik would know the term I was choosing to omit.

"It was. They instantly knew they were mates." His smile was audible.

"That's your world, not mine. When they met, my babcia thought my grandfather was a *shmuck*. They spent just over four decades together," I said.

"Are you asking me to date you like a human would?"

That stopped my thoughts. He had never offered to date me as a human, and when he bit me, he didn't know I was a witch. He was trying to change, to make himself open to more, which I hadn't thought possible for him. The salt packet in my palm had gone cold and the mezuzah around my neck was no longer burning. That told me much. He was willing to stop some of the alpha posturing and try to meet me halfway. Would he be willing to know me as more than a mate? I knew Nathan was waiting inside and that I should get back to him, that I was being unspeakably rude. Would have to be evasive because it was not in my nature to lie.

"If you come correct, Erik, we'll see if we can make it work. Act like a person, not an animal," I conceded.

"That was uncalled for." His voice was a playful growl this time.

"If you're going to try… dating me, you'll have to get used to my humor. I'm going to try for a clean slate, if you'll do likewise. In the meantime, can you let me live my life?" I hated how much pleading bled into my voice.

"I'll have to let the human touch you?" His voice had become a snarl again, and I swore I heard his teeth grow over the phone.

"If Nathan wants to touch me, I won't stop him. I also won't let him do anything I don't want him to do. I'm not a five-dollar whore," I said. Yet another pedestrian whipped their head in my direction as they passed. I was causing all sorts of scandal tonight.

He chuckled. Across all the distance, Erik chuckled. "Your words, not mine, Jakob."

"Oy gotenu. Hashem must have—" I stopped myself, I had shifted into Yiddish.

"One of these days, you'll have to teach me to swear as you do. The human can touch you." Erik was magnanimous.

"Fine, we'll set up a time later." With that I ended the call and was shocked to see just how long it had taken. As I reentered the restaurant, my glasses fogged up, and it took me a few moments to find Nathan, his arms crossed at the table.

"Are you going to tell me what that call was about?" Another demand, and the hairs on the back of my neck stood on end.

"It was deeply personal and involved a situation that's dominated my life since May," I offered. It was as much of the truth as I was willing to give.

"Is that all you're willing to tell me?"

"That's all," I said.

"Well…." Nathan finished off his current glass of wine. "Despite everything, this hasn't been my worse date ever."

"I need to hear this story," I said as I leaned forward.

My parents tried to set me up with Emilia Choi. It… didn't go well."

"When was this?"

He didn't answer, just raised his glass and drank deeply. Nathan proceeded to tell me about what had to be one of the worst blind dates I had ever heard of. I laughed easily throughout and offered one of my dating misadventures in turn. The waiter came back as I wrapped my story, and we placed our orders.

"You're really not going to tell me anything about your phone call? I am a lawyer—I might be able to help if you've found yourself in a bad contract," he offered. I laughed, more to myself than anything else.

"It's not a contract issue, per se," I said.

"You play your cards awfully close to the chest."

"A gentleman should be allowed a few secrets," I said with a grin and a wink.

"A man of mystery. You must be beating off suitors with a stick."

An image of Erik in his wolf form, branch between sharp fangs, flashed in my mind, and I bit back a laugh. "Hardly, but thanks for the compliment."

"You really don't like compliments much, do you?" His tone had gone serious, and I knew I wouldn't be able to evade the question.

"When I feel I've earned the compliment, then I accept it. I'm not as mysterious or as handsome as you think I am," I said, shrugging a single shoulder.

"We'll have to agree to disagree," he said as he rested his chin on steepled fingers.

"I know my strengths," I said, "and how I look, well, that's not my strong suit. I wasn't homecoming king for a reason."

"You should ask Nicole about the shit show that was our homecoming court our junior year of high school." Nathan shivered as he finished.

"Would it be appropriate for me to ask her?"

"She'll tell anyone willing to listen about it—and a few people who haven't been willing got the story anyway." Nathan smiled again. Then our waiter came back with our dishes, and we ate in a comfortable silence.

CHAPTER 8

THE MORNING after my date with Nathan was the first snow of the season. Anyone who has ever lived with lake effect snow knows that the first snow of the season can be serious business. Everyone was driving more slowly, and there were a few times on my commute in the predawn darkness when I looked out the windshield and saw the distinct, almost anchor-gray sky of early morning that warned of heavy snow ahead. It sent a shiver down my spine and made me wish I had invested in a car with heated seats. When I exited my car, the shivering intensified. No matter how many layers you wore, this was the sort of cold that sank into every exposed pore and sank deep. But the deep cold wasn't the only thing messing with my head. Several gravestones in Toledo's Ottawa Hills Memorial Park had been shattered. It was more than malice.

The first thing I heard after the echo of the metal back door was Cara's distinct soprano. I was too busy removing my coat, scarves, and gloves while unfogging my glasses to pay attention to what she said. It was only as I pulled my phone out to see notifications about the first schools being canceled that I really picked out the rhythm of Cara's voice. Whatever she was saying, she wasn't saying it in English.

In my years working under and then with Cara, I hadn't ever heard her use a language that wasn't English. She spoke in staccato bursts. From what I could hear, I knew it wasn't part of the Semitic language family, and it didn't sound like any of the Slavic languages I knew. It also wasn't one of the Romance languages, or it at least didn't sound like my high school Spanish. I stayed still and tried to hear more. Cara's high voice carried, but the words were alien. The sounds ran together, and there was a rhythm to them, but I had never heard the language or any member of its family before. It was musical, haunting, and in its tone there was potent sorrow. Liquid grief glided over every syllable, each word a dirge. It reminded me of the way the book of Lamentations sounded when read in Hebrew. This was Cara in pain.

As the conversation ended, I began my work. Even if we wouldn't open to the general public, there were still orders we had to fill. I had my tablet out and was gathering ingredients when Cara exited her office and looked at me. I lifted my head and offered a small smile. She arched a brow but moved to her own space, and we didn't say anything to each other as we worked. Eventually I lifted my head and, over the whir of fans and mixers I asked, "What language were you speaking?"

"My mother tongue," she replied, not lifting her head.

"Which is?"

"None of your business," she answered, a slight lilt in her voice, but only for the briefest of moments. "Let's keep focused before the power goes out."

"We're going to lose power?" I asked as I grabbed coffee grounds for the mocha cupcakes ordered for an anniversary dinner.

"According to the forecast, it's probable." She raised a shoulder. "And even if we don't, there's going to be at least one driver who crashes into a utility pole, or something else. You know how people are with the first snow of the season," she said, still not looking up. I nodded. I had lived in cities with snow my entire life. No matter how long the winter, at least one person forgot how to drive in it every season. It would be only a matter of time before Cara made a bet about where the first accident would be and how bad it would get.

We worked together in silence, and I could distantly feel the snow falling outside. As opening approached, I walked to the front of the house to see a decent accumulation already on the ground. The streets were packed with parked cars, all covered with at least two inches of dense snow. I turned the sign, unlocked the door, and stared for a long moment. While there were a few pedestrians, the streets were mostly empty. I pulled my phone from my pocket and saw more snow and falling temperatures were both likely. I bit my tongue to prevent myself from cursing.

"You might want to get out of here while you can," Cara said. I spun, surprised I hadn't heard her moving.

"I don't need to—" I tried to object. Cara just laid a small palm on the center of my left shoulder blade and made a sweeping gesture with her other hand.

"Look outside, Jakob," she said. "With the weather as it is and the roads getting worse, I don't think we're going to be getting lots of people coming in. I've already gotten my fair share of texts asking to reschedule due to the snow. Besides, with that car of yours, do you honestly think you could get home in this?"

"Are you sure?" I asked. Cara worked through everything. Snow, sleet, hail, thunderstorms—even Black Friday hadn't slowed her down.

"Get out of here while the getting is good, Kuratowski," she said with something resembling a fond smile. "Or do you feel like waiting hours for AAA to respond?"

Not one to question, I nodded and took my phone out of my pocket. As much as it pained me to admit it, knowing my car—and not having AAA—there was a chance I would need help. Erik had wanted to get to know me as a human, and what was more human than dealing with car trouble? I sent a quick message. *May need your help.* I didn't wait for his response as I headed out into the falling snow. As before, the shock of icy air reminded me of lashes sticking together and the bitter, frigid burn that could crawl from your nostrils straight into your lungs.

As I suspected, when I reached my car, the engine sputtered but didn't catch. My father and eldest sister were doubtless laughing at me. I had never been mechanically inclined, but I knew that I needed at least a jump-start.

"Nieszczęścia chodzą parami," I spat, the old Polish warning that loosely translates to "misery loves company," as I re-entered Siren's Sweets through its metal door. Cara looked up, one of her brows quirked.

"What language is that?" she teased me.

"Język mojej babci," I replied, deciding not to translate. It was the same sort of nonanswer she'd given me, and she bowed her head, the fine lines at the corners of her eyes and mouth more obvious with her grin. "You don't have the ability to jump a car, do you?" I asked, somehow already knowing the answer.

"I do not," she confirmed.

I fumbled for my cell phone. By the time I finally extracted it, Erik had replied. *What do you need help with?* I rolled my eyes as Cara handed me a mug of what passed for coffee, and I gritted my teeth. I would have given anything to have texted Nathan, but he drove a brand-new Tesla, and I didn't trust those in the first snow of a Cleveland winter. I still didn't understand why he had gotten a Model 3 out of all the hybrid and electric cars that were available. Then again, considering my car, I wasn't in any place to judge. Teeth still clenched together, I pressed in the all-too-familiar digits of Erik's number and waited.

Of course, he answered on the first ring. "A call means you do need me, doesn't it?" His rich voice echoed in my ear and I saw Cara tilt her head at me. Had she ever seen me this emotional?

"Get off your high horse," I said. "You're the one person I know in this city who has a car that can handle the snow. I need a jump."

"As far as I understand, this isn't traditional dating by human standards," he half joked. I rolled my eyes and did the most basic of breathing exercises, all the while feeling Cara's eyes on me. She was clearly far too amused.

"Can you help me or not?" I asked. A heartbeat of silence was swiftly followed by another, and Cara was leaning against the wall, arms crossed over her chest, grinning to beat the Cheshire cat.

"I'll be there when I can. Do you have jumper cables?" he asked.

"I do," I said. "I'll meet you out back." I proceeded to give him the address, followed by directions so he could find the small lot I had parked in. I shuddered and took a sip of the coffee.

"You had to ask an ex to jump your car, didn't you?" she all but cackled, and I wondered if I should have left my car buried beneath the snow, grabbed a rideshare, and dealt with the car later.

"It's… complicated," I said.

"It's complicated?" She raised her brow impossibly high. She had to have practiced that in the mirror. "That's some Facebook bullshit."

"This isn't any of your business," I parroted her words from hours earlier, and she laughed.

"At least you're quoting me correctly." She moved from the wall and back toward the kitchen, and when she looked over her shoulder at me, even in the dim hall light, I saw a gleam in her eye. "You know, I don't think I've ever heard you swear, Jakob, unless it was in one of those other languages you know. Just how many languages do you speak?" she asked.

"You don't remember?" I answered.

"Humor me."

"With any real skill? Three," I answered as I followed her and filled the mug she had brought me with more coffee. If I was going to wait, I was going to be armed.

"Do you just not swear in English, then?" She took the carafe from my hand and poured for herself.

"I try not to curse," I answered honestly.

"Why?"

"Just how I was raised, I guess."

"Did your mother wash your mouth out with soap?"

"Something like that." I hoped that would be the end of the conversation, and Cara just shrugged and went about her work in the kitchen, continuing as if the first snow of the season weren't falling outside. She was almost liquid, the way she glided about, not stopping for more than a fraction of a second, instinctively knowing where everything was. Her gaze was on the bowl in her hands, not whatever ingredients or tools she might need. All that existed in the world was that bowl. She cracked an egg with a single hand in a way that would have made any *maître pâtissier* cry.

"Soufflé?" I guessed as she grabbed an orange and a zester.

"Soufflé Grand Marnier," she answered still not looking up from her task. "If I have a day off from the demanding customers, I want to practice. It's been too long since I've made one of these."

"It might be a while before my 'it's complicated' shows. You need a second pair of hands?" I offered.

"Thanks, but no thanks. I want to do this on my own." She lifted her head, flashed me a genuine smile, and then returned to her work, the orange moving across the zester in controlled, precise motions. Cara was an artist in the kitchen, and I watched, enthralled by the lightness of her movement, the fluidity, and the way she simply existed in her kitchen. Working without a recipe, trusting instinct and memory... I remembered the first time I had seen her working on the day I came to interview.

She had just put the oven on preheat when I felt my phone vibrate. I waved to Cara, who was focused on cleaning. She never half-assed anything, and I always loved watching her work. But I didn't want Erik coming into Siren's, so I stepped into the lot and saw at least a half inch more snow on my car. Erik stood next to it, looking at me and then at the back door to Siren's Sweets.

"Doesn't feel right, you working here," he said.

"How many times—" I stopped myself and just moved to him. He kept his gaze focused on the building, as if it might come to life and bite him. I moved past him and fished in the back seat for my jumper cables and a small shovel. "Help me, will you?" I asked. He shook himself out of whatever had taken hold of him and cleared snow as I popped the hood.

"Ready when you are," he said as he returned to his pickup. "Although feel free to take your time. I am enjoying the view." I was bent over, making sure the connector points were as clean as I could get them.

"Must you be so crude?" I scowled as I stood.

"When it comes to you, Jakob, I must," Erik answered. My Judas heartbeat fluttered in my chest and I turned my face so he couldn't see my rising blush and prayed the snow would obscure my scent. Once the cables had been correctly placed, I returned to my car. As I turned the key, the engine sputtered and the lights flashed on, but I didn't hold for too long, not wanting to cause any damage. It hadn't caught. This was more than a dead battery. "Piece of garbage," I yelled loudly, feeling the Yiddish words echo around me. It wasn't a curse; it was an accurate description.

"Well, whatever it is, the battery may be only the beginning," Erik said. I pulled myself out of the car and wondered how much magic it would take to have him frozen solid and if that would classify as my great working.

"What else can you detect with your keen powers of observation?" My tone was sharper than needed, but with the snow falling and no way to easily fix my car, I couldn't summon energy for civility.

"Can't you—" Erik hunted for words as the snow caught on his magnificently golden hair. He looked every inch a Viking, and I averted my gaze as my thoughts traveled back to his house and the fireplace I had briefly seen there. This was the sort of day when lying in front of a fire, a lover's arm around your middle, would not be at all unwelcome. Erik wrinkled his nose and smirked. He was smelling my lust and I chastised myself. No time for such thoughts. "—use your talents to fix what's happening?" he finally finished. It was a genuine question, and it shocked me out of open hostility. I had been expecting him to tease me about my scent, to ask me what I was thinking.

"My... talents don't extend to most forms of modern technology. It's part of why I've gone through as many cell phones as I have. I don't want to know what would happen if I tried anything with the car," I said.

Erik approached my vehicle and bent over to study the engine. It was my turn to admire his rear, although I shifted my gaze quickly so he wouldn't catch me.

"Aren't you a carpenter?" I asked.

"My youngest brother is a mechanic, and so is one of my uncles. I might not know as much as they do, but I know the basics," he answered. "And you're allowed to look, you know." My cheeks were ruby and it wasn't solely due to the cold.

"I—" I said, then tripped over my tongue. What could I say?

"Jakob, you are talented, sexy, and sharp as a whip, but you'll never be a professional gambler." Erik chuckled as he continued looking over the engine. I didn't move any closer, as I wouldn't have the faintest idea about what he was doing.

"T knows I'm not a good liar," I said, not catching the fact I had used the teen's preferred nickname again.

"One day, one or the other of you will have to tell me how you got him to let you call him T," Erik said. "Even if you were a talented liar, you'd have to work hard around my… group to be convincing."

"Do lies have a smell?" This would be useful information for the grimoire I rationalized.

"No, but we can smell sweat, nervousness, and hear slight variations in heartbeats if we focus. We're generally more accurate than polygraphs," he boasted.

"Considering how inaccurate polygraphs are…."

He went back to work as the snow continued to fall and the wind picked up. I almost called on magic to warm myself, but I didn't. Erik turned his head and moved away from the car. "What news do you want?" he asked.

"What are the options? Bad or worse?" I cringed, imagining how expensive this might be.

"Not nearly that dire. Your engine is in good shape for a car as old as yours. How many miles do you have on it?" he asked.

"Just over 180,000," I admitted.

"You've done well taking care of the car. The bad news is your battery is completely dead. *If*—" Erik let the emphasis on that two-letter word hang between us. "—you trust me, I'll call my youngest brother. His shop's just outside of Shaker Heights. He'll give you the family discount if I ask, but with the weather, it'll be at least three hours before he can get here."

I weighed my options. Shaker Heights wasn't far at all, and every penny saved would go a long way. "If it's not too much trouble," I said. Erik nodded and pulled his phone out of his pocket. His thumb moved faster than my eye could follow across the screen, and I pulled my coat tight around me and headed from the small parking lot.

"Are you really going to try taking a bus in this weather?" Erik yelled.

"I could always try getting a rideshare, but I don't think I'll have more luck with them," I said.

"You could let me drive you back home."

I stayed statue still. How close did I want Erik to come to my sanctuary?

"I would even be willing to drop you at the closest intersection if you'd be more comfortable with that. Although, for the family discount and the ride, I think a cup of coffee would be fair," he continued, a glint in his eyes. I almost groaned but stopped myself. There was only so long I would be willing to wait, and I knew that if I went back into Siren's.... I marched toward Erik but waited a foot from the cab of his pickup.

"If you try any funny business on the ride or push your luck—" I said.

"I won't, I swear. You have my word as the alpha of my pack that I will do nothing to you unless I hear you ask for it," Erik answered.

I believed him. I knew how much those words meant and how serious the oath was.

"Thank you. You've—well, it was very decent of you to help me," I said. I moved past him to the passenger's side. The cab was chilly but warmer than the air I had just left. He got in moments later and looked at me.

"I'll tell you where to turn and where to stop," I said. He nodded and started his truck smoothly. As we drove out of the parking lot, I noticed that the snow had slowed down. I snorted.

"Something amusing?" I didn't need to turn my head to know he was smiling.

"Of course the weather improves just a little after I get in your truck," I said.

He chuckled. "Who knows? We may yet get more snow."

"We may indeed."

"You're agreeing with me, Jakob? Is the world finally coming to an end?" Erik probed.

"We're only talking about the weather, Erik. Even Superman and Lex Luthor might have agreed about the weather."

"You're gloriously nerdy sometimes." He flashed another smile. "In your telling, am I the Joker to your Batman?"

There was something heavy in his question, even with the playful tone. Erik patiently let the silence sit between us as I thought over my answer.

"You're not my Joker, but you're also not a Selina Kyle or Wonder Woman," I answered.

"Where do I fall, then?" he asked.

"Turn right at the next intersection," I instructed.

"That's not an answer, Jakob."

"I know."

"Any chance I'll get one?"

"As soon as I've brushed up on my Batman," I promised, and he snorted. When I told him we'd be turning left at the next light, he immediately shifted over to the left-most lane.

"I don't remember you being this jumpy as a driver," I said.

"In this weather, it's better to be on the safer side," Erik said.

"My babcia, aleha hashalom—" I said.

"Are those the same language?" he asked.

"No, babcia's Polish, and the aleha is Hebrew. Anyway, my babcia, my grandmother, she would have agreed with you about how to drive in this weather," I said.

"You loved her, didn't you?" Erik's question was unexpected but I didn't need time to process the answer.

"Deeply."

We turned and he swallowed.

"Have you—did you—could you have—" He was searching for words, and I vehemently shook my head.

"That's strictly *farboten*." I slipped into Yiddish without thinking. "It's the most dangerous thing anyone like me could do. Necromancy is as old as it is dangerous—and necromancy might be the oldest of magicks. It was referenced in the Tanakh. The price for that sort of magic is astronomical. Even if I had the raw power—"

"You do," Erik interjected.

"How would you know?" My whole focus was on Erik.

"My pack knows it. *I* know it. We can smell it on you when you're… what's the word you use for it?"

"Working or casting."

"When you cast, you're an inferno. You smell of ash, ozone, a storm at sea, and just a hint of the earth after an earthquake. It's a scent you don't forget. It's why some of my pack are scared of you," he explained. My mouth fell open and I almost missed the next direction.

"Did you smell that on me when we met? Shouldn't that have warned you about what I was?"

"You only smell that way when you're working with magic. When you are not, you smell—"

"Of pine, cedar, freshly fallen snow, and just a hint of juniper and sage? Like spring on the border of summer?" I butted in.

"You remember?"

"How could I forget?"

"Have you decided where I fall in your cast of characters yet?"

"I told you, I have to go through my comics," I said, and he let the silence rest between us until I told him to make the next turn. I looked out my window at the small cemetery I had driven past hundreds of times. I righted myself suddenly, and Erik was too busy paying attention to the road to look at me. I saw, or thought I did, a twisting, spectral, half-real shape near one of the stones—a mass of snow made solid, something umbral, something with a primal darkness at its core before it winked out. I blinked hard and it was gone. It couldn't have been there. I must have been looking for some ill omen to warn me away from Erik.

We were nearing my street, and I tried to decide how close I wanted Erik to my home. My wards were strong, my protections growing with each night I passed in the house. It came from time, from familiarity. The more familiar I was, the stronger the protections—at least, if I was right in my translations of what one of the ancestors had written. While the snow wasn't as bad as I had feared, steaming up my glasses and having my lashes freeze together didn't sound like my idea of a good time, even given how used to the cold as I was.

"You're more than a mistake fueled by bottom-shelf tequila," I eventually admitted.

"I can live with that," Erik said, "for now."

"You—" I stopped myself, thinking about the words I wanted, *needed* to use. "You represent something I don't know if I should take on. Even in a minimal capacity, it's a big commitment, and I'm already trying to keep a lot of balls in the air. When my uncle Danny was first dating my aunt Eva, he knew she had two children from her first marriage. He knew what he was getting into. With you, I don't know what I'm getting. It's a lot more than two preteens, though," I said. He just nodded and turned when I told him to. We were less than a half mile from my house and I thought I saw the fine hairs on the back of his neck rising.

"What is it?"

"We're getting closer to your house, aren't we?"

"How did you... you can feel that?"

"I can." I wondered what would happen as Erik got even closer. Even I wasn't picking up on the familiar hum of magic at this range.

"What are you thinking, Jakob? You're trying to knit a sweater with your eyebrows right now," he said.

"Keep your eyes on the road," I instructed. "I'm trying to decide just how close I want to let you get."

"Could you—what could you do at this range?" he asked.

"A gentleman is allowed his secrets," I answered. A nonanswer, but not a lie. Erik rolled his eyes. We made another turn, and the thrum of magic pushed at the edge of my awareness.

"I'll let you know this. Here, I'd know if there was anyone who intended me harm," I said.

"Do I mean you harm, Jakob?" We came to a rest at a stop sign, and I knew he wouldn't move until I answered him. From there I could walk if I had to. But did I want to? Or did I want him to take me farther, closer to my home? I closed my eyes, focused on the thin tangents of power, and let them blend and bleed through me.

"You mean me no harm," I answered, my voice almost lethargic.

"Can you sense what I intend?" he asked as his truck moved again.

It was faint, distant, a distorted echo, but it was there, dim and flickering. "I do." It wasn't just my connection to the ground, to the area around me.

"You know what that means, don't you?" His voice was lower, a near growl.

"I do."

"Do you have any opinions about that?"

"Honestly… I'm too shocked that I can pick it up over all the ambient noise."

The fatal moment was upon us. I made the decision and opened my eyes. "Right here, into the cul-de-sac. I'll tell you where to pull over and you can come in for a cup of coffee. As you said, it's the least I can offer," I said.

"Only a cup of coffee?" He had gone back to being playful and teasing.

"Don't press your luck," I said. "Besides, fair is fair. I've seen your bathroom, bedroom, and other parts of your house. You can at least see my kitchen."

"I'd rather—"

"I know what you'd rather, and I'm *this* close to revoking my invitation." I emphasized my words by holding my thumb and forefinger less than a half inch apart. He slammed his jaw shut and made the turn. Even in the adverse conditions, Erik parked smoothly and easily. I was impressed but wasn't going to give him the satisfaction of showing it. As I exited the cab of the truck, the wind bit into me and I shivered. My house was only across the street, but as we crossed, I felt my feet slip. I would have planted my butt on the concrete, but Erik was behind me, his arms around me, and his lips next to my ear. We stayed like that for a long moment before I righted myself and pulled away, still feeling his heat as I trudged through the drifts to my door.

I pressed my fingers against the mezuzah on the doorframe and home rushed through me. He remained distant, on the edge of my property. It took me a moment to negotiate with the wards I had set. My intention to keep him from my home had been strong, and the magic had acquired a will of its own, but I haggled, bartered, and all but begged the wards to lower. I reminded them silently that this was still my home, that if I didn't want him there, all I had to do was say the word. Snow fell on my bare fingers, but I was focused. I felt Erik waiting with a predator's patience. It didn't make the work any easier.

I pulled my fingers from the metal and saw him relax a little. As I pulled the key from my pocket, I made a gesture, and he bounded through the snow. I opened the door and made a sweeping gesture, all too aware of how close he was to me. "Welcome," I all said. "Welcome to my home."

CHAPTER 9

MY HOUSE was nowhere near as imposing as Erik's. Mine was a modest two-story pseudo-Victorian with a full basement. With only three bedrooms and one and a half baths, I doubted it would ever be on the cover of *Better Homes and Gardens*—or any other magazine or website. Still, I was proud of it and I enjoyed the large bay window and functioning fireplace. The cat lifted its head from its paws, jumped up, and wrapped itself around Erik's legs. I unlaced my boots as Erik bent over and scratched the cat between its ears.

"You realize you're living up to every stereotype about witches that exists?" Erik asked, not looking up from the furry traitor.

"The cat's not mine, not really," I said.

"What do you mean?"

"The cat just showed up one day. It ran inside during a rainstorm, and I fed it. I took it to the vet, but it doesn't have a chip. I haven't named it."

"How very *Breakfast at Tiffany's* of you," he said. I managed to collect my jaw from the floor and he smiled. "One of my uncles on my mother's side teaches film criticism at Carnegie Mellon," he said. The cat left Erik, rubbed against my legs, and then moved over to its bed, where it promptly fell back asleep.

"That's... well, I don't know what I expected."

"Just because my brothers and I decided to go into the trades doesn't mean the rest of my family did. My mother has a master's in counseling and only didn't go for her doctorate because she didn't need it for what she wanted to do long-term." It was hard to tell if he was boasting or not. I had been put in my place, so I nodded. As much as I claimed that he didn't know about me, I was as guilty and knew shockingly little about him.

I collected myself. "Take your shoes off and make yourself comfortable," I instructed as I removed my coat and moved down the hallway, trying not to acknowledge the blush crossing my face. As I entered the kitchen, my fingers flitted to the doorpost mezuzah and then to my lips. Every witch had a space that was the heart of their home, my grandmother had explained. Like her, I had chosen the kitchen. It had been in her kitchen where I had learned how to channel magic. Most of my ancestors who had been magic-touched had favored kitchens for their seats of power. Like the entrance to my house, the kitchen was heavily protected and warded.

I had to spend a little longer negotiating with these wards—as the heart of my house, it was where the magic was strongest. Eventually the wards fell, and I turned to Erik to find him barefoot in his jeans. I stared at him, and he gave me a broad, genuine smile, though perhaps just a bit embarrassed.

"In case I had to shift," he said, and I made a gesture to the round, secondhand IKEA table in the corner of the kitchen. Erik moved nearly silently, and the cat trailed after him. As soon as Erik sat, the cat hopped into his lap and curled itself into a small ball. The traitorous feline was purring loudly, and I turned to focus on making coffee.

"Is all of your house against me?" Erik asked. I was busy filling the carafe and measuring the ground coffee.

"After our night together, I may have gone a bit overboard with my home protections," I confessed.

"Was this before or after you found the cat?" He asked, patting the sable head of the little Judas.

"I didn't find the cat until July, or was it June, when you called asking me to help—was that Nick?" I tried to remember.

"June, I think."

"Right." I finally sat opposite him, and a beat of silence passed between us at the table. "How much do you understand about magic?" I finally asked.

"Only what my pack's witch told me when I was still a kid," he said.

"What did she tell you?"

"She said magic is what lets my pack—any wolf—feel the call of the moon. It's what lets us shed our human skin," he said.

I nodded and caught a hint of my grandmother's perfume, as if it floated from the grimoire. If Erik noticed it, he didn't say anything.

"That," I said, and was surprised to hear the slightest hint of Polish in my voice, "is what magic does. My question for you is, what is magic?"

He shrugged, more focused on the cat than my question. I snapped my fingers and the stove clicked to life. Erik lifted his eyes from the cat, and I extended my hand to the gas-burning stove opposite us. I narrowed my eyes and a spark of blue flame leaped to my fingers. It danced as it moved from one fingertip to another, winding serpentine around my wrist. I rejoiced as it caressed and raced over bare skin, changing from blue to the otherworldly jade of witch's fire.

"That's impressive," Erik admitted, "but that doesn't tell me what magic is."

"Magic is will made manifest. It is the will of a person or nature itself. Magic is how will bends the world. Everything that has ever lived, everything that has ever breathed, all of it had will, had the potential for magic. It's in the reaction of atoms, the unfolding of life. What we do—" I stopped myself for a second to let my words sink in. "—is an exercise of our will. My call to the flame or your shedding of human skin is an extension of our will."

"I don't know if I would agree with you," he finally said. The cat leaped from his lap, clearly upset that it was no longer the center of attention.

"What's your definition of magic, then? Not just what it can do, but what it is at its heart, at the core?" I asked.

He brought his brows together and looked at the table. The coffee maker went off and I poured us two mugs. I placed one before him, and he nodded his thanks. "I'm not a philosopher," he finally answered.

"I'm not asking you to write a thesis." I brought my mug to my lips and cooled the liquid with a thought. "Just asking from one magic-touched to another, how do you think magic allows you to walk as a wolf?"

"Is it something supernatural?"

"When you shift, isn't it the most natural thing in the world for you?" I interrupted.

"You really should have been a lawyer, not a baker." He lifted his mug in a small salute, and I mirrored the gesture but kept a distance between our mugs.

"I didn't want to hate myself," I said simply.

"I honestly don't know if you're joking with me."

"When I was growing up, my parents tried to point me toward law or medicine, professions that would support them in their old age. I didn't have the right mindset for it, though. As I grew, I saw how unhappy the lawyers in my family were. I knew it wasn't going to be a good match for me," I said.

"Too much stress?" he guessed.

"Too much time potentially in the public eye. Witches—at least the witches of my family—we try not to draw attention to ourselves. Siren's gets more than enough attention, and I don't know how I would have lived with the public eye on me if I had become a trial attorney like my parents wanted," I said.

"Such a modest man, it really doesn't become you," Erik said. I heard him begin to push back from the table. Holding my mug with one hand, I made a quick gesture with the other and the chair slid forward and touched his knees. A shocked expression crossed his face and I sipped my coffee, smirking behind my cup.

"What did you just—?" Erik asked.

I arched a single brow above my glasses. "This is *my* house, the seat of my power. You might not have smelled me casting because this entire place is fused with my magic," I said. "Even though I let you into my home, I don't fully trust you yet. As I told you, when I warded my house, I was thorough, and magic is an extension of will, of intention. I intended to keep my home safe from you," I explained.

He sat in silence for a long moment and then brought his mug to his lips, his eyes on me. I looked back at him, and the tension between us hummed with things unsaid. I didn't know if this was feeding his fantasies of my power, but in this house, I was a prepared witch. I wouldn't be a dead witch. But I was all too aware of Erik's gaze. He wasn't looking past the window to the snow falling on the street, creating a scene from a Rockwell still life. He was entirely focused on me.

"I won't be able to cross your threshold again—not unless you want it—will I?" Erik asked. I raised my mug in a silent salute. While his pack's witch might not have taught him much, he was catching on fast.

"Like any good home security system, all I need is the right combination, and you'll be locked out," I confirmed.

"Well, now I'm here, what else would you like to know about me? What did you ask that human you went out with last night?" he asked.

"Is that what you think all human dating is? Asking questions?"

"Am I wrong?"

I decided not to attack the question. Besides Nathan, my last real date had been... well, longer ago than I cared to admit.

"Do you think this is a date?" I asked, making a gesture between us, taking in the two mostly empty mugs of coffee, the scarred tabletop, and the off-eggshell tiling I had finally gotten clean.

"Well, it would be a lot more like a date if—"

"Stop what you're saying right now, or I promise by all my ancestors I will use a piece of string to have your entire body bound," I said.

"You're into rope play?" He leaned across the table, pearline teeth flashing in the light of my kitchen.

"Not what I meant." I blushed all the way down to my collarbone. There were so many ways he could have followed up, but he didn't. I guessed he found my threat somewhat credible.

"Am I at least allowed to ask about your other date?" He quirked a single brow.

"Not if you're going to be uncivil," I answered.

"Civility is overrated," Erik scoffed.

"My house, my rules," I reminded him.

"I'll try to be civil, but only for you."

"Thank you."

"I've noticed... you think of yourself as closer to humans than to a wolf. Why is that?"

It was a genuine question and I took my time trying to find an appropriate answer. "Witches are human, at least physically. We don't have accelerated healing or the alleged life span of a wolf. Also, if I don't have something on me that I can use to cast, calling to magic is more of a pain than it's worth," I answered.

"You didn't need anything to work here," he pointed out.

"As I said, this is the heart of my home. I poured a lot into it to have ready access to magic. Outside of here, trying to cast without the appropriate fuel would be a bad idea, to say the very least. My babcia—" I caught myself on the Polish word.

"Your grandmother?" he asked. I nodded.

"She could do workings without any material components, but it always took a lot from her. Even with magic, you can't get something for nothing. By the time she started teaching me, she had been practicing for decades. I might reach her level of skill one day," I offered.

"Was I really the only person in your contacts who could give you a jump?" He was teasing again, and I glared daggers at him, but nothing more.

"If you're asking why I didn't call Nathan"—Erik looked like he wanted to hiss at the name of the other man, but he didn't—"he drives a newer Tesla. Do you really think that would have been able to handle the streets in these conditions?" I made a gesture to the window, where snow fell lazily.

"Why did he buy that car?"

"He said it was a gift to himself."

"A very impractical gift. If this were San Francisco, San Diego, or even Portland, I might understand."

"Also known as places that don't have real winters?" I couldn't help but grin.

"You said it, not me," he said back.

"Horror of all horrors, I think I agree with you."

"Not the worst feeling in the world, is it?"

I didn't answer. Instead I chose to stare at the last of the coffee in my mug and wondered if it would be worth the energy to heat it. I raised it to my lips, killed what was left, and put it down with a small clink. "No," I admitted after a pause that had lasted a lifetime.

"Jakob, I admit, our night... I shouldn't have done what I did. I'm sorry," he said, and I would have dropped my mug if it had still been in my hands. I hadn't thought I would hear those two words from Erik, at least not anytime soon.

"I can't have heard you right," I said finally.

"I did wrong," he repeated. "My wolf reigned that night. You answered in the heat of the moment. It was wrong. If you had a wolf, you might understand how it could feel to know you have what it needs before it," he reasoned.

"That's not much of an excuse. Is it something your pack does often, biting those of us who should have known better?"

"Only when—" He bit his lip and looked up at me, the arctic ice of his eyes piercing into me. I knew what he had been about to say, and he had stopped himself. He continued to surprise me by showing restraint. I thought back to our first night, when I had called him unlife. If he had been one, he would have been a creature of feral hunger and pure instinct, unable to restrain himself at all—in anything.

"Are nonwolves rare in your pack?"

"Not as rare as you might think. My maternal grandmother was human, claimed by my grandfather under the Buck Moon."

"Which one is that?"

"July's. I thought you'd know all the full moons."

"How did she adapt?" I asked.

"The way my grandfather tells the story, she was far from happy. She fought, spit, and even tried unloading a 12-gauge into him."

"A woman after my own heart."

"Would you shoot me?" Erik's pout reminded me of a scolded puppy.

"I might just," I replied, my lips twisted into a grin. Comfortable silence sat between us as he brought his mug to his lips and emptied it.

"Your grandmother tried to shoot your grandfather." I shook my head in amusement. "How did he survive?"

"He ran low to the ground and wove quickly," Erik said, and there was a genuine smile on his lips. Despite myself, I mirrored his expression. He was charming when he needed to be, and it wasn't all just sex appeal.

"How long will I need to run from you?" he asked, and I sensed the easy comfort of seconds ago flying from the room.

"My grandmother had rules for almost everything in life. One of the first things she taught me, something she repeated to me on her deathbed, is 'an unprepared witch is a dead witch,'" I said in a deadpan imitation of her.

"Is that why you're so cautious? You don't want to be caught unprepared and end up dead?"

"The last time I went anywhere without being prepared, I met you."

"You're not dead, though."

"I could have been."

"You need to stop dwelling on what might have been and accept what is." Erik was leaning across the table, if only slightly.

"I do, which is why I won't be caught off my guard again." I was mirroring his body language, G-d help me.

"Am I truly a fate worse than death?" His voice was just above a whisper.

I swallowed as I hunted for the right words. "You're not worse than death, but I had no choice, no freedom. My babcia also taught me the importance of both choice and freedom."

He seemed to take this in stride, but he didn't say anything. His tongue darted over his lips, and my eyes followed its track, though I knew I shouldn't have. I should have gotten up, made the appropriate gestures, and asked him to leave. I should have closed my eyes and extended my will into the bones of the house and *made* him leave. But I didn't. Instead I swallowed and thought back to what he had told me less than a minute before. "Your own grandmother fought back. She did more than I am doing by trying to kill your grandfather. I don't want you dead, Erik, but you can't make the choice of a pack for me. Have you ever asked your grandmother for her side of the story? What her world was like once she was bitten?"

He sat in silence—for exactly how long, I don't know. How often had his grandfather told him his story? Had his grandmother ever been allowed to be the author of her own history? He looked at me, and there was something in his eyes I couldn't make out, but it sang at the edges of my awareness, raced along my neck, and hummed near the base of my skull.

"She realized she loved him… eventually," he offered, and there was fondness in his voice.

"How did she put it in her own words?" I had to know.

"In her words, she 'came to love the mangy bastard,'" Erik answered. I didn't need the senses of a wolf to know he was telling the truth. His grandmother had come to love his grandfather, even if she had tried to shoot him at first. I stopped myself from thinking about the parallels between his grandmother and me. She had used a 12-gauge; I had favored witch's fire and improvised chemical weaponry.

"She came to love him," I echoed, letting the words sit between us. "Is that what she wanted?"

"She wanted a life with love, yes. What is it you want, Jakob?" The question was open, direct, and I was glad I was seated. What was with this man and his ability to metaphorically knock me off my feet? What was it I wanted?

"I want a life with as few secrets as possible," I eventually answered.

"In a pack, you wouldn't have to hide being a witch," he reminded me.

"How many secrets would I be responsible for in your pack, Erik? Just how many members do you have?" I asked.

He thought for a second, and I could almost feel him tallying up the total membership. "You'd be free to do as you wanted in the pack," he offered.

"That's not an answer. Besides, how many times since the bite have I been called, pulled to help you and yours. That's not freedom, it's a different form of servitude," I countered.

"Jakob—" Erik said.

"What?"

He rested both of his hands on the false wood of the tabletop. There was less than an inch between his fingers and mine, and I felt heat radiating from him. His eyes were dark with things I didn't want to interpret, and I almost wished my will wasn't as strong as it was. It would be so easy to give in, to surrender, to give up the dream of freedom for a flash of comfort, for the pleasure I knew he could bring from my body.

"I want you, Jakob, however I can have you. I want you," he finally said.

"Is that really the case, Erik?" I asked, a hollow echo in my voice I hadn't expected.

"Why is that so hard to accept? Can't you believe someone would want you? That I want you?"

"We're… not in the same league. We're not even playing the same sport," I said at last.

"Is that the best you could come up with?"

I shrugged. "You live in Cleveland long enough, you start picking up the local slang."

"That's another thing we agree on."

"Questioning other people's car choices and agreeing about a language are not enough to build a life together."

"I've told you how my grandparents met. They didn't share much. What did your grandparents share?" he countered.

"A history, a faith, and the experience of loss," I said.

He was silent as he processed this. There were questions he wanted to ask—I felt them, running silently along the back of my neck and under my skin. It was uncomfortable. There were so many ways he could break the silence, ease the itch that only seemed to grow. But he didn't do anything. Instead he let the silence linger, perhaps longer than he had to.

"May I…?" He stopped himself.

"One question," I allowed, "and then I will show you the door."

"How many—" He swallowed. "How many did your family lose?"

"My grandfather—my father's father—he was the only one in his family to escape. They were taken to Terezín in 1943. He survived. His siblings, his parents…. My mother's family, they were already here, and my babcia's family left Poland before it got too bad. They know just how lucky they were," I answered. We stood and walked toward the front door, and I was surprised the kitchen wards didn't slam back into place immediately. I had to feed them a bit of power. Erik's nose wrinkled. He could smell my magic again, and I wasn't sure how I felt about that. The cat left where it had been sleeping and wound its way around Erik's legs again. The fuzzy turncoat didn't stop as Erik sat to lace up his boots. I adjusted my glasses, as they had slid down my nose, and I tried not to think about how domestic the entire scene was.

Erik stood and leaned in. I might not have had the enhanced senses of a wolf, but I picked up hints of tobacco, bay rum, and something deeply and purely Erik. I should have made a gesture and forced him from my home, but he leaned in, his lips almost brushing against my ear, and his hot breath raced down my spine and sent spikes of sensation throughout my body. He could have closed the distance, and I don't know if I would have been able to fight him off. A part of me wanted it, wanted him to slam me against the wall and claim my mouth. "Thank you for the coffee, Jakob," he all but whispered.

"It was the least I could do," I said finally, after what felt like a lesser lifetime. The cat was now batting at one of the aglets, and worlds of silence were between us. Erik wouldn't do anything unless I asked; he had promised me that and he was going to be a man of his word. He turned and put one hand on the doorknob, but he stopped himself, leaned down, and lifted the cat. He passed the purring Judas to me, and the cat rubbed its head against my chin. It was a poor substitute for what my body craved, despite what I knew I should want. Then Erik turned back to the door, opened it, and stepped into the night.

I watched him walk down the path and then cross the street. He didn't look back. If I had whispered it then, he might have heard me and… what? I had to be stronger than this. I put the cat down and it ran to the couch, positioning itself so it could watch as his headlights turned on and he pulled away and rounded the end of the cul-de-sac. I told myself I waited only to make sure he was gone. There was a heartbeat of silence, followed by another, and I made my way back to the kitchen.

I would clean—that would keep my mind from spiraling.

CHAPTER 10

"PLEASE, G-D, take me now," I all but begged as beads of sweat ran down my neck. Outside it was chill November. Inside Siren's Sweets it was at least eighty-five degrees.

"Die on your own time, Kuratowski," Cara said. Her hair was bound in a loose ponytail, and there was a thin sheen of sweat on her forehead. We had been in the kitchen for hours, rushing an order for a client who wanted to ensure their great-grandfather would be able to make it to their wedding. It was a sweet gesture, and the family was willing to pay for our trouble, which was a pleasant change from some of the entitled customers we had to deal with. Neither Cara nor I had it in us to say no, but we had been working ourselves to the bone, and blood, sweat, and tears had been shed. Or at least, my blood and tears. I had yet to see Cara either bleed or weep. Starting well before dawn, Cara and I were now nearing the finish line, and I, at least, was feeling the distinct ache that came from completing a job well done.

"Cara," I began, "do you honestly believe you have any sway over G-d?"

"In my kitchen, maybe," she answered. She closed her eyes and leaned against a wall, and I couldn't stop myself from chuckling. I knew she was dead serious.

"Well, as long as we don't have any other fires to put out...."

"Don't finish that thought. We don't need to tempt fate," she lectured.

"Here I thought you had sway over G-d," I taunted. She wasn't even able to summon one of her famous murderous looks, but there was a hint of a smile on her lips. "Shall I go get the van?"

"In a second. We still have—" She looked at her wrist. "—ninety minutes before we need to get this to the site. I'm going to bask for a moment."

"Basking sounds good."

"It is."

I slumped next to Cara against the wall and took in how it had come out. Cara and I had called in every favor we had with almost every florist in a ten-mile radius to get the right collection of rose petals. While it didn't match our original description, considering the limited time we'd had to work with, I allowed pride to rush through me, if only for a quarter of a second.

"You never told me what happened the other day, during the first snow," Cara said out of the blue. I turned my focus from the cake to my partner, but she was still totally focused on the cake.

"You never asked."

"I was hoping you'd tell me. It's been a lifetime since either of us got any action, and if I can't live through you... well the man who came to help your car was hot enough to forgive for eating toast in bed."

"You were watching?" I almost yelled. Cara flicked her gaze toward me and winked. Red rushed up my cheeks, and I turned away. "How do you know anything about the state of my sex life?" I couldn't believe I was having this conversation with Cara.

"You work almost as much as I do. If I haven't been getting lucky, I know you also haven't gotten some strange either."

"I don't know if I follow your logic."

"Am I wrong?" Cara's grin would have shamed any wolf's.

"Since when did we become the sort of people who discuss my sex life? I don't even think about my lack of sex all that often."

"Since now. So, what happened with the Viking?"

"Viking?"

"He looked like a cover model for one of those historical romances—you know the ones—either a Highlander or a Viking."

I hated to admit she was right on the money with the description of Erik. My blush still hadn't gone down, and I doubted it ever would.

"Nothing happened—at least, not what you're thinking," I clarified when I saw the look on Cara's face. "He drove me home, we shared coffee, and the cat likes him more than me now."

"Nothing more?"

"He promised he wouldn't do anything if I didn't ask, and I didn't ask."

"Oh, so you're holding out for the cute brother of that bride? What was his name? Nathan? Did he come over after the Viking left?"

Of all the times for her to demonstrate a near-encyclopedic knowledge of my life, why now? I looked at the floor, knowing my cheeks would have shamed rubies. My hands trembled as I slid my glasses up my nose, doing anything I could to buy a few fractions of a second. "He didn't," I confessed. "We haven't even set a second date."

"Busy schedules. I didn't think accountants would be slammed until February."

"How did you even see Erik?" I had to know.

"A Viking name indeed," Cara crowed. "You were so busy trying to rescue that sedan of yours that neither of you were looking back toward the door. He was looking at you like you balanced the world on your finger, Jakob. If he had come to my rescue through a blizzard like he did for you, I wouldn't have let him go so easily. At least not until I had thoroughly thanked him."

I had known Cara for years, had known she could be bawdy and crude, but having it directed toward me? That was a first, and I couldn't say I was enjoying it.

"I'll give you my week's paycheck if you promise to drop this right now."

"Jakob, we've been working together for over six years. You're a partner here now. You've worked tirelessly, helping me build up this business. The least I can do is make sure you're getting some sort of satisfaction."

"And you don't think I find my work satisfying?" I tried to tease, tried to lighten the mood, as the tone had shifted. I would take her teasing over the somewhat somber look I now saw on Cara's face.

"I don't doubt you enjoy working here with me, but you need more out of your life than your job, Jakob," she said. Her expression was unreadable, and I shifted slightly. I wondered if this had anything to do with the rushed wedding cakes. Cara wasn't the most sentimental of people, but perhaps a wedding so close to an impending funeral might make her maudlin?

"You think you can cover the bakery for the next twenty minutes or so? I have an errand or two I need to run," Cara said.

"No problem. Will you be back to help me load the van?" I asked.

"Sure," she said, and then she left me standing in the kitchen with the completed cake. I watched her as she walked away, sweat still dripping down my back. Then she exited out the back, and I was in the process of loading our industrial dishwasher when a spike of cold ran from my feet straight to my heart. It was how my babcia described the sensation of the Unliving. I felt my phone vibrating in my pocket, and the chill subsided as quickly as it came. I removed it and didn't recognize the number. It took me a moment before I was able to decipher *Nd ur help, emergency.*

Who is this? I texted back.

Its T. Before had I finished reading the four characters, I saw the icon indicating another text was incoming. *plz. Nd ur help.*

What's wrong? I typed back. Since Erik had been in my house just under a week ago, I hadn't heard from any member of his pack—or from him.

I can't feel my wolf, Terence's text read. Blood froze, and my heart might have missed a beat. I wasn't a wolf—I couldn't know how that felt—but I had the distinct impression this was a big deal. It also meant something that Terence's first thought had been to come to me, rather than to his alpha. *Get to Siren's ASAP*, I texted. Then I raided the different spices we had available. I hoped that Cara's errand would be a longer one because I was about to start doing magic in the bakery—something I hadn't ever thought I would do.

C U in 10. I didn't reply. I was too busy grabbing ginger, crushed lavender, peppermint, salt, whatever I thought might be useful. I even stole a rose petal from the cake, hating myself as I did so. I would have killed for sage at that moment, but I would make do with what I had.

I was waiting at the front door when I saw Terence running down the sidewalk, hooded sweatshirt pulled tight around his body. That was bad. Then I saw his face. I saw genuine fear, and I managed not to curse, but it was a very near thing. I unlocked the door and pulled it open. Terence stopped, inches from the threshold, seemingly unable to move across it.

"Get in here," I all but commanded. He was rooted to the spot and his nose and brow wrinkled.

"I can't. Did you ward this space?" he asked.

That made me pause for a second. There were wards here? How had I not felt them?

"Give me a second," I said as I laid my hand on the lintel and closed my eyes. For the first time in the years I had worked with Cara, I actively tapped into the flow of magic where I worked. Focusing on my breathing, I let my awareness spiral outward from me and downward, working through layers of metal, concrete, and earth. It was there, deep, buried strong and rooted in a way I had only encountered once before. It thrummed as soon as I touched it with the edges of my awareness, sending a shiver down my spine.

"You feel it without your wolf?" I asked, my voice slightly accented with a hint of Yiddish. The barrier that Terence felt—it was the sort of magic that made my hair stand on end. I knew it instantly—from my own experience and the generations who had come before. This was fae power. The last of my ancestors who had directly worked with fae power had been back in Poland, sometime in the early nineteenth century. Only remnants and fragments of fae power remained, or so I had thought. To the best of my knowledge, the fae had never made it to the New World.

"It's heavy." Terence sounded a little uncertain, and I got what he meant. Apparently the look on my face as I concentrated was enough to make him quiet. After my first year in culinary school, when I had taken a summer to work in the kitchens of Prague, near the Staronová Synagoga, I had felt power like this. I hadn't pushed then because it was an area thick with pedestrian traffic and I didn't need to be seen letting my guard down to have a conversation with deep magic. I almost wanted to tell Terence to leave, but he had asked for my help. I would do what I could for the teen.

My mouth moved as I went over my great-great-uncle's formula for working with old magic. It was a Hebrew formula, and moments passed before the humming of fae power responded to the incantation. My fingers dug into the wood of the doorframe as the ward crushed into me, but I was able to keep my feet, if just barely. How had a power like this escaped my witch's senses? I could hear my grandmother's voice reminding me not to be unprepared, that I had been foolish for not knowing this about my surroundings. She would have been right, as she was about so many things.

The will animating the ward was slippery and danced despite being bound in the earth. This was magic that would have taken me a lifetime to learn to cast. I opened my eyes, and I heard rather than saw Terence take a step back. Witch's fire—my eyes and skin would be alight with it. I didn't have time to pray that no one would notice or to cast a concealment charm. For once, I was thankful that Siren's was slightly off any of Cleveland's main drags. My mezuzah pulsed, sending out waves of flame in time with my heart, and I focused the fire on my skin—and in my eyes, veins, and bones—downward.

The ward reacted and fought me, but I had fingertips touching salt and silver singing on my neck. These were enemies to fae power, or so the grimoire claimed. I was willing to play with fire—metaphorically, if not literally. The barrier trembled and shifted, responding to the repeated mantra. Three choice words in biblical Hebrew and I felt the barrier shatter. I stumbled back, and Terence fell in after me. I collapsed on the floor, and while Terence stumbled over me, he kept his footing. I had expected amusement or judgment when I looked up. Instead there was something that almost approached awe. He extended a hand to me, and I accepted it. No one would ever accuse me of being proud. As much as I wanted to pant, to catch my breath, I had a job to do and didn't want whatever had played with fae power to come back and find that I had disrupted its work.

"What did you just do?" Terence's awe was audible.

"I fought with a fae barrier. I had to use some old magic, stuff I generally try not to use, to get it to cooperate," I said as I got to the door and turned at least the physical locks.

"Alpha Erik said that our pack's witch, the one when he was a cub, said that fae magic was dangerous, that it was hard to master," Terence said. "He said that the witch then didn't have the power to break a fae line unless the pack was with her."

"They're hard to break but not unbreakable. All depends on how stubborn or stupid you are. She probably downplayed her power. I could talk more Magic 101, if you really want, but you came to me for some help," I said.

"You still have the strength to help me after dismantling fae magic?"

"You asked me for help, T. Where I come from, friends help each other," I said. Terence smiled so broadly it threatened to split his face. I made a gesture with my hand, indicating that he should get behind the counter and out of the line of sight of the general public. The front of house was supposed to be closed today, and I didn't want anyone getting the wrong impression.

He made his way into the kitchen and I followed him, turning off the lights and closing the door. I was tempted to text Cara, ask her how long she would be, but that might set her "something's wrong" alarm off. I didn't need to have that conversation with her right now. I took the salt from my pocket and laid down a crude circle. It wasn't much, but it would work. I then reached for the lavender and the rose petal and crushed them between my thumb and forefinger.

"What happened that made you lose contact with your wolf?" I pressed the rose/lavender mixture against my palm.

"I was in gym. There's this boy—"

I looked up to see his cheeks darkening. "Did he catch your eye?"

"He's cute I guess, but—"

"You're still hung up on Erik."

Terence's continued silence spoke worlds more than anything he could have said.

"What happened with the boy?" I prompted, needing to know more of the story so I might be able to help him.

"We were the last in the showers. We were just shooting the shit, then he leaned in and kissed me. I didn't know he liked me like that. I thought my wolf would have alerted me, sat up, snarled, warned the boy away. My wolf didn't. I can't feel him—"

"Your wolf?" I needed to confirm. Terence nodded and continued.

"It's like he's stone. He's there, but I can't feel him, not really. I didn't want Alpha Erik to know," T babbled.

I brought my finger into my mouth, sucked it for a second, then dipped it in the crushed flower petals. Muttering in Yiddish, I drew two small sigils on Terence's forearms. He looked like he wanted to object—wanted to yell at me for doing something gross and crossing into his personal space—but I shot him a look that would have served Cara proudly, and Terence twitched but shut his jaw. As I made a third small sigil on Terence's throat, I noticed the light in the room change. Hues of emerald, peridot, jade, and malachite danced and cast twisting, shifting shadows. Witch's fire had come unbidden. Apparently, I was doing something right. I made a last sign on his forehead, which continued to glow as I lifted my finger. Then I reached for the sprig of peppermint. I held it in front of his mouth, and Terence stared at me with open puzzlement written large across his features.

"Put it under your tongue, don't swallow," I commanded. This time he listened to me without a gesture of defiance. He took the herb and made a show of opening his mouth and putting it beneath his tongue. His jaw slammed shut as I chanted in earnest. The four sigils all glowed, mirroring my witch's fire. I extended a hand and a knob of fresh ginger flew into my palm.

I snapped it under his nose before he had time to react. The symbol on his forehead blossomed gold and light cascaded and pulsed as his eyes rolled back. I closed my eyes and switched to Hebrew for the last part of the formula. Given that it was something I was making up on the fly, I was pleasantly impressed by my ability to improvise. The light continued, growing brighter, brilliant, a star contained in Terence's skin that flared, almost blinding me. I chanted of hearth and home, of stories passed across generations, and of the unity of man with beast. I recited words of balance, of completion, of being whole.

Then it came—a howl that was low and plaintive at first, but rose, grew, and merged with my chant. It was a song of pride, of triumph, of raw animal power. The lights exploded, fracturing and splitting, vanishing and running. I shut my lips, and Terence's primal howl continued. I could see his eyes clearly, and they bled with black, purely animal. I extended my toe to the line of salt and smudged it, and the gathered energy torrented out. He was smiling again, and he looked younger than his seventeen years. It was all too easy to imagine him as a child, unwrapping presents on his birthday.

"Thanks! Thank you so…." He stopped himself midgush, and his nose wrinkled. The joy that had been on his face vanished as quickly as it had blossomed.

"I know, I know," I apologized, admitting defeat. "Erik's told me what I smell like when I'm working."

"It's not that." He was snarling, and I wondered if I had gone too far and should have asked him to wait so I could triple check my family's collected magical knowledge.

"What is it?" I couldn't keep the fear from my voice.

"This place, it's like the way that line felt. If it was bad without my wolf—" He didn't finish.

I was going to ask him another question when I saw Cara standing at the back door of the kitchen. All was still for a moment, and the air was suddenly thick with tension. I had the distinct impression that I was in a scene scored by Ennio Morricone, the sort that went right before the gunfight. Cara's eyes narrowed, and Terence's mirrored the gesture. His eyes had become abyssal night, and his mouth opened, revealing lupine fangs in the place of human incisors. I snapped my gaze back to Cara, who opened her lips, just barely.

For a fraction of a second, everything was still and quiet. Then the world exploded. The sound that came from Cara was something of deepest grief, of purest loss. It was the scream of a mother holding her dead child to her chest. It was the cry of a widower, seeing his wife's coffin being lowered into the earth. It was pain and despair. It consumed everything, drowned out the memory of any sound other than the high, keening wail. It was agony for me, and I was selfish enough to own I didn't want to know how bad it must be for Terence.

Instinct guided my hand, and I grabbed the salt. It felt as if blood were dripping from my ears, but I knew what I had to do. The circle I had used to reunite Terence with his wolf had been worthy of Giotto compared to the scattering I did now. Speed and intention were more important than accuracy. Terence was hunched, curled in on himself, and I did see blood on his ears. As the last grain of salt completed the circle, I shouted a single command in Hebrew. Cara's lips were still partly open, and I knew outside of the circle, the deafening, maddening, soul-rending cry was continuing. I hated myself for what I was about to do, but I leaned over, dipped my finger in the trickle of blood, and then grabbed the ginger root. A hasty sigil and a command word in Yiddish made both of Cara's hands fly to her midsection and her face turn green.

Aside from the night with Erik, I hadn't done any offensive workings. My theory of offensive magic was sound, especially with as much time as I had invested in the grimoire recently, but theory and practice were two different things. I looked at Cara as she tried to keep herself from spewing all over the tile of her kitchen. The ancestors who wrote about offensive magic had made it clear that if you had to use it, you needed to be willing to fight for your life. You had to fight dirty. Terence moaned and I shifted my focus back to him. His teeth looked more human, but he was still on the ground, unable to get up.

I flicked my gaze back to Cara and saw her right herself, the color returning to her cheeks. I pulled out the mezuzah from beneath my shirt, and it flared and cast oblong shadows as ghostly greens pulsed and radiated. Cara took a small step back and saw that I still had my hand on the ginger root with the blood sigil. Despite the situation, I swore she smiled.

"Jakob," she said.

"*Ben side*," I countered, naming her. While none of my ancestors had directly met a wailing woman before, it was easy enough to tell what she was. I was a little furious at myself for not piecing it together earlier. After all, a fiery redhead with a stratospheric soprano range, who had named her bakery after another kind of fae infamous for their voices. If I had been paying attention, if I had been a prepared witch, I would have known.

"I was wondering how long it would take you to find out," she admitted. "I'm—"

"Displeased that it took me so long?" I interjected.

"I'm impressed you got your act together, named me, and were able to almost make me puke, although you know what a hell that would have been to clean up. You never did cast at work, so I can't be too shocked it took you as long as it did."

"You knew?" I was stunned.

"How could I not? You reek of magic, Jakob, although you've been more careful than I thought."

I was stunned into silence. Cara didn't hand out compliments lightly.

"The name of the bakery should have told me I was working for a fae."

"You're handling this remarkably well," she said.

"Considering I just found out that my business partner is fae, that the fae are in the Americas, and that not only are you fae, you're a wailing woman, I'm proud that I'm not having a full-on panic attack," I yelled, far past caring.

"That's more of what I was expecting, to be honest," Cara admitted. Despite myself, despite the situation, I couldn't keep back a laugh. It soon became hysterical. Terence looked up at me from his fetal position, and Cara didn't move from where she stood. This was just typical of the year I was having. I don't know how long I laughed, only that when I pulled myself together, I was feeling much more composed.

"Let me guess, he's one of the pack of the alpha who railed you? The Viking?" Cara asked. I nodded.

"What did he need you for?" she asked.

"He lost contact with his wolf," I said.

"You aren't the pack witch yet. I would have felt it in your magic," Cara said. "So, why did you help him?"

"He asked," I said simply.

"You're far too giving, Jakob." Cara rolled her eyes. Terence had managed to pull himself up to one knee and was staring across the bakery at Cara, a combination of respect, anger, and fear on his acne-scarred face.

"If I promise not to scream, will you dispel your circle?" she asked.

"What will you swear by?" I shot back. A smile of pure pride flickered across Cara's face. Despite the fact I had almost made her vomit—or perhaps because of it—and regardless of not remembering the correct forms on how to deal with what I had thought was an extinct species, she was pleased with me. What I wouldn't have given to curse freely then, but I had been better trained and I held myself back.

"You've done your research." The smile was in her voice too.

"I guess because I haven't gotten out much in the last five months, I've been able to catch up on my reading," I explained.

"No need to be modest, Jakob," she all but crooned. "I wouldn't have hired you and then offered you a partnership if you weren't clever." Her voice was soft now, like a bell. She brought her finger to her mouth and tapped one lacquered nail against her lips. The Morricone score that I had been imaging a lifetime ago came back in deafening stereo. Terence was all but pressed against me, waiting to see how I would react. I just watched Cara as she went through her options. She lifted her head and there was childlike glee written boldly across her features. "I swear by the crossroads I will not scream unless I am attacked... or a hearse goes by," she said, making a swift gesture I didn't recognize with her right hand near her heart.

Terence looked up at me as I bit my tongue and tried to go through everything I could remember from the grimoire about different oaths and how they might apply. I hadn't spent nearly enough time in those sections of the tome to know how serious or binding a crossroads oath would be to a death fae. For the second time that day, I was left with pure instinct. My toe moved slowly, and I was careful to make sure both Terence and Cara could see my movements. I smeared the salt circle again, and when Cara clapped her hands, delighted, I wondered if I had made a wrong move. Rather than press any advantage, however, she sat opposite Terence and me. Terence looked between the two of us, as though trying to figure out what had just happened.

"I suppose this is the wrong time to ask for a bigger stake in Siren's?" I ventured. It might not have been the best question to open with, but I wasn't in my right mind.

"We can talk about your share in Siren's after we figure out what to do about him." She made a small thrust of her chin at Terence. He had the good grace to blush deep red. "He won't be able to keep this from his alpha, and the last thing I need is a pack of wolves beating down my door."

"Why do you think my pack would want to be around you?" Terence couldn't stop himself from asking.

"It's nothing personal, kid," Cara said, "but wolves—or any shifters, for that matter—don't tend to be fond of the fae. It goes back generations, and I don't understand it fully." There was a sympathetic smile on her face. "As soon as you could feel your wolf again, what was the first thing you did in my space?"

Terence didn't answer, only turned a deeper shade of red and averted his eyes. Cara turned her focus back to me. "I can't afford to have any more wolves on the doorstep, Jakob."

"I promise I won't take any pack calls on company time," I swore. "And once I find a way to break my bond with the alpha...."

Cara sighed and I stopped myself. "You're powerful, Jakob, don't deny it." Cara raised a hand to stop any objection before I could even form one. "However, even your power can't undo a binding to a pack. The only way out of the bond is if the alpha dies or if you die."

I swallowed. "Is that why you were encouraging me to think about the type of life I wanted?"

"I don't want to scream for you, Jakob, not unless I really have to." Any sense of play had gone out of her, and she was somber again. I had only thought about what it was to hear the scream; I hadn't thought about what it would mean to be the screamer, to feel it ripping through my body. The loss, the raw pain of Cara's wail—it was enough to shatter a soul or break a heart. You couldn't give a scream like that unless you knew what that pain was. It was something that had to be felt at the very core of your being, and I wondered just how many times Cara had had to scream throughout her life.

"You won't scream for Alpha Erik, will you?" Terence asked.

"I don't want to scream for anyone, kid, but your alpha can't know about me. If a whole pack came at me, I might have to scream in earnest," Cara said.

"That wasn't a full scream?" I couldn't stop myself from asking.

"That was barely a whisper." Cara turned back to me and there was a small half-smile on her lips. She wasn't boasting. It was simply the truth. Besides the ritual glass of wine each Friday, I had barely touched alcohol since my night with Erik. Tonight, though—tonight I would be reaching for the Luksusowa I kept stashed in the back of the freezer for emergency situations. I was going to be needing it.

"If my alpha asks," Terence said, but he stopped himself. We knew what he was thinking. Disobeying the alpha would take levels of self-control and strength the teenager might not have.

"Erik can't come here. If he does... it might start a War," I said. Both Terence and Cara heard the capital letter and nodded. If the grimoire was to be trusted, no one could walk away from a War once it started. I had privately surmised that the fae had gone extinct due to some War or other, that the blood feud had continued until the last fae had died. I was man enough to admit when I was wrong—as was evidenced by a banshee standing less than twenty feet from me—but we were at an uneasy impasse. While I didn't think Erik would willingly come onto Cara's territory with ill intent, even he might not be able to fight off his instinct, and I didn't want to know the sort of damage that Cara could do with a true scream. The whisper had been bad enough.

Terence worried his bottom lip, and Cara rested one of her lacquered nails against her top lip. If the situation had been less dire, less potentially dangerous, it could have been funny. Instead, a witch, a banshee, and a teenaged werewolf sat in a crude circle, trying to think of ways to avoid a War.

"He'll drag it out of me, like about your date," Terence said. This confirmed my suspicions, but I still felt sorry for the kid. It was then that a scrap of paper caught my eye. Terence shifted his gaze from me to the counter and then back to me, clearly not seeing what I had or understanding its significance. Cara turned her focus, and the smile was back on her face.

"Fucking clever, Kuratowski. Very fucking clever." She almost laughed as she grabbed the scrap and found a pencil. Terence still looked puzzled, his gaze darting between Cara and me as if we were playing some sort of tennis match. Cara crossed toward me and Terence retreated. I didn't blame him. She passed me the paper and the pencil and I put it down and drew hastily, the tip flying over the paper as I scribed a formula. It was simple, but it would work.

"Write what you saw on the piece of paper, and then hand it to me," I instructed as I turned to Terence. He arched a brow but came over and wrote on the blank piece of paper. He took his time, and his handwriting was barely legible, but I wasn't going to complain. When he finished, he passed me the piece of paper and shuddered as he felt the spark of magic flare.

"What…?" he asked.

"You just gave me your words," I told him, wondering why I hadn't thought of it before. It might have been a common expression, but like most things, everyday rituals could come from places of real power. "You can't tell Erik what happened because you gave it to me," I finished.

Terence stared at me and then at Cara, his mouth hanging wide open. "What will I say if he asks?" he eventually said.

"That you gave your word," I said. "If Erik is half the alpha he thinks himself, he won't press you any further than that. If he tries, he'll have to come through me, and I have ways of resisting him," I reassured.

"You are entirely too clever, Jakob," Cara praised. "Now, let's get things cleaned up here and send the whelp on his way. We're pressed for time and need to deliver a cake."

CHAPTER 11

"OF ALL the holiday treats you could have popularized, why did you choose fruitcake?" I asked. December was in full swing, and the lake effect snow was back. I was waking even earlier than usual to shovel out my driveway. December weddings, holiday gift baskets, a gingerbread house competition with a $20,000 prize, and requests for New Year's Eve goodies meant that December was one of the busier months for Siren's. Both Cara and I were burning the midnight oil. Even after the holidays, we'd be slammed with Valentine's Day prep work. Only after that would Cara or I sleep easily. We likely were both planning our vacations. Me, I needed a vacation, not only to get away from Erik's attentions and the bakery, but also to get away from the news. This time it was from Sandusky, in the Cholera Graveyard. Four graves had been dug up, and the bodies had been... well... gnawed upon.

"It was something most of the other bakeries weren't doing. It had become a punchline and I wanted to see if there was a way to make it into something people actually wanted." Cara shrugged as she continued to chop almonds. She hadn't looked up from her cutting board. To be fair, I felt the shrug more than I saw it, also elbow-deep in preparation. Even if we were closed to the public today, the kitchen was firing on all cylinders. She put down the knife and expertly poured from a half-empty bottle of bourbon, the third one so far. There would be heaven only knew how many more by the time we stopped.

"Did you bring the fruitcake back out of spite?" I asked.

"Is there a better reason to do anything?" she replied. I didn't need to see her lips to know that she was smiling. Spite was a great motivator. Part of why I had hit the grimoire as hard as I had was to spite Erik and his talk of mate and pack. It wasn't the only reason, but it certainly added something to my search. Erik had texted me since Thanksgiving, only briefly, asking when he could next see me. It was more than Nathan had done in a long time.

"No, there really isn't." I reached for some fresh ginger, grated it, and then moved over to the cloves and cinnamon. My hands reeked of spices—they likely would for the next couple of days. Cara and I worked in companionable silence next to each other and moved in time. I felt my phone rattle in my pocket, another alert about an incoming order most likely. We were already working as hard as we could to meet demand, and I honestly thought we would need front-of-house help, at least through Valentine's Day.

The constant business might be a blessing—it would give me space and time to think and get my head in line with my heart. I tried not to listen to the latter too much, but now I had a feeling it was trying to tell me something. For the last few days, I had awoken in predawn darkness from dreams of a decidedly carnal nature. In them, I saw Erik looming over me, remembered his hands running over my body, and the almost-feral smile on his lips when he first kissed me. Each time I woke, my shoulder and cock throbbed in time with my heart. I'd had to be very careful about what happened after I woke. I didn't need half-formed spells and oaths flying from my mouth in a moment of passion.

"You're thinking about him, aren't you?" Cara asked. I managed not to cut myself, but it was a near thing. I kept my head down, but like I knew her, she knew me. She would be able to feel the flush rising up my neck and crawling over my face.

"I'd rather we didn't," I said.

"Jakob," Cara said. I stopped what I was doing only because I felt Cara's own stillness. I looked up to see her, the sad look on her face and something flitting through her emerald eyes. Now that we both knew what the other was, we had stopped wearing so many masks, at least when no one else was around.

"Even banshees don't live alone," she said.

"I'm not alone. I could see my family in less than three hours if I wanted," I said.

"What do you share with your family? What do they know? Do they know that you're a witch?" she asked.

"No, but it's been something of a tradition. The magic remained secret with the one who had it until they could train the next member of the family. My grandmother once told me that she thought the magic would die with her," I answered.

"Did she?"

"She did. She even said she had prayed on it once."

"An odd prayer."

"She might not have been the first," I said. While we were more open with each other, there was only so much I was willing to tell Cara about the grimoire, about the way I had been trained.

"I've met other witches. At least for them, they didn't bother with all the cloak-and-dagger shit your family seems to be fond of."

"That's their family. In my family, the power bounces around. It's traveled across bloodlines and through different members of the family over generations. For us, our first priority was keeping ourselves out of sight, even from those we are closest too." I shrugged.

"That's a very hard life to live," Cara said bluntly.

I chuckled, resisted making an *Annie* joke, and turned back to my bowl. "You said that even banshees don't live alone," I pointed out.

"I have my sisters and my brother. I can always feel them, call to them without using a phone—although phones do make things much easier. I might not see them often, but I know where they are, how they are, and what they're doing. My family is always with me, and we can't have secrets from each other. We can't lie to each other. Do you remember that you had to wait two weeks after your interview before I hired you?" she asked.

"I didn't think it took too long. I've known people who had to wait over a month before they got news one way or the other," I said. She smirked.

"Any bakery worth their sugar would have hired you on the spot. You know you're that good, Kuratowski—own it," she said. I averted my eyes for a second. Nathan and Nicole had both been right about my lack of self-confidence. Eventually, I'd find a therapist to help me deal with it, when I wasn't eyeballs-deep in supernatural shenanigans.

"Thanks," I said. Cara made a noise but I still didn't look up.

"I almost didn't hire you because my family *knew* what you were. They felt you as soon as I did. I was on the phone with them the second you left the building. They argued with me, tried to tell me I would be inviting trouble by bringing a witch into my place of work. I flip-flopped on whether or not to hire you until the day I made the call. To be honest, I still hadn't made up my mind by the time I called you," she explained. She was moving again, pouring another generous amount of bourbon over candied fruits. She swiveled, moved low, and emerged holding two shot glasses. She was as generous pouring into the shot glasses as she had been pouring over the fruit.

I stared, first at Cara, then down to the liquor. When I lifted my eyes to Cara again, she raised the shot and took it smoothly. I couldn't help but mirror her. I figured if Cara wanted to start day-drinking, I wasn't going to stop her. I could afford to join her, if only this once. Warmth from the shot spread rapidly in me, and I coughed. Cara laughed at my inability to handle the bourbon.

"The point being, my family knew about you, knew the risk I was taking. They were constantly calling me. It took you almost six years before you brought trouble here with that wolf. My eldest sister, Bridget, she's still amused as all hell by how clever you were in solving the problem of the whelp. They knew. And I have an active support network, which is not something you have for your magical self," Cara finished.

"As I said, it's the way my family is. I learned young to be unseen, unnoticed. If you get noticed, it tends to make you dead," I offered. Cara nodded.

"Very old-school."

"It's not just the magic thing, though," I continued, emboldened by the whiskey. "It's a Jewish thing. Do you know how many anti-Semitic slurs I've heard in my life? I'm Polish on top of that. I think I know every dumb-Polack joke because they've all been hurled at me. Let's not even talk about what happened when I came out of the closet."

"Did your family disown you?"

"No, but I did have to change schools." I shrugged a shoulder as I said it. Cara grabbed the bottle again and poured another set of generous shots, then quickly downed hers. I matched her again, and we touched the rims of our glasses. This time, the shot was smooth, almost silken as it went down my throat. I hadn't anticipated this when I got to work. I had anticipated an assembly line, focusing on getting as much done as possible.

"I get that. The world's a scary place, and you do what you can to avoid trouble. Still, you have to have someone beyond me to talk to about this—or just someone besides the cat. Fae, human, shifter, or witch, we're all social. Even the undead congregate," Cara said.

A single word instantly killed my buzz. "The undead?"

"Someone in your family had to have seen them. The undead are more trouble for you than for me. Granted, death fae, but still, the undead hate witches."

"My babcia, she called them *dybbuk*, demons or unlife," I said.

"I've heard them called dybbuk but not unlife. It's as apt a description as any. What did she tell you about them?"

"That only the most powerful of their kind could resemble something close to humanity, and even then it would be a strain for them. She said that it was in the way they moved—that their voices would always have a rasp, as if they couldn't get enough air to fill their lungs. She said that you could always smell the rot, no matter how much cologne or perfume—" I stopped when I saw the look on Cara's face.

"Your grandmother sounds like a smart woman," Cara said as she poured herself a third shot. I lifted my brows at her and she quirked a single brow at me.

"I didn't know that fae tolerance was so high." I wasn't sure if I was complimenting or scolding her.

"I'm just an experienced drinker," she said and then emptied the glass. Then she put it down and picked up her knife, solid as a rock.

"Moving away from the undead," Cara said and half shivered. She was still an artist with the knife. Her slices would have done a surgeon proud. "I get why, in an ideal world, you might want to try being alone and not have Erik as part of your life. This, though—this isn't an ideal world."

"I know that." I moved to one of the ovens and slipped on mitts just as the timer went off. I removed a tray of gingerbread persons. In addition to the contest we'd be entering, we were hosting a decorating night and it had already sold out. There were also families who wanted their own gingerbread person for home decoration. I knew by the end of December I would swear off ever baking gingerbread again. I also knew that a year from now I'd be doing this same thing.

"I know you do, Jakob. You were with a werewolf, and that's almost like catching an STI. It's not a death sentence, though, and I would know," she said, her voice rising. Learning morbid her sense of humor/worldview was proving a bigger adjustment than the reality of her being a banshee. I was almost tempted to pour myself a third shot but refrained.

"I don't know if I'm ever going to be able to get used to this," I said honestly.

"Gallows humor is the best sort," she countered, "and joking about death, well, it helps."

"Was what you just said really a joke?" I couldn't stop myself from asking.

"You want jokes, do you? I have plenty. What's a skeleton's favorite instrument?" I looked up, wondering if she was serious. She had schooled her features into a perfect poker face and I held my breath.

"A trombone," she finished with a perfect deadpan. I groaned.

"I will pay you to stop," I said. She tilted her head back and laughed at me.

"Like you have enough money to bribe me. I know just how much you take home, Jakob," she said, her voice a near singsong.

"You're not as funny as you think you are," I groused.

"You don't need to be so grim. After all you're a witch, not a reaper."

We fell back into companionable silence, her dicing fruit and soaking it in liquor, me mixing spices and flour together, going between proper gingerbread and the far more popular cookies. As I held a cookie cutter above spread-out dough, I looked to Cara. She was back in the zone, totally focused on her knife work. Her liquid-smooth motions sparked something, and I almost dropped the tool I was holding. I can't say what it was about watching Cara with a knife at that moment—all I knew was that the realization had come suddenly, and would not let me free. I knew what I had been doing wrong. I was thinking like a human.

In trying to deal with Erik, I had been trying to think about blunt force, shattering the bond. If I could understand more about the bond, understand how the magic worked in his pack, I might be able to mirror Cara's surgical precision. I might find a way to snip it without either of us dying as a result. I was mentally using every insult and invective I could think of, being careful not to put too much intention behind any one of them. While Erik wanted me to serve as the pack's witch, I still didn't know what a pack's witch did.

I stepped back, and Cara watched me as I fished my phone out of my pocket. I had to think of something believable, some way to get back on Erik's good side. While he had been persistent with his texts, I knew he might find it a little suspicious if I was all gung-ho about a role I had been fighting for the past few months. When I put my phone back, Cara looked at me with a puzzled expression on her face.

"Don't text a werewolf while tipsy," I explained.

"Not bad life advice," she agreed.

CHAPTER 12

I BRUSHED my fingers against the wick of the *shamash* candle, eyes closed as I recited the blessings for the first night of Hanukkah. I took my time as I formed each syllable and only lifted my hand as I finished the last of the prayers. The wick sputtered, a burning sunset as I guided the shamash to the first candle. The world outside the bay window was dark, and some of my neighbors had turned on their various holiday displays. Curled atop the couch, the cat ignored the small magic and the holiday peacocking. I had left work only after I sobered up. We were ahead for the day, and Cara had seen my need to leave.

I looked at the heart of the small flame and my mind drifted. This, the lighting of candles, had been my first working, three years before I became *bar mitzvah*. The flame was mildly hypnotic, and I let it work through me. I hoped that watching the fire would bring me to a moment of clarity because, while I knew what I needed to do with Erik, I still didn't know how. As my mind drifted, the strongest image that arose was my grandmother's face.

I remembered her last day, her face pale, the light in her eyes fading, only half there. For the first time I could remember, there was no iron in her grip, only velvet. Tears were flowing down my face. Outside the small hospital room, my parents, cousins, aunts, and uncles all waited. She wanted to say goodbye to each of us individually, but it was taking its toll, and there were now nearly minute-long pauses between each sentence. I felt it, the faintest spark as she drew on the last of her power. It would keep her only so long, and we both knew it. The power that had been with her since her girlhood was ebbing and now, as she mustered the last of it, we both knew what that meant.

"Jakob," she said. I squeezed her hand to let her know I was there, not trusting my voice. My tears were free flowing, but on her face, there was only a small, contented smile.

"Do not mourn for me, my clever boy," she whispered, her voice as frail as winter sunlight.

"Babcia...." I couldn't say more. How do you summarize a lifetime of love? How can you let someone know how much they mean to you? Everything I felt for her was summed up in the single word, what she had been for me—would continue to be for me even after she was gone.

"It is time. Do you have the book?" she asked. I squeezed her hand and then opened my backpack, where the grimoire had been living since she first came to the hospital, nearly a month before. She had told me to look after it the day she went in. She knew what was coming and tried to prepare me as best she could. She had felt the cancer and knew there would be no fighting it through science or sorcery. I fumbled as I searched for a pencil or pen. It had taken me longer than I wanted to open the tome, to hold my pen steady.

"My clever boy," she praised. I saw her lips move but didn't hear anything. This was it—her last working. I was the last family member she wanted to see. To this day, I knew that at least one of my cousins resented me for this, but Babcia had lived with my family for at least half my life at that point, and they didn't say anything to my face. She drew in one breath, then a second, and the lights flickered—a last call to power.

"My great working happened shortly after your father was born," she said. There was no hesitancy, no drawing of breath. She spoke fluently—granted, not in English, but she was wholly there—composed, present, and aware. This was what she had marshaled the last of her strength to do. She needed the words to be understood, spoken firmly, and I put pen to paper, prepared to record her words. It was what she had done for her uncle, and he for the witch before him across the generations, possibly going all the way back to the first witch.

"Of all the children, I feared most that your father would be touched by magic," she said, going on. "Of course, he does not know, nor do any of his siblings." Her eyes closed and I knew that while her body lay in the sterile, white sheets, her mind, her soul—they were back on the day of her great working. She was in the past more than she was in the present. There she was, a young mother, at the height of her power. But it wasn't just memory; she was living it again, and she might be feeling the faintest hint of that power.

As she spoke, I felt her magic bleed from her hand into mine. It crawled up my arm and seeped into my bones and blood. It seared itself into me. Even though I had called to magic before, even though I had done workings since the age of ten, my eyes stung in a way that had nothing to do with tears. It was the witch's fire. For the first time in my life, my eyes burned with it. I had seen the jade flames from time to time when my babcia worked and had once asked when they would come to me. She had told me they would come when I was ready. I looked at my grandmother as my eyes burned, and saw her as she had been—a young mother, just out of her maidenhood—and as she was now—the crone who had protected and guided the family. The magic continued to pour from her into me, and as much I might have wanted to reverse the current, as much as I wanted to put life back into her, I knew I couldn't.

"Your father was sickly. All the family knows this or has been told. What I haven't said is that when your father was five months old, he should have died." My grandmother's voice was steady if cautious. Even on her deathbed, she was still a prepared witch. She was not a dead witch yet and wouldn't be one until she absolutely needed to be. She squeezed my hand, and I blinked, the tears refracting the flickering emerald in my eyes. I closed my eyes, matched my breathing to hers, and squeezed her hand back. When I opened my eyes again, the tingle of fire was gone. Her lips twisted into a small smile. Even with her eyes closed, she had felt me banish something that might reveal us.

"I was home, folding the laundry downstairs. I felt—did not hear—felt deeper than my bones and blood—that there was something nearing your father. I had prepared the house well with wards. Jakob, what is a witch who is unprepared?" she asked.

Despite myself and the situation, a faint chuckle escaped my lips. "An unprepared witch is a dead witch," I repeated.

"My clever boy," she praised me, and I leaned down and brushed my lips against her knuckles. There was a beat of silence before my grandmother inhaled a steady breath and made herself continue.

"I went to the crib where your father slept. He was lying still, but standing over him was a great and deep shadow. Not the shadow of death. Death now is an old friend, waiting for me. The shadow standing over your father was a dybbuk." A shiver passed through her body. The machines attached to her responded, their beeps harsh and shrill. I paid them no mind; there was nothing I could do about them. My whole mind was on my grandmother. Having seen a dybbuk, my grandmother had been deeply scarred, and the experience never fully left her.

"I froze, seeing the dybbuk standing above your father's crib. Even in the old country, dybbuk were rare, and I did not think they could follow us to the New World. I should have known better. Wherever the greed is strong, there will be dybbuk, and greed has always been strong in this land," she said, shaking her head.

"You mean that my father was—" I said, not sure if I wanted to continue.

"Your father would have been a meal for the dybbuk, Jakob. It was taking his core. They always favor taking the young and the innocent, because they are a source of infinite potential. However, any witch, or any of the magic-touched, are always in danger. This is why you need to be a prepared witch, so you do not become like them." Even then, my grandmother had the mind to admonish, to warn me. Even as she bled the last of her power into me, she had enough of herself left.

"The dybbuk was so focused on your father that it did not sense me. I had a knife in one hand and a sprig of juniper in my other. I held both out and I called. I had never called to magic as I did on that day." She then proceeded to tell me what she had said, the formula she had used. My hand, the one that held the pen, flew over the page in the grimoire, my chicken-scratch Polish blending in with the other lines of text throughout countless generations. "The knife and juniper, they burned brighter than the sun, and the dybbuk turned to ash before me. It had already done its foul work. Your father was still, and it was almost the stillness of the unliving. Seeing him so still, his skin all but blue—

"I screamed then, my clever boy.

"When my mother and father died, may their memories be a blessing, I was an orphan. When your grandfather died, I was a widow. As your father lay there, stiller than the dead but not among them… there is no word for this. It is a pain too great to be put into words. I pray you never know this pain, Jakob.

"I pulled your father from his crib and put him to my chest. My tears fell, and I didn't think they would ever stop. I was rocking back and forth, holding your father's cold form against my beating heart. I should have prayed then, but I was trying to accept what I had seen. A dybbuk had been standing over my youngest son, had wanted his life for its own, and had almost taken him from me. I carried your father down the stairs into my kitchen, all the while wailing, my voice threatening to go raw."

My grandmother paused, and her breath shook for the first time since she had worked her magic. I squeezed her hand, but I couldn't say anything. This was the last story she would tell me, and I didn't want to stop what would be the last words she spoke to me. Outside the room, I knew my family waited, sipping lukewarm coffee, flipping through pages of books or magazines they weren't really seeing. A part of me wanted to be with them. As my grandmother's power bled into me, I tasted death, felt it crawling up the back of my throat. I knew I had to be there, to accept what she was giving me, but it was not something I would wish on anyone, although I knew someday I would have to do this as she was doing it to me.

She went on, and I resumed writing, my hand slanting to fill a blank space at the corner of the page. She told me about the sigils she had drawn, and I mimicked what I thought they would look like. She told me the incantation she had recited, how she had called on Sarah, Rivka, Rachel, and Leah. She told me of the herbs and flowers she had used, the way she had meshed lavender and thyme and broken a piece off the cedar table, the one my uncle still had in his home. She didn't tell me how long she was bent over my father's body, drawing, chanting, and sprinkling. When a witch does a working, we can lose track of both where and when we are.

What my grandmother did remember, what she did tell me, was of my father's sharp inhale of breath, the small mewling cry that grew and echoed around her. As she lifted him to her chest again, he was warm and squirming, not the frozen doll that would have become dybbuk. Her tears mingled with his, and they cried together, mother and son.

The pen fell from my hand, and I cried again. But she had no more tears left to shed. I squeezed her hand as firmly as I dared, but she only gave the faintest squeeze back, barely a touch of pressure. That was how I knew it was over. The last of the magic had left her. It was in me now, a fluttering, flitting thing. One day this last part would leave me as it had left her.

"No more tears, my clever boy. Your last sight of me should be a pleasant one," she commanded. The innate weight and authority were gone from her voice, and her eyes were closed. I brushed my hand across my own eyes, put the grimoire and pen back into my backpack, and then brought my lips to her cheek. I kissed her, and she muttered a faint blessing in Hebrew. The intention was there, but the force to drive it forward, to make them more than words was gone. I lifted my head and stood. The hand that had been holding hers let go slowly. Then I turned and stepped out of the room. I couldn't look back. If I did, I would cry. She had told me she didn't want any more tears, and I would listen, would not let her see me crying again.

I would give her the last sight she had asked for.

My parents were around me as soon as I crossed the threshold. I wrapped my arms around my father and we held each other, neither of us able to say anything. We breathed together, both of us doing what we could not to cry. There were so many things I wished I could have said to him. I wished he could have known how much his mother had loved him, how intensely she had fought for him, and most of all, what she had done so he could be where he was now. But I would never be able to tell him. So I cried—for all the things I would never be able to say to him, for what he could never know.

A few of my relatives joined us. Someone, I still don't know who, whispered in my ear, peeled me from my father, and guided me to a chair. Seconds or maybe hours later, my hands were filled with a paper cup of the worst coffee I would ever drink. It wasn't just the situation; hospital coffee never tastes good. Whether you're waiting for good news or bad, no matter why you're in a hospital, there is no such thing as a decent cup of coffee there.

My babcia died as she wanted, surrounded by her family. She had said goodbye to each of us on her own terms. My uncle Eli, her oldest son, said something to his wife just out of my hearing. I don't know what he said, and if I am honest with myself, I don't want to know. They weren't things I was meant to hear; I know that much. My grandmother closed her eyes after she told me of her greatest working, of how she had fought back unlife. Even with her eyes closed, I tried not to sob too openly, tried to obey her last instructions to me.

At 4:32 in the afternoon, my grandmother exhaled. Her breathing had grown ever more uneven. The room was still as we waited to hear her inhale again. Five seconds passed, then ten, then twenty. At the end of a full minute, she still hadn't taken in air. I don't know how she had talked the doctors into turning off the hateful beeping of the machines, but she had. By 4:35, her chest still hadn't stirred, and the eldest of my grandmother's children, my aunt Judy, leaned over and pressed her head to her mother's chest. Again, stillness descended on the room. Aunt Judy shook her head, and my father stood, as calmly as anyone could, and went to get a doctor to confirm what our family already knew. I heard my uncle Eli reaching for the hem of his shirt and then the distinct sound of cloth ripping. It was soon echoed by every member of the family still in the room. As the doctor came in, I was in the middle of the *kel maleh rachamim*, one of the numerous prayers for the dead. I knew it would be recited again during her funeral service, but it was one of the few pieces of liturgy I could remember at that moment.

We were escorted out of the room so the medical staff could do what they needed. When my grandmother had received her diagnosis, she had remained a prepared witch, even as she went to her death. She had made sure that her final arrangements were in place. Even as my mother called the funeral home and then my grandmother's synagogue, I admired my grandmother's foresight. She had trusted her youngest child's wife to be the most clearheaded in the aftermath of her death. After all, my mother was a nurse; she worked alongside death. I reached for my mother's hand then, and she put hers in mine. It shook as my mother hung up with the synagogue and reached out for the burial society. Even though my mother knew how to handle death, this was a death that stung for her.

I was one of the *shomrim* after my grandmother had been wrapped in the burial shroud and placed in the coffin. It was one of the longest nights of my life, although I couldn't remember any of the details. I knew we read from *Psalms* and *Lamentations*, but which particular verses are beyond my memory. I just needed to be near my babcia for the last time. Even if it was just an unmoving shell that held nothing of the woman I had loved, the woman who had trained me as well as she could, I owed her. While my lips moved in official liturgy, I spent time going through the private rites that are owed to a witch who chooses burial. My grandmother had fought unlife and won; she would not want to become one of them. I can't say anything about the eulogy or about the graveside service. When the time came, I threw my three shovelfuls of earth on the coffin, and the sound still echoes somewhere deep inside me.

It was only in my parents' home, where my grandmother had lived for so many years, sitting on a low stool with a plate of pierogi, that I came back to myself in a real way, and I had to steady my hands so as not to spill the pierogi over my black suit. These were store-bought pierogi.

I didn't feel any of the love, any of the comfort, that my grandmother had poured into every one she had ever made. As I held the plate of dumplings, I remembered the numerous times I had worked next to her in near silence, mixing the fried onions, potatoes, and sauerkraut together. I recalled the first time she had shown how to fold the dumpling and her voice at my ear, telling me how everything needed to be balanced for the pierogi to be just so.

A smile crossed my lips then—a brief, flickering thing—but it was the first time I had done so since her death.

IN THE present, I looked at the flickering candles of the menorah—their golds, shades of vermillion and ochre, and at their heart, the faintest hint of emerald. I knew then what needed to happen. If my grandmother had been in the room with me, she would have scolded me for not being her clever boy, for taking so long to find an easy solution to a problem, for making things more complicated than they needed to be. I pulled out my cell phone and finally sent a text to Erik. I offered him latkes and pierogi and the lighting of candles.

He responded with a single word—*When?*

CHAPTER 13

"I WAS beginning to think you were serious about not wanting to see me. Tell me, Jakob, what made you change your mind?" Erik asked as I opened the door to him. As with the last time, lowering the wards of my house to admit him was an act of negotiation, though it was less strenuous than before—almost shockingly so. Magic could be incredibly intuitive and adaptive. I looked up at the slate-colored sky, rolled my eyes, and stepped to the side, silently inviting him in.

"Remember, wolf," I said, trying to narrow my eyes in a threatening manner, "this is still my home. Push your limits and see just what I will do to you." Erik was already across my threshold and removing his peacoat. As with the first time he had been in my home, the traitorous cat was wrapping itself around him, weaving between his legs. He reached down, stroked the top of the cat's head, and let it play with his laces as he undid his boots. I waited as patiently as I could. When he finished, the cat meowed its displeasure at no longer being the center of attention but left to find one of its many resting places.

"Noted. You still didn't answer my question, though," he pointed out. Sighing softly, I turned and led the way to the kitchen. If like truly attracted like, then ending up with someone as stubborn as Erik was something I could not have avoided, even if witches could meddle with the strings of fate.

"*If*"—I emphasized the conditional word as strongly as possible—"and it is a big if, I decide to step into the role of pack witch, I need to know more about it. None of my ancestors ever were. I also need to know more about the last pack witch. Who were they? What were they like? Do you have access to their grimoire?" I peppered him with questions as I pulled out a mixing bowl. While witches—at least the witches of my family—didn't lie, we had been known to play with different versions of the truth. I put the mixing bowl down next to the ingredients and began working with my hands. This was one of the many recipes I had learned how to do by feel, by memory, by touch alone. If I was going to have Erik eating my latkes, I had to be serious about them.

"The grimoire?"

"A book of shadows?" I tried. I looked up and Erik still looked puzzled. "The spell book," I clarified. Erik shook his head.

"It was burned with her. Our pack's witch, she wanted to be cremated, and her—what did you call it? A grimoire?" His mouth was awkward around the word, as if trying it on for the first time. He was standing in the doorframe, looming into my kitchen, and looking at the small table, probably remembering how I had manipulated his chair the last time he had been in my home.

I nodded at the news. While forbidden to us because of our Jewish heritage, cremation was fairly common among witches. It was a way to ensure that a witch could not be forced back as unlife. If the body was burned, then there was no way for it to be animated, to be made to serve the hunger that kept unlife walking. Also, without a successor, someone to train in the practice, I could understand wanting to burn a grimoire. It was better for the knowledge to be lost than to fall into the wrong hands.

"Despite the whole thing about burning witches, there are some who prefer to be burned rather than buried," I said.

"She was quite clear about what she wanted to happen with her body. My great-uncle was the alpha at the time—he made sure she got what she wanted. We had to fly to Colorado and then drive for hours so we could legally have an open-air pyre for her," Erik said. I lifted my brow at the dedication of the pack. "She had been with the pack for forty years, through three alphas, including my great-uncle. The other thing she asked was to be cremated close to a new moon."

"She wanted it done at the dark of the moon—it's the best time." I didn't look up from my latke preparation.

"Why?" he asked.

I exhaled and there was a moment of silence. If I was going to tell him this, I was going to be sharing more about witches than I should. But nothing ventured, nothing gained.

"A new moon—the moon's secret face—for a witch, it's like a full moon is to a wolf. It's the period when all things are possible, when one thing has ended and something new is about to start," I said. I moved away from my bowls and held a potato and a mandoline with a grater attachment. This was not something I did by muscle memory alone. I had more than my fair share of scars due to the vengeful kitchen implement.

The one time I had done anything that might have classified as an offensive casting before meeting Erik had been because I cut myself on a mandoline. The blade had fallen from the plastic housing less than a microsecond after the curse left my lips.

"Want me to help?" Erik asked. I didn't need to look up to know he was close to me. I smelled him, felt the heat radiating off his body, was entirely too aware of his breath teasing the top of my head.

That morning the newspaper had reported that another grave was desecrated, this time in Monroeville, Pennsylvania. The news attributed it to fans of George Romero taking things too far... but I knew otherwise. Erik's heat, the steadiness of his breath, drove away the creeping cold, the sense of wrongness that had been in my tailbone since I saw that report. I kept my eyes downward as I manipulated the potato over the mandoline. If I was going to use a piece of machinery, now would be the time. I could put down the bloodthirsty mandoline and throw the potato into a food processor. But I had promised Erik homemade latkes, and for me, that meant handmade. I was nothing if not a man of my word.

"Thanks for offering, but I don't need you bleeding in my kitchen. Feel free to raid my fridge. I got a six-pack of Great Lakes," I offered. Much to my relief, I felt Erik move out of my space and toward the refrigerator. I heard the door open, glass clinking, and the sound of a bottle cap popping off. It didn't hit the floor, and I looked up to see a claw extending from Erik's thumb, bottlecap in his palm. He grinned at me and I turned my face down so he wouldn't see the smile that crossed my lips. It was a cheesy way to show off for a werewolf, but I wasn't going to deny that I had enjoyed it.

Finished with the potato, I touched my finger to the wick of a votive candle. It flickered to life with no invocation, and I grabbed an onion. The candle flame wasn't a foolproof method, and it might have been more my belief in the candle than anything else, but with it lit, I managed not to cry as I worked with the vegetable.

"I know I've said it before, but I'll say it again—I don't ever see myself ever getting tired of you doing that," Erik said. He was all but leaning against me, his forearm less than a half inch away from mine, and I stopped moving. I didn't trust myself around blades with him so close. Heat was spiking in my body, and it had nothing to do with the flickering votive. I knew what I should have done, but I couldn't make myself. Then he pulled back, dragging his thumb over my forearm, leaving a trail of gooseflesh in its wake. I felt heat linger where he had touched, but I focused on my breathing and steadied myself before I continued working the onion over the mandoline.

"Thanks," I said when I was able to speak. "It's one of the first things my grandmother taught me to do. Did your pack's witch ever tell you about her first working?" It might not have been the smoothest segue in history, but it would serve. My ears thrummed as I heard Erik's arm move as he raised his bottle. I looked up in time to see his Adam's apple bob, the beer tilted just so. When his lips popped from the bottle's mouth, his tongue flicked out over it. I was grateful that I was pressed against my kitchen counter. Erik was playing dirty, and he knew it.

I warred between my desire to learn more, to throw him from my home, or to do something far more carnal than I was supposed to. Luckily, logic won out.

"I can't remember, to be honest. Elaine—" He said for a second, his face transforming from sinful to fond at the mention of her name. "—was willing to show me a few tricks, but I was still a pup. She was busy with my great-uncle. At the time, I wasn't the first choice to become the alpha."

"Becoming an alpha, how does that work?" I couldn't stop myself from asking.

"It's... not easy to understand. It's not genetics—not always. My great-uncle was an alpha, as was his mother before him, but she was elected to the position when the alpha before her died without naming an heir. It's a bit like how you explained your magic to me," Erik said. I nodded, my latke mixture temporarily forgotten.

"I think I get it," I said. "Alpha status, like magic, likes to hop around and doesn't always adhere to a straight line."

"So, any of our children could be witches, or none of them could?" he asked, arching an eyebrow.

"Have you been reading trashy fiction? I don't have the power necessary to make either of us carry a pregnancy to term. In the over four hundred years that magic has lived in my family, none of us have even heard of such a thing being done." I chuckled. When I felt safe, I worked the onion over the mandoline, finished as quickly as I could, and put the evil instrument to one side.

I moved the shredded onions and potatoes into a towel and squeezed hard to strain out the liquid. Erik might have easily done it with one hand and barely tensed his forearm. I wasn't gifted with the strength of a werewolf and turned just slightly so he wouldn't be able to see the strain on my face. I might have used magic, but my babcia had always told me that using magic in the kitchen was the last resort of the lazy. Besides, food made with magic never tasted as good or as sweet, or was as filling, according to her. I wasn't going to argue with her wisdom, not now.

With the potatoes and onions strained, I mixed them thoroughly together. Once they were blended, I added the other ingredients and then pushed my fingers back in to mix by hand. You had to feel the texture—it was something you knew by touch alone. I heard Erik take another slow sip of his beer, but I didn't look up to watch the show this time. I was in the zone.

"It's my sister, actually, who has a small library of trash fiction. When I told her about you, she all but squealed and then went to find some of her favorite titles. There have been a few nights when she's gotten as tipsy as a werewolf can get before she read passages aloud." Erik raised both his brows. "There's a lot of laughter. Humans have the strangest ideas about us."

"When I was in ninth grade, I read *Macbeth* for the first time," I said, my hands still a blur in the mixture. "It wasn't the first time I had seen witches in fiction, of course, but I remember asking my grandmother if she thought that Shakespeare had known witches—real ones, that is." I moved away from the batter and toward the sink and used an elbow to get the water flowing. The look on Erik's face wasn't predatory, much to my shock. No, it was pure interest and curiosity. He was leaning forward as if he wanted to hear more.

"What did your babcia say?" he asked, and I was surprised to hear the Polish word fall from his lips. His pronunciation needed a lot of work, but he had tried.

I collected myself, rinsed off my hands, and grabbed a clean cutting board. "She said it would be hard to tell. She thinks he might have. She said he might have even been touched by magic, but was likely not a witch. It's hard to know that far in the past," I offered. "Want to come over here and try your hand at making latkes?"

Erik moved across the small kitchen almost faster than I could observe. He was smiling, his arm almost pressed against mine, and I forced myself to stay where I was, even if a part of me was screaming to press myself against him.

"Have you ever made meatballs?" I asked.

"My *mormor*—grandmother—she made sure all of her grandpups knew the right way to make Swedish meatballs. I admit, it's been a while, though," he said. I nodded, gathered some of the mixture, formed a rough sphere, and placed it on the clean board.

"That's about the size we want. A little bigger, a little smaller—neither direction will kill you. All latkes are beautiful, in the end," I offered.

"Latke positivity?" Erik asked, and I let myself snicker briefly.

"Latke positivity," I affirmed. There were still dozens, if not hundreds, of questions I wanted to ask—so many things I hadn't said—but I was content to work alongside Erik in silence. When the bowl was empty, there were about twenty of the balls waiting for the hot oil. I had been generous with my portions but doubted there would be any left for tomorrow's dinner. Erik moved to my sink without me having to ask, mirrored my motions from earlier, and used his elbow to get the water flowing. He washed his hands quickly in a way that wouldn't have been up to my grandmother's almost surgical standards. I was tempted to make a joke about being raised by wolves, but I didn't know if we were there yet. I followed him, rinsed my hands more methodically, and then turned on first the small hood fan over my stove and then the burner over which I had a set a pan of oil.

Erik sat in silence as I worked. When each latke was a golden brown, I removed them from the oil and set them on a serving plate. I repeated the initial steps with three more balls of batter, but when I dared to look at Erik, I could have sworn he was sulking, his toe working its way across the tile of my kitchen floor. This was something I would have never expected of him, and it made him almost human. Almost.

"How did you become the alpha of your pack?" I asked, trying to break the silence. It might not have been the most important of the questions, but there were things about Elaine that Erik might not have known, and the only way I could find out would be to talk to the pack elders. The only way I would manage that was if I learned more about pack hierarchy.

"It wasn't some sort of trial by combat, if that's what you're thinking," he stated. I briefly rolled my eyes.

"I didn't think you pulled a Hamlet until you said that," I said.

Erik took another pull from his beer bottle. "There are things I can't tell you, Jakob—not right now, anyway. *If*"—he mirrored the stress on the word I had used earlier in the evening—"you decide to serve as the pack's witch, then you get to learn how alphas come to power. If it takes me surrendering my position as alpha to have you join us, well, I would be happy to do so."

I was stunned at the offer and almost forgot to flip the latkes. But the bubbling of the oil forced me out of stunned silence and I got back to the pan. He was willing to give up the status of alpha for me? That was a lot to swallow, and I wasn't sure how to process it.

Eventually, I had all the latkes plated, and I brought the large serving dish over to the table. The sour cream, horseradish, and applesauce were already laid out, each with their own serving spoon.

Erik joined me at the table and his hands were a blur as he heaped his plate high first with the latkes and then with the condiments. By the time I had finished plating my first latke, Erik had devoured three. Instead of spreading applesauce and sour cream over the still-steaming latke, I watched transfixed as Erik shoved a fourth and fifth latke into his mouth. Erik lifted his eyes from his plate with a dollop of sour cream at the left corner of his lip. I brushed the corner of my own lips, and instead of using a napkin, his tongue darted out and circled his lips, quickly and roughly. He winked at me when he had "cleaned" himself, and I rolled my eyes.

"Just for your information, that was pretty close to the polar opposite of sexy," I stated firmly.

"Was it now?" He was teasing me, again.

"It really was." I nodded. He tilted his head back and laughed. The deep sound echoed through my kitchen, and I tried to remember the last time laughter of any sort had filled my house. Was it the last time he had been here? My babcia's kitchen had always been alive with the sounds of arguments, tears, and conversations, but most of all, laughter. It had echoed with streams of gossip from next-door neighbors or conversations with children and grandchildren far distant. While the kitchen was the heart of my home, her kitchen had been the heart of a family. The silence of my kitchen was deafening in comparison. The only sound to fill it most of the time was my poor attempt to sing along with the radio or the sounds of me cooking. Occasionally I would stream a podcast, but actual human voices were rare.

It was not a comforting thought. I remembered what Cara had said—that she always felt her family, that she was never alone. I had grown too used to the silence, I supposed, and had accepted it out of necessity. My kitchen was more of a mausoleum than a metropolis.

"If your cakes are as good as your latkes, it's no wonder that bakery of yours is successful," Erik said as he grabbed yet another potato pancake. I wasn't sure if it was his seventh or eighth. I had just finished my third. I wondered if I had made enough for the two of us. Apparently, the legendary appetites of werewolves were matched by the reality. For the first time since meeting him, I wished I had seen Erik, or any wolf, eat. Terence and I had only shared coffee and spell work. I was perhaps out of my depth and it was not a comforting feeling.

"I'll let my business partner know. She might be more generous with my share of the profits," I said, a smile on my lips. I wondered how much Erik's compliment would mean to Cara. She might think he was only saying it to find his way into my bed, and perhaps she would be right. But she might agree with him, and that was a scary thought.

"Speaking of," Erik said, and a dagger of icy fear plunged straight into my heart. I was thankful in that moment for the magicks of my kitchen, which apparently muted his senses around me. I focused on my breathing, trying to regulate it, trying to restart my heart. It certainly felt as if it had stopped. Erik, however, was more focused on blending horseradish with sour cream, smearing both of them over his next latke and then popping it into his mouth. He soldiered on, not acknowledging any of the physical stress I was going through. "What exactly happened with Terence when he came to see you? All he says is that he gave you his word not to talk about it."

I reached for a glass of water and took a long, deep sip. It was a crude play for time, but it was the only one I could use at the moment. When I had all but drained my glass, I grabbed another latke. I knew I could only stall so long, and his eyes were heavy on me, unflinching. I was out of time as I finished the potato pancake. I exhaled. "Well, that's between me and Terence. I promise you this; it's nothing that would be a threat in any way to you or any member of your pack," I said. It was the truth. As long as Cara was left alone, as long as they didn't invade her space and force her to scream, she wouldn't be a threat to them.

He nodded and grabbed yet another latke, holding still for a second before he shoved it into his mouth. "Were you also the one who warded the entrance? I felt something in the parking lot, and I thought it might be you, but—" He stopped himself.

"That wasn't witch's power you felt. It was fae," I said. Erik's eyes widened. It wasn't the whole truth. I didn't tell him how I had been able to manipulate the line—shatter it, according to Cara. We had done some repairs, but I knew she wanted more and stronger lines. I couldn't blame her.

"There are fae? In Cleveland?" Erik's curiosity was palpable, his latke forgotten for the moment.

"From what little I know, fae aren't tied to any particular spot, and I have no way of knowing exactly how old the line is. Why wouldn't a fae live in Ohio?" This was another nonanswer. I hadn't asked when Cara had put down her wards, though I could guess, but as I had said, I didn't know exactly. Eventually, Cara might have to reveal herself to the pack, and I hoped to heaven it wouldn't start a War, but if I had learned one thing about Cara, it was that she would act in her own time and on her own terms. I just hoped I wouldn't be the one to force her to reveal herself.

Rather than answer my question, Erik took his time eating the latke on his plate. He was up to at least ten or eleven when I grabbed two more for myself. The serving plate, which had been filled to the brim, was now all but empty. I wondered if I would need to call out for a pizza. I hadn't invited him over for pizza, but it would take less time for it to get here than it would for me to make another batch of latkes.

As I weighed which one of the local pizza places to call, Erik lifted his eyes and focused on me. His stare was narrowed, and fear ran through me again. "Have you had direct contact with the fae?" I wouldn't be able to stall, not like before. I looked down, unwilling to meet his eyes.

"I have, but this is something I get to keep to myself, at least for now," I said. My ears were filled with the rushing of my blood, and I didn't look up for several heartbeats. When I lifted my head, Erik nodded slowly and took the last of the latkes from the serving plate. I almost let out a sigh of relief, but I had better self-control than that.

"You said Elaine was the pack witch for forty years?" I asked, hoping he'd be willing to answer, hoping I hadn't derailed things too much, hoping he was still willing to share, to give me something I might be able to work with.

Erik paused on his penultimate latke. He shrugged. "At least forty. I know my great-uncle wasn't her first alpha. She... officiated the ceremony when his mother stepped down and he became the alpha. I don't know if my great-grandmother was her first. As I said, she was willing to entertain the pups, but she didn't tell us much about herself. I don't know exactly how many alphas she served, especially with the lifespan of a wolf," he said.

"So, wolves do live longer than us mere mortals?"

"There's nothing 'mere' about witches. Couldn't you use your magic to extend your life span?" he asked. I almost dropped my fork as I shivered, and he looked at me, shock written large across his objectively handsome features.

"That's one of the biggest taboos for us. If you want to become a dybbuk, you use your magic to do something like that." I was aware of the Yiddish only after it had escaped my mouth. Erik tilted his head slightly. "The unliving, undead, whatever you want to call them," I translated. While Erik didn't shudder as I had, a visceral look of disgust crossed his face.

"That's a great reason not to use magic like that," he agreed.

"What do you call them?"

"My mormor—she called them *draug*...."

"Like in *Skyrim*?"

Erik laughed again, and it echoed as it had before. I hated to admit it, but I was growing used to Erik's laughter. Not that I would say it out loud. "Close enough," he clarified.

"One of my ancestors wrote about another witch who used their magic to extend their life, back in the old country—"

"Poland?" he asked.

"Not in modern Poland, no. This would have been in what is now Lithuania. I'm not a hundred percent certain of the dates," I admitted. "The account is vague, but what they do have was enough to give me nightmares when I first read about it." I shuddered. "To spare you, just know that when someone becomes a dybbuk, it's something you don't want to be around for. Even with all the euphemisms that ancestor used, it's nightmare fuel, pure and simple."

"Just how many languages do you know, Jakob?" I felt Erik's earnest curiosity, and it was something Nathan hadn't bothered to ask about during our date.

"With any degree of fluency?" I thought about my answer. "Three—English, Polish, and Yiddish. I can speak and read Hebrew well enough to cast, and I know basic Lithuanian and Czech. Are you fluent in Swedish?"

"You remember." His smile reached his eyes. I was thankful that I was seated or my knees would have given out under me, traitors that they were.

"How could I forget?" I responded.

"Not fluent, not really. I speak just enough Swedish to order a beer. Now, if I remember correctly, you promised both latkes and pierogies. We've had latkes. Where are the pierogies?" Erik asked, his eyes twinkling and his lips twisted into a wicked grin. I resisted the urge to moan. Of course he would remember that. I stood and moved to the freezer.

"I was wondering if you would remember that. I was debating whether I should actually order a pizza. Only you'd remember the pierogi," I groused as I bent down and dug through the different containers. I finally found a plastic container next to a bag of brussels sprouts. Despite my organization, despite knowing that being prepared could be the difference between life and death, my freezer and refrigerator seemingly had minds of their own and would reorganize without my consent. I placed the pierogi on the counter and then went for a pot to the right of the stove. As I filled it with water, I saw Erik's all-too-predatory smirk.

"You're not going to show me how to make them from scratch?" he almost challenged.

"You're lucky I let you help in making latkes. You haven't earned pierogi yet," I answered. It took a few minutes for the water to come to a boil. I introduced the dumplings to the pot and then waited, actively not looking at the alpha werewolf at the table. His eyes were heavy on me, and I attributed the flush rising on my neck to the steam from the pot. Would I ever get used to him looking at me like that? Was that something I *wanted* to get used to? Despite what I had promised myself, I was seeing new possibilities, things I hadn't dared admit. I strained and plated the pierogi and brought them over to Erik. "I'd recommend either the horseradish or the sour cream as toppings," I said. Erik devoured the pierogi with the same speed with which he had consumed my latkes.

"At least one of the champion speed eaters has to be a werewolf," I said, more to myself than to him as I watched his fork fly from the plate to his lips. It was close to a blur.

He waited just long enough to swallow and then looked to me. "Not to the best of my knowledge," he said. He grabbed his napkin and dabbed it at the corner of his lips, where there was a small dollop of sour cream. I thanked heaven that he had decided not to repeat the display with his tongue.

"That makes sense, I guess," I said.

"It would be too obvious?" Erik was teasing me again.

"Exactly."

"I do have table manners, you know. I can eat like a gentleman. I even know which is the salad fork," he boasted.

"Really?"

"Really. Last week, a teenager in my pack was admitted to Davidson College through early decision." Erik was smiling as he told me, pride lighting his eyes. Whoever this werewolf was, Erik was excited for them, that they would be stepping forward and seeing more of the world. I thought about Terence. If he was able to get over Erik, would he want to go to college? I knew he wanted to make something, to have something he could touch. As a graduate of a culinary school, I knew traditional college wasn't for everyone. I would have to ask him when I saw him again.

"That's, what, four states from Ohio? The parents must be worried sick." I had gone to culinary school two states and a time zone away from where my parents were living. They had argued with me about it constantly, and my mother had stuffed an entire suitcase with underwear and socks, convinced I'd forget to do laundry. During my first year, she called me almost every other day. The calls added at least an hour to already exhausting days, and there had been times when I had almost yelled at my mother. She loved me, but that love had been suffocating. My father's worries were quieter. He'd send me small emails, all less than a hundred words long, but each of them demanding a response of some sort. It had taken me staying in Chicago over a summer for my parents to get the idea that I was not only surviving but also thriving.

"It's not as much of a strain as you might think. There's a bit of a tradition, like Amish rumspringa," he explained, the plate of pierogi almost empty by then.

"Werewolves go out and about and try to decide if the werewolf life is the right one for them?" I asked.

He chuckled, lifted the almost-empty beer, and killed what was left in a single swallow. Then he got up, retrieved a second beer from the six-pack, and effortlessly popped the cap off. He sat opposite me and leaned a little over the table. "It's not like that," he said. "I can only tell you so much because you're not a full member of my pack yet, even with all you've done for us. But basically, there comes a time in each werewolf's life when they decide if they want to stay with their natal pack or find a new pack to call their own. For example, before we met, a wolf in my pack wanted to go wild and live in Oregon. I called an alpha I know in Boring—"

"There's seriously a town called Boring in Oregon?" I interrupted.

"It's not the worst town name I've ever heard of."

"What would that be?" I knew I was derailing us, but I had to know.

"Toad Suck, Arkansas. My brother, sister-in-law, and their kids stumbled across it as part of a road trip a few years ago. They bought me a T-shirt to prove it."

"You've got to be kidding me."

"Nope." He popped the *P* and I couldn't help but smile. "So when this member of the pack wanted to go exploring, I called the alpha I knew. Boring isn't too far from Portland, where they had family. For the teen going to Davidson, it was something similar."

"This sounds like a werewolf exchange program."

I enjoyed the way his laughter echoed around the both of us. "Not the best analogy, but it's far from the worst," Erik confessed.

"Is there some sort of central werewolf government?" This was something that I actually had to know. If there was, then I would be dealing with more than Erik and his pack. There would be webs I hadn't yet explored that I might have to unravel. It would be hard enough to extricate myself from one pack. Facing an organized bureaucracy would be more than I could handle. Even Cara, with all her resources and her siblings, might not be able to stand against a werewolf government.

"There's only so much I can tell you," Erik said. That was not reassuring.

"Now you have me worried about a werewolf IRS." I wasn't sure if I was joking or not. Erik had devoured the last of my pierogi and I was half wondering what I had left to eat. I felt the sun set without needing to look out the window and the prickling at the back of my neck intensified as the need to stand grew. It was time. I moved silently, the chair gliding behind me with a thought. Erik was transfixed. He didn't say anything as I moved to the menorah, in sight of the bay window. "I promised you the kindling of light, didn't I?" I asked.

"You did," he nodded.

"Follow," I commanded as I made my way to the menorah. I heard Erik's footfalls, felt him standing behind me, but didn't smell him or notice his heat. He was keeping a respectful distance. My gaze was focused on the candles, not on our reflection in the mirror. I extended my fingers and touched the wick of a candle. My voice was strong and sure; the Hebrew echoed in the space between us. I lifted my fingers and the wick sprang to life, faintly green for a fraction of a second and then transitioning to the standard oranges, reds, and yellows of normal fire. I then gripped the body of the candle and guided it through its purpose. When I brought the shamash to the center, I finally lifted my head and turned back to Erik. He was standing at what my uncle would have called parade rest, his head bowed slightly, a show of respect for my house, my rules.

"That's one of my rituals. I know I'm still not a part of your pack, but can you tell me about what a pack ritual is like?" I asked.

He lifted his head and there was his smile again. Despite what I wanted to feel, my heart fluttered in his chest as he took a seat. The cat instantly jumped into his lap, and Erik began to talk.

CHAPTER 14

DRIVING THROUGH predawn darkness, there was a smile on my face, even if I hadn't gotten the best night's sleep. While I hadn't learned everything I wanted, I had fully enjoyed my evening with him. When he wasn't pressing the "mate" thing down my throat, he had a good sense of humor, an honest curiosity, and didn't mind being the cat's preferred sitting place. When he finally got up to leave (much to the cat's displeasure) he held himself at my threshold and scuffed a toe at the lintel. To my shock—and his as well—I wrapped my arms around him and gave him a tight hug. In that instant, despite the fabric between us, I felt his heartbeat, strong and steady, and I pulled away quickly, my head spinning. He didn't say anything, only grabbed my hand, raised it to his lips, and, with his eyes on mine, leaned in and pressed a brief kiss to it. My skin tingled long after the wards had bent back into place.

Snow fell as I drove, and I took my time. I might be a little late, but better late than dead. I doubted that we would get a snow day. While the first snow had caught Cleveland unprepared, it was December now, and snow was to be expected. With finals so close for so many students, schools were unlikely to close. I pulled into the space behind the bakery, turn off the engine, and watched a few flakes dance in currents of air, suspended in the dim glow of a streetlamp. I moved across the lot as quickly as I could to avoid the knives of moist cold carried by the wind.

Once inside, I quickly hung my jacket and scarf and barely nodded to Cara as I headed to my station. Fruitcakes and panettone. We would be working nonstop today. Cara moved past me, her eyes downcast into a bowl as she grabbed ingredients.

"Is that some sort of fae superpower?" I asked, locating the dough I had let rise overnight.

"Is what a fae superpower?" she replied, not looking up from her work.

"Knowing exactly where everything is without needing to look," I clarified. Cara scoffed but still didn't bother to look up.

"You've been working with me long enough to know that my kitchen is my domain. I don't need any power to make it the way it is. I could move in this kitchen with a blindfold. I know where you are because you make more noise than an elephant. Granted, you're an elephant that knows where the zester and vanilla are, though," she said. I didn't bother to roll my eyes.

The rest of the dawn hours were spent in silence—or as close to silence as I could manage, being an elephant in her estimation. Eventually Cara left her station and headed to the front of the house to get everything set up for the general public. I was getting ready to remove yet another tray of panettones from the oven when Cara stepped back into the kitchen. I paused only once I had put the tray down to cool.

Cara generally had an excellent poker face. The fact I could see concern written in the crinkling of her brows—that was a kick square in my ribs. "There's someone here to see you," Cara said. She kept her voice steady, but I wasn't able to stop the fear from spiking in my body. It was the same sort of fear you'd get when you saw a text from a lover that read *We need to talk* or if a teacher asked to see you after class. I tried to focus on my breathing.

As I exited the kitchen, I went through the short list of individuals who would try to see me at Siren's. I doubted it was Terence, and it wouldn't be any of the rest of Erik's pack. Cara and I had been working on the wards, building them back together, our magicks feeding each other and layering with each other smoothly. In the first session, I had paid a great deal of attention to Cara—the way she drew magic with little more than a twitch of her lips. It made sense that her magic would be more verbal than my own. After all, a banshee's power was her voice.

I entered the front of house to find Nathan standing there with a nervous grin on his face, which only enhanced his already handsome features. If anything, it made him seem more human and gave him a slight boyish quality. There was a faint rose tint on his cheeks. As I looked past him to the trees on the street, I saw wind whip the branches. He wasn't blushing because of me. As I crossed the room, he quickly flicked his eyes down, averting his gaze. I stood just on the other side of the service counter and didn't cross my arms across my chest, as much as I wanted to. I stood still and waited for him to say or do something more than smile. He kicked at the tile flooring with a stylish black leather shoe—the sort that was impractical for any real walking in Cleveland at this time of year. Eventually he tried, "I don't suppose you serve humble pie?"

"We're all out, I'm afraid," I said, "although I know it won't take long to prepare." My tone was neutral, balanced. I waited to see what else he might say. His total radio silence since Thanksgiving hadn't made him seem like someone worth fighting for. Even if I did manage to separate myself from Erik and his pack, I no longer saw Nathan in any romantic light.

"I figured, since we haven't been connecting over the phone, I would just come in," he said, and I bit back a sigh. I felt Cara's gaze digging into the space between my shoulders. How long had she been standing there, I wondered? I turned back to her and, in the second of silence between us, I felt the full weight of a banshee's stare. She moved from where she stood, a mug of what passed for coffee in her right hand, which she gave to me with a smile. She flicked her gaze at Nathan and he took the smallest possible step back. He might not be magical, but he could feel the ill intention of my business partner. Having Cara on my side was a good feeling.

I motioned to the same table we had used at the cupcake tasting, and he sat slowly. Outside, snowflakes descended languidly, and I watched them more than I did Nathan as I made my way to the table. He had interlaced his fingers and was running his right thumb over his left. His chin, with two or three days of stubble, rested uneasily atop his knuckles. I raised the bad coffee to my lips and sipped it slowly as I waited.

"I don't know where to start," he confessed, the words rushing out.

"It's all right. Say what you need."

"I should have told you that I wasn't out to my family. It wasn't right for me not to let you know that," he continued at the same, almost frenetic pace. I debated whether I would need to draw magic for this but realized that as long as I knew Cara had my back, I would manage. I would be okay. I had something close to a friend for the first time in too long. I would survive without magic.

"Nathan," I said, and my voice was level, firm, and surprisingly solid, "we only went on one date. We were still figuring out whether we wanted a second date, and let's be honest, when we didn't so much as kiss at the end of it, we might both have guessed what was going to happen."

"I know, but still. I should have let you know." He bit his tongue and looked down at his hands. "It wasn't fair to you. You deserve someone who's out, someone who wouldn't have been afraid to kiss you at the end of the night or hold your hand throughout the dinner. I was more focused on the door, worried that one of my relatives or a friend of the family might come in. That wasn't right," he said.

"You're right," I agreed. "I do. You're also owed someone who can be honest with you."

He looked up then, and there was something in his eyes that I couldn't identify. "Is there something you weren't telling me?"

"Let's just say we both have our share of baggage, and ours aren't matching. You need someone whose baggage matches yours." Nathan looked puzzled and I bit back a sigh. "It's a reference to *Rent*." He nodded but still didn't look like he got what I was saying. I could have made a poor joke about him being straighter than he was gay, but I didn't think that would be fair to him. I lived up to several stereotypes. He didn't.

"I *did* have a good time with you," he asserted.

"And I had one with you," I agreed.

"Is there any way—?" he almost asked, but I narrowed my eyes.

"Nathan, I'll say this once and only once. I'm not going to cause friction for you with your family so close to her wedding, and I'm not going to stand in the background, pretending to be something I'm not. When—if—you come out, you have to do it for yourself. You can't do it for someone else. I know it's scary, but the entire world can feel like a narrow bridge sometimes. It's up to us to face that fear and walk on across," I said slowly.

"Those feel like lyrics to a Christian rock song," he tried to tease.

"Not Christian." It was both a statement and a reminder. "I would offer you the original expression, but—"

"But what?" he interrupted.

"Is it really something you want to hear?" I asked. His eyes fell again and he finally unlaced his fingers and tapped out an irregular staccato on the surface of the table. He worried his lower lip with his teeth. It was still charming, still cuter than it had any right to be, but my heart remained steady.

"I don't know if I can do that, be that strong," he confessed after several seconds filled only by the frenetic motion of his fingers on the table.

"You might be able to find it, if you look hard enough," I said.

"Is this going to screw things up with Nicole?" he asked. It was nice to know that he was still concerned about his twin, even now.

"I'm enough of a professional to let this slide. The question for you is, will it be weird for you to see me at the reception? If you can handle me being there, I can handle seeing you with someone else on your arm."

"I'm sorry, Jakob," he offered, averting his eyes again.

"As I said, it was only a single date, and it was far from the worst one I've had. I was able to walk out without blood being drawn or threats being made," I said, a sad grin on my lips.

"That sounds like a hell of a story." He waited to see if I would follow up my comment, but I only stood, and he mirrored my motion. We stared at each other across the table and he extended his hand. I took it and gave a firm handshake but didn't reciprocate the squeeze I felt from him. When I pulled my hand away, I saw defeat in his handsome features. He turned and went out the front door and headed down the street without a backward glance.

My skin was cool before I lost sight of him, no ghosts lingering where his touch had been. I sighed and turned when I felt a hand on my elbow. Cara stood there, holding a shot glass filled with an amber liquid that smelled as sweet as it did strong. I took it and downed it in one fluid motion. I didn't sputter this time, and she gave me a proud grin.

"Sucks, doesn't it?" she asked, looking past me at the street, still mostly empty save for the falling snow.

"It could be worse," I answered.

"What will you do about Erik?" she asked. I was shocked to hear her use his name. I didn't trust any words that would have come to me so I shrugged the smallest of shrugs. In the reflection, I saw her nod sagely. When I felt her hand tighten on my bicep, I offered the most genuine smile I could. It wasn't much, but it was something.

We turned together and headed back to the kitchen. We needed to bake.

CHAPTER 15

SNOW WAS packed hard on the ground, and the night air whistled, carrying drifts that danced under the streetlamps. It was starkly beautiful, even if I shivered a little as I exited my car. I could still turn, could still run away, I told myself. But I was here, at the same trailhead I had used months ago when I had treated Zoe. I pulled my jacket as tightly around me as I could. I was rail thin, without any natural insulation, and my coat could only do so much, and I was diving into the deep end. I might not be able to come back from this. Since seeing me light the shamash, Erik and I had been exchanging regular text messages.

Although Nathan wasn't a part of the equation anymore, I wasn't ready to step in and be a pack's full-time witch. But if I was going to try and find a way out of the role, I had to know what the role was. There had to be something I could do besides kill either Erik or myself, and if I felt the magic, I would know better what strings to pull, metaphorically and magically speaking.

Erik had asked me to join them for their full moon celebration in January. When I accepted, he called me, wondering if I was joking or if he was having a stroke. Apparently even werewolves, with their enhanced healing, could suffer a stroke. That went into the grimoire too. I confirmed and he told me when to get to the trailhead. Here I was, standing, looking at pristine snow, seeing neither human footprints nor the distinctive tracks of a wolf. I resisted the urge to pull my cell phone from my pocket and check the time. I was here. Now I had to wait.

When I heard the stirring of branches behind me, I spun on my heel, pulled up my reusable Kroger bag, and let it hang just below my heart. My gaze immediately went down, looking for a hunter's eyes, a wolf's gleaming eyes. Finding them, I inhaled and tried to slow my thundering heart. Golden orbs locked with mine, and it stepped forward. In the darkness, I couldn't make out its coat, but I had the distinct impression that the tail was darker than the body, although I couldn't say why. Even through the darkness, I swore I saw a lolling tongue and fangs that shamed the snow. I was a dead witch, I thought to myself, despite the supplies in my bag. I would not have time to grab salt.

I *felt* the fur beginning to melt away. Through the shadows I saw the muzzle shorten and the paws grow broader, the nails growing shorter and thinner. The scar on my shoulder, Erik's bite, thrummed as the transformation continued. I stood awestruck as I heard bones reshape inside the lupine body. I lost any sense of time while I watched the wolf become a woman. Before me, naked as the day she was born and seemingly not minding the cold, was Alicia. She shook her head, and her hair achieved a gloss only capable through the use of the right bathroom products—or so I had been told. I thought I saw a smile on her lips, no sign of the whiter-than-white fangs as she stepped forward.

"Impressed, brujo?" she asked.

"Very," I replied, not even thinking about lying. There would have been no point in it, even if I had been someone who lied. She was showing off, and I had been too busy trying to remember the *viddui*. While a part of my logical mind knew that any wolf I saw tonight was likely to be a member of Erik's pack and thus unlikely to hurt me, I was only human. I could make mistakes with the best of them. I wondered if hers would be the only shift I saw tonight. If I saw more, I might understand more, and it would be easier for me to manipulate the strings—or that's what I told myself.

"I'm surprised you finally accepted one of Erik's invitations." She quirked her head to one side.

"*If*—" I said, remembering how much the word had weighed between myself and Erik in my house. "—I decide to become this pack's witch, I need to understand exactly what that means.

"Basically, you'd be doing what you're already doing for us— solving shit Erik can't. You'd at least be getting laid regularly," she said. I knew she wouldn't be able to see my blush through the darkness, but I wondered if she would be able to smell it. She cackled as she led me down an almost familiar trail, and I noticed that she didn't leave any footprints on the snow. How had I not noticed the lack of a trail before? Unlike the last time I had come here, her pace was leisurely, and at several points, she turned her head to make sure I was following.

"You'll need to tell me how you can walk about without any clothing on. Even with a lifetime of true winters, I'm a little chilled,"

I confessed as a breeze knifed through the trees and hit my nose. The sound of her chuckle almost echoed in the dark January night.

"You should know just how hot a wolf's blood runs. After all, you've slept with one," she teased. I think she was trying to embarrass me to death. I stopped and debated whether I should head back to my ancient sedan and drive back home. While it was still early, all things considered, I might have a chance for more than six hours of uninterrupted sleep if I got home soon, the cat of course permitting. Instead I followed Alicia but didn't acknowledge what she had just said.

Moonlight spilled through the branches, and there were a few stars—ones I had never learned to name. We got to the same clearing, off the beaten paths, that I remembered from each of the times I had been roped into helping Erik. Logs were gathered in the fire pit, waiting to be lit. I lifted a brow and saw a smirk on Alicia's lips and a glint of gold in her dark eyes. I heard the snapping of branches, the snuffing of chill air. I saw glinting eyes as wolf after wolf emerged from the tree line, and I had to focus on my breathing. My hand went into the Kroger bag and I held the salt, ready to throw a crude circle, but I managed not to.

The largest of the wolves—arctic white, a massive beast that wouldn't have been out of place in a George R. R. Martin novel—stepped forward. I knew Erik, even in that shape; I felt it in a place deeper than my bones and blood. I watched as he shifted, his transformation a smooth, liquid thing. I was transfixed, seeing it, feeling it. This was primal power, like Cara's scream. Perhaps that was why wolves and fae didn't mix? I would have to ask Cara about that later. As Alicia had done, Erik shook his head at the end of his transformation. He stepped toward me, the cold doing nothing to impede his impressive size or the smile on his handsome face.

Nudity was not the cultural taboo for werewolves that it was for humans, I guessed. It made sense, but that didn't mean I was comfortable with it.

"When I was last here, you had already lit the fire," I said, trying to fill the silence between us without my eyes flicking downward.

"The last time you were here was an emergency. You're here to see what it's like to be a pack's witch. One of the duties of the pack witch is to start the fire," Erik informed me as he took another step forward. Like Alicia, he left no print on the snow. There was only so much my brain could process at a time, and for some reason it was fixated on the reality that neither Alicia nor Erik left human footprints. I could understand not leaving any lupine trace, but not leaving a human sign? It just didn't click.

"Why's that?" I asked, hearing the slight squeak in my voice, knowing that I must have sounded like a five-year-old.

"Tradition. Fire is a strictly human thing. When the pack's witch lights the fire, it's a signal, letting us know we can be both human and animal. As you're fond of saying, you're much closer to human than a wolf is, but when you light the fire…." He said, letting me have a moment for his words to sink in. I shivered, and it was not strictly a response to the below-freezing night air. His stare was intense and it went straight to my heart. "You'll be telling all the wolves that they can walk that middle way, that place between humanity and other that a witch embodies," Erik finished.

"I don't suppose I get to use a match?" I asked. Behind me, Alicia laughed, and there was another chorus of wolfish amusement. I was willing to have Erik laugh at me, but Alicia? For some reason, that spurred me forward. I shifted my glasses up the bridge of my nose, removed a glove, and placed bare fingertips to the log. Then I closed my eyes and chanted. In a whisper, I spoke of an ancient birthright, of feast and play, and of the need to reduce forests to ember. Heat pulsed through my body and traveled down my arm. I wrinkled my nose as I smelled the first smoke, and my words came faster and louder. There was no amusement, not now. I didn't need to see awe to feel it. I pulled my hand back and there was an eruption of sparks from deep in the center of the pile, a column of malachite flame. Then it crashed down and shifted to the usual reds, golds, and oranges. I turned and opened my eyes. There were yips of surprise and even a few steps back from some of the wolves. My eyes were burning with witch's fire.

Shifting my gaze, now tinted emerald, I locked with Erik's golden eyes. For the eternity of a second, I was aware of only him. Then he tilted his head back and loosed a howl that sent shivers through my body. They had nothing to do with the temperature. The wolves in the circle around us mirrored their alpha with a symphonic keening to the moon floating high above us. At that moment I *saw* the tendrils of power, the cords of magic rushing between Erik and the members of his pack. I saw the weave of the world shift and strain as wolf after wolf began to lose four legs and walk on two. Snout after snout shortened to become a simple nose. I saw smiles on a few faces but smelled the distinct, almost rusty tang of fear.

As soon as I smelled fear, the fire disappeared from my eyes. How had I known that smell? Moreover, how had a human nose picked up the amorphous scent? I flicked my eyes back to Erik, who had turned and was speaking to a woman with one of the worst haircuts I had ever seen. He was dealing with pack matters, and I would leave him to it.

I felt the rush of blood in my ears, but over it I heard the stirring of night birds, flickers of conversation, and the yips of wolves who had yet to shift. I swore I heard the crunching of snow under paws that left no trace as a pair of wolves ran through the underbrush, chasing each other. There was cinnamon and a hint of sandalwood—desire, more potent than the fear I had picked up on moments ago. I all but stumbled to a snow-covered stump, not bothering to clear it off. The cold seeped through my jeans and slammed me back into myself. Erik had told me that I would be able to pick up on things, that my senses would be enhanced by being bound to him. Was this what was happening? I didn't need to look up as I heard the unsure gait of a teenager. It had to be Terence.

"I honestly didn't believe Alpha Erik when he said you had finally agreed to join us for a full moon," he joked. Even without the whirlwind of new sensations, I would have known the smile in his voice.

"Here I am, at least for the moment." I tried to smile back at him, but I knew it was only a half-felt thing and hadn't reached my eyes, not fully.

Terence crouched next to me and put a hand on my back. Even crouched, he was somehow taller than me. I had long accepted that I would never be a power forward for the Cleveland Cavaliers, but this was slightly demoralizing. Terence probably hadn't even finished growing, and he was already taller than I was and had muscles I would likely never develop unless I spent what little free time I had in a gym. His hand on my back sent a small shiver through me, and there was more than heat to his touch. He was offering me his strength. I looked over at him. Our glances locked and I asked a silent question—Did he know what he was willing to give me?

When I was a teen, shortly after I had become *bar mitzvah*, my grandmother had shown me how to share magic, how to open the flow of power. It was an abyssal thing; it would let another person into the deepest part of your being—what I knew as a soul. It was an act of absolute faith and trust. Terence was next to me, looking at me, offering me his strength, his power, and there was a small smile on his face. What shocked me more than the offer he might have been making unknowingly was that I was willing to take it. I would let this teenager into my soul if he was willing to offer the same to me. I almost pulled away but managed to keep myself in place.

"What's got your boxers in a twist?" Terence asked. I gave a short laugh and it broke the somber mood between us. A naked teenager teasing me about my underwear—the night couldn't get much stranger. If I was laughing at this, I would need time off. It would have to wait until after Valentine's Day of course. While there were a few March weddings, there were more in February or April. March wasn't a marrying month, at least not in Cleveland. I had yet to take any sort of real vacation in the years I had worked for and with Cara, excluding my yearly fast for Yom Kippur, which while restful, was not exactly a day to relax. I needed a real vacation.

"Earlier, for just a few seconds—" I said, knowing what I was about to admit, but not wanting it to be the case. "I smelled fear. Someone was afraid of me, and I smelled it." The admission was out in the open. Terence's warm, dark gaze was firm and his hand was warm against mine.

"You must really be Alpha Erik's mate, then," he sighed. There was resignation and hurt in his voice, but it was balanced with a sort of genuine happiness. I almost snapped at him for using the m-word, but my need to know more outweighed my desire to object to something that might be truer than I wanted to own.

"Why did you say that, T?" I asked.

"When a mating, a true mating, happens between a werewolf and someone more human, the mate gets some of the wolf's senses. My aunt said that happened to her when she became my uncle's mate." Terence finally turned his head, and I followed his gaze to where a large wolf rested its head on the thigh of a woman wearing a jacket thicker than mine and what looked like a pair of very comfortable sweats. I blinked, shocked to see someone actually wearing clothes. I noticed a few others at the edge of my vision. All wore practical boots, but that's where the similarities ended. They were of different ages. Some were as old as the woman who cradled the wolf in her lap, with more salt than pepper in their hair. Others were young, running alongside wolf pups, yelling happily, playing as only carefree children can.

"Those are the human children of some of our pack members. They also get the senses from their bonds with their siblings and parents," Terence said.

"Werewolves can have human children?" I asked. This was another thing I'd have to find space for in the grimoire.

"It's roughly equivalent to a recessive trait," T said. "In some packs, if a child is human, they're adopted out. Alpha Erik's never insisted on that. Says it's because their children might pass on the power to shift. Going back to my aunt Charlene, she was freaked out when her senses started spiking. You'll have to get her to tell you the story about the time she was on a flight and she heard someone half the plane away using the toilet. Not a good time." Terence smirked at the memory, and I grinned. "While her senses aren't as sharp as a born wolf, she's learned how to use them better than a few of the other wolves I know."

"Is the brujo complaining to you, T?" Alicia's voice came from over my other shoulder. Terence didn't move his hand as we both turned to her. What was more surprising was that she rested her hand just above his. Both of them were touching me, passively offering me their strength.

"Apparently he's finally getting some of the enhanced senses and was having a mini freak-out," Terence explained.

"Damn it!" Alicia yelled, but her hand remained in place and so did her smile. "I thought your control would be stronger, brujo. I had twenty dollars riding on it." Terence flipped her the bird so fast I would have missed it if I hadn't been looking.

I sputtered, not used to being someone other people bet on. Apparently my night could and would get weirder than talking to two people naked as the day they were born. I smelled the blush rising up my chest before it reached my cheeks, and before I could do anything about it, my ears rang. Distantly, past the crackling of the central bonfire, I heard hushed, sharp whispers. I picked up the hostility, the derision, and knew that the words—many of which I couldn't catch—were about me. It was a female voice, an older one—the one that often said it wanted to speak to a manager. Karen clearly wasn't happy that I might finally be acting like a pack witch.

With breathing exercises I might have stolen from a pay-what-you-can yoga class I had once attended, I tried to pull my hearing back. My fingers flew to the inside of my Kroger bag, and as I found the salt, I exhaled low and deep. Both Terence's and Alicia's currents of power closed off as I pushed downward and called to the earth. The sounds of wolves and humans faded for a moment as the earth sang around me. I inhaled and heard Karen's sharp intake of breath from wherever she was. It was matched by a few others. Even Alicia gave a small sound of surprise. I didn't need to open my eyes to know I was wreathed in the eldritch light of witch's fire—not the best way to make a good impression with a pack of werewolves. As the fire on my skin and on my clothes flickered out, I was centered, calm. Burning power did sometimes have fringe benefits, apparently.

"You could have warned me you were about to do that. Although, I'm not going to lie, that's very badass," Alicia said. Even if her tone was light, there was concern on her face and in her eyes.

"That was an accident?" I tried.

"Bullshit," Terence said. "If you want, I'll go grab my aunt Charlene or one of her kids to talk you through this. Even with magic, there's no shame in needing help handling it. I mean, the whole wreathed-in-fire thing is seriously cool, but—"

"I'll try not to do it too much," I offered a small smile.

"With your ability to… work—" Alicia said, silently asking if she had used the right word; I nodded and she continued. "—magic I thought you'd be able to handle enhanced senses. After all, isn't magic something you feel?"

A valid question. I thought for a moment, wondering how I could best explain to wolves what it was to work magic, how similar it might be to the shift. The wolves had never told me much about what it was to shed their human skins. That was another thing I would have to ask and find a place for in the grimoire. "Working is an active thing. Passively I might feel something, but unless I'm opening myself and actively calling, the flow of magic is at the back of my mind, in a place that's neither awareness nor thought, but just *is*. Sorry if that's not too helpful. Also, as you said, Alicia, I 'feel' magic. I don't hear it or smell it. It's something in my skin, in my blood, in my bones," I said.

The two werewolves nodded as they took in what I explained. I wondered if Alicia had known Elaine and how Elaine had experienced magic. In my great-uncle's writings, he had "seen" the flows of magic—diamonds glittering against a sable backdrop. My grandmother had "tasted" magic—a potent mixture of onions and garlic just beneath her tongue. The first author described "smelling" magic, saying it was the mixture of lavender and an oncoming storm. Even the others who "felt" magic described it in different ways. For me, it was like a limb that had fallen asleep, returning to life.

"Say the word, Jakob, and either Terence gets his aunt or I find one of the other humans of the pack to talk you through this. They can tell you how long it takes to adjust, how to cope with smelling things no one ought to smell. Just be thankful there isn't a skunk out tonight. If you think it's bad for human noses, you don't want to know what it's like with the borrowed senses of a wolf." Alicia wrinkled her nose at a memory.

I turned my head her way and said, "I'll manage. It's just overwhelming and unexpected. Besides, the position isn't official. Maybe this will go away."

"You told me that you try not to lie, Jakob. Does that only apply to other people, or does it also apply to yourself?" Terence raised a brow at me. I was flat-footed, unable to say anything to the teenager. "Your senses are going into overdrive." He inhaled, and I could see that a part of this was still painful for him. "It means your heart has already decided, even if your head is fighting it. Your heart knows what it wants, where it needs to be. You can keep fighting it, but hearts are generally stronger than heads. Do you want to spend that much time fighting what your heart knows?"

Was Terence right? Had a part of me already decided and was I just being too stubborn to accept that decision? Was I really giving in to Erik and accepting that I was to be his pack's witch? When had I surrendered? Was my decision to learn more the thing that had doomed me? I felt my jaw moving but didn't hear myself saying anything. I must have looked like some sort of horrid fish. Alicia's hand moved up my back and ruffled my hair. I managed not to sputter audibly, but it was a near thing.

"I come by my stubbornness honestly," I offered. "And when my head's made up, there's precious little even my heart can do to convince it otherwise." Both Alicia and Terence gave me commiserative pats.

Before either of them said anything, we all heard a rustling. My nose wrinkled, and from the corner of my eye, I saw Terence's doing the same. A pair of wolves loped into the clearing, reeking of musky, sweaty, passionate sex. If I hadn't been able to smell it, I thought I would have seen it. Even in their wolf forms, they had the sort of light step and glow that appeared only after a couple had been truly intimate with each other. The larger of the two stepped forward, and his shift was slower than Alicia's. Eventually, Micah stood before us. Past him, Zoe's return to humanity was smoother, but only barely. Both had shy smiles on their faces.

"Witch," Zoe said, stepping toward me, resting a hand on Micah's arm.

"Jakob. Please, call me Jakob." I held up a hand. Their smiles shifted from shyness and potential embarrassment to something warmer, more genuine and open.

"Jakob," she continued, "the last time you were here, my grandmother thanked you. Neither of us were in our right mind, and well...." She blushed. In that moment she looked more a girl than a woman.

"It was nothing," I tried to offer, not sure if there was an appropriate thing to say. What was werewolf etiquette at an occasion like this? My lack of knowledge was truly staggering. Even if I wasn't going to be a pack witch, I could at least be polite. I felt out of place and off balance.

"You brought Zoe back to herself, even when Alpha Erik couldn't," Micah said. "That's not nothing. When we're ready to have pups—" He stopped himself and placed his hand in hers. There was only affection on his face and on hers. Their love was almost a tangible thing. I felt Terence lift his hand and step away. The loss of his warmth and his unexpected offer of power stung for a fraction of a second, but I didn't blame him for leaving. I was surprised he had stayed as long as he did. A crush of his had died tonight when I confirmed that my senses were going haywire. A first heartbreak is never easy to recover from. At some point, I'd have to find out what happened with the boy who had kissed him in the shower. For the life of me, I couldn't remember if Terence had told me his name in the moment.

"When we're ready to have pups, we want you to be with us, to help us—me—through it, along with my grandmother," Zoe said, and there was a weight in her voice that I would have sworn hadn't been there moments ago.

I didn't have a chance to put my foot in my mouth, as Alicia was standing, digging her fingers firmly into my shoulders. I looked up to see a broad smile on her lips.

"He would be honored, when the time comes," Alicia said. Zoe and Micah looked at Alicia and then at me. I just nodded, not sure what I had been signed up for but knowing it was something I had to say yes to, based on Alicia's reaction. Micah and Zoe turned, still human, still holding hands, and stepped past the central bonfire and into the tree line. I looked up to Alicia, and she was staring at me, still smiling.

"Sorry I answered for you," she said, "but you really didn't want to say the wrong thing there."

"What exactly was that?" I asked.

"Basically, you're going to be the godfather to one of their children. It's a big deal," she told me. "Zoe's grandmother is going to be midwife, and you're going to be the first person to speak to the baby."

"That's a really big deal," I agreed.

"Normally, it's something asked of a parent or another member of the family. You, being a nonfamily member and yet to accept your place in the pack? That's their way of saying that they fully accept you. More than that, they trust you to protect the next generation of their family. It's saying they accept your authority," Alicia explained. If I had been standing, my knees would have gone out from under me. A family in this pack trusted me to protect them, accepted my authority? This night was officially the weirdest one in a very long time. Alicia disappeared—for how long, I don't know—and returned with a bottle of water. I chugged it all in less than three seconds.

"I know, it's a lot to take in," she said, and her voice was as kind as I had ever heard it.

"I need to get out of here before any more bombshells go off," I said. She extended a hand to me and I took it. I was shaky on my feet, but she didn't laugh at me, didn't comment on the fact that I needed to shake my legs out or how it took me a second to find my footing. We walked from the bonfire, but when I heard Erik's booming voice asking us to stop, my foot hovered in the air, as if I were about to tread on a land mine. I saw the tension in Alicia's back as she turned, and anticipation, dry leaves in autumn, reached my nose. Alicia stepped to the side to give Erik and me a moment of privacy, even as his broad palm landed on the center of my spine.

"Running away already?" His tone—there was no teasing in it. Rather, there was something genuine there, but what it was, I couldn't say.

"This," I said, "is more than me showing you what it's like when I light candles in my home." As an excuse, I knew it was frail, that it wouldn't hold much. But Erik nodded.

"I understand, but I hope…," Erik said.

"You hope…," I repeated.

"I hope that you'll be willing to come to our next meeting, stay for longer. I can come over, help talk you through some of this. I know there's a lot to handle, but please… think about it?" He was earnest. Even without the heightened ears, I would have known that. At least, that's what I told myself. I swallowed as I searched for words. Would coming bring me any closer to what I wanted? What I thought I wanted, anyway? I had seen so much, felt the flow, but there was still too much I didn't understand about this world and the magicks in it, at least not yet. "Meet me on the dark of the moon," I said, my voice level. "We can talk then."

Erik nodded, then he leaned down. I froze but didn't say no, didn't throw up a barrier, didn't ask him to stop. He brought his lips against the pulse point of my neck, inhaled deeply, and then gave it the softest possible kiss. He straightened himself then, smiling. I knew I was redder than a beet, redder than even a ruby. I turned and began to walk. Alicia continued two or three paces ahead, and I swore I heard her whisper, "Fucking finally."

CHAPTER 16

SINCE SEEING the new moon rise just before sunset, my nerves had been incredibly high. Now I was on the couch, head tilted so I could look out the window. The cat had retreated to one of its many hiding spots. On new moon nights, the cat was never near me. A survival instinct, pure and simple. All things were now possible—at least for me. Erik had met me on a full moon, when he was most in control. Tonight, I would be at my strongest, and he would be without his pack. Tonight I would stand as over four hundred years of my family had stood, under the influence of the moon's secret face.

The sun had only just set, and the night was heavy. Streetlamps glowed, and in the homes across the street, lights were on. My house was an island of darkness. Even the headlights of cars as they drove by didn't seem to touch my window. There were things I could be doing, should be doing, but I waited. Erik had texted me that he would be a little late because he needed to finish a project. I was as ready as I was going to be, and in the stillness, I gathered myself.

When I had told Cara earlier that Erik was coming to my house, she cackled with glee, even as she applied chocolate fondant to a five-tier hazelnut cake—we had been asked to do something that resembled Nutella.

"Are you going to tame the wolf tonight? Going to make him howl?" Cara's eyes gleamed. I liked it better when she hadn't been pressing into my personal life.

"Why did I tell you anything? I must be going crazy," I said more to myself than to the banshee working next to me. She had laughed again, and I couldn't make myself reconcile her laughter with the soul-rending effects of her scream. She had done it again—this time in earnest—only a few days ago, when a hearse drove by Siren's. She had fallen to the ground, and the scream still echoed in the deepest part of my body. I was able to create a quick and crude circle, but I still had seen her, mouth forced open, eyes rolling back as a wail of heartbreak and despair ripped through her body. It had been less than half a minute, but thirty seconds can be a lifetime.

"Nothing's going to happen," I told Cara, but even as I said it, I knew it for a lie. While my head might not want anything to happen, I didn't know if my head was still in control.

For the last three days, as soon as I got home, I cleaned, dusted, and brushed every square inch of my house. I knew that this time, when Erik entered my house, it would be different. Cara hadn't needed to call me on my lie.

At the edge of my hearing, I picked up the distinct motor of a large pickup truck. I smelled the faint hint of exhaust, then wood shavings and sweat. Erik had exited the cab and was coming down the sidewalk. When Cara and I were combining the ingredients for the fondant, I'd had to step out of the kitchen briefly. I was used to the strong smells of a kitchen, but the chocolate, bitter and dark, had proved too much for me to handle for a moment. It wasn't the only time in the last two weeks when my senses had spiked. There wasn't a rhyme or reason to the episodes, and I had developed crude coping strategies to manage them when they flared up. At some point I was going to have to talk to Terence's aunt, learn from her directly. What I had now was a stopgap at most.

I got to the door without looking through the window as soon as I heard Erik's footfalls on the small walkway to my house. The wards of my home fell with barely a thought, and I opened the door to find Erik at my threshold with his hand raised. For a heartbeat we looked at each other and said nothing. We had been exchanging frequent texts; he had even asked if he should bring anything. Although Cara and I had started our marathon for Valentine's Day and I closed myself off to the rest of the world, Erik had found a way to reach me, to try to make me laugh, to be present.

Backlit by streetlamps, I couldn't make out his face, not at first. His shadow fell over me and merged with the darkness of my home. Then I saw his lips twitch and become a smile. It wasn't the predatory smile I associated with him. If anything, it was shy, uncertain… almost human. Our eyes locked, and I saw flashes of emerald reflected there for the briefest of seconds. I had been unaware of witch's fire dancing beneath my skin, so close to the surface, ready to come and play.

I stepped back, giving him nonverbal permission to enter. He took it and made sure to close the door once he was fully inside. In the darkness of my hallway, I turned and moved into the house without making a sound, on a beeline to the kitchen, and Erik followed. His footsteps almost echoed as he trod toward me. "Is this what you're like every new moon?" he asked.

"I haven't had anyone in my space during a new moon since my babcia died," I confessed.

"How did you manage that in culinary school?" Erik was incredulous.

"Rashid was very chill. He got that I needed my time to myself. He joked about my monthly visitor, and I made myself scarce anytime he brought over a girlfriend or boyfriend. We balanced each other out," I answered, my lips quirking slightly.

"So," he said, leaning in.

"So," I responded, mirroring his body language. I wasn't sure of where to head next, what I might say. Now we were on my turf, in my time, and the silence was like the darkness—heavy, omnipresent, filling the space between us almost tangibly. I counted seconds in my head, slowly, timing them by my breath. Erik scuffed the ground with his toe, and I wondered if that was his tell. Would he always do that when he was nervous? And why was I allowing myself to think of it as cute?

"Your first meeting, your first time filling some of the duties, was it—did you—" Erik stumbled over his words at the end, and I knew that if I tried to rush through anything, I would be as tongue-tied as he was, if not more so. I could see the ridges of his cheekbones, the set of his jaw, the way he kept his eyes downcast, trying to avoid mine. I stepped closer, into the silence and the darkness, and filled it with my presence, with my will. It was familiar to me, something I had known from birth and would know until my last breath.

"It was overwhelming to me in the purest sense of the word," I answered.

"I saw Zoe and Micah with you, and Terence and Alicia. You're beginning to gather some support in the pack," he said, his lips quirking up at the corners.

"Most of them are still afraid of me. I heard—" I stopped myself, not sure whether he knew already. The cat would be out of the bag soon enough. Alicia and Terence might have kept this to themselves, but I hadn't extracted their words on it.

"What did you hear?" Erik asked.

"Whispering," I said. "I couldn't make out the words, but I heard the tone. I knew what they would have been saying, and it was unnerving, to say the least."

"You mean—" He was going to ask a question. I was ready with his answer.

"I'm picking up some of your senses. It comes and goes in waves. I haven't been able to find a pattern yet." I averted my gaze. For him, I knew what this would mean.

He was in my space, a delicious combination of summer rain, sandalwood, musk, and the faintest hint of bay rum. I tilted my head up and, unbidden, the house was filled with a viridian glow as witch's fire sprouted over my skin. He didn't back away, though, even as the fire leapt from my skin to his. This was a cool fire, a heatless fire, a fire of will, and I did not will it to become an inferno. The fire ran up my nose and adjusted my glasses in response to a thought. Erik grinned and leaned down; less than a handsbreadth of distance was between his face and mine.

"Would you let me kiss you?" Erik asked.

"Not now." He lifted his palm and the fire chased him instinctively. I called it back to myself and then pulled it inside. The darkness and silence settled into the place where there had once been heat and spark. In it I could see him narrow his eyes and bite his tongue. There was so much he wanted to say. I saw it in the twist of his lips and the faint hint of gold flashing in the darkness. With a gesture, I would be able to keep him bound in place, a statue. In a move, he could have me pinned against a counter, his teeth at my throat. With an impulse, I could call to all the wards and walls of my home and force him from it, but I knew I would need more than an exhale this time. With a thought, his human skin would fall away, and he would be the predator again. It was a standoff, and there was no easy way forward.

"You're finally accepting the bond," he said firmly.

"At least parts of it. It's making work inconvenient, to say the least," I said. I raised a hand and silenced him with a gesture rather than through any act of magic. "Even if I do accept becoming the pack witch for you, I'm going to keep working with Cara. I like my job."

Erik nodded, accepting my decision. "What was it you heard that made you run, Jakob?"

"I didn't hear words—not exactly. I was more aware of the tone, the venom in it. You know I've been hated for many things, Erik. I've been hated because of my orientation, my faith, and my ethnic background. I've grown used to hate—I had to in order to survive. The hatred in their voice wasn't for any of those reasons. They hated who I was as a person."

"Do you remember anything about the speaker, anything about the voice?" He was immediately concerned and defensive.

Thinking back, I closed my eyes. "It was a woman's voice. I think it belonged to the woman with one of the worst haircuts I've ever seen. It was badly dyed, the bangs were poorly layered, and she had the sort of voice that demands to speak with a manager."

Realization crossed Erik's face and he reached out and stroked a thumb on my forearm. I shuddered without meaning to, more of the fire dancing over his skin. "That's Yvette. I know why she would hate you. For her, you're the end of a cherished dream. When I became the alpha, some members of the pack had hoped that my previous flings with men were nothing more than experiments—me taking pleasure without the risk of getting a girl with a pup before I was ready. They thought I might grow out of it, that once I was alpha, I would do what a good alpha should do—find a nice girl and start a small den of my own, be a model for the rest of my community. Yvette's daughter just graduated college, and even knowing I'm gay, she's all but thrown Celeste at me."

"She named her daughter Celeste?" I didn't know why I had difficulty accepting that part of the story.

"Celeste's twin is Genevieve," Erik went on, and he was smirking.

"I thought my parents were cruel when they named me."

"Even with a *k*, your name isn't unusual, Jakob."

"My middle name is almost as Polish as my last name," I warned.

"You're going to have to tell me now."

"Wojciech."

"Bless you."

"Trust me, I've heard that before."

"I can imagine," he said, smirk audible. "Even if I wasn't gay, though, Celeste wouldn't be on my radar. She's too much like her mother, too immature for her age, still far more a girl than a woman."

My jaw dropped. "You know Britney Spears?" Erik just smirked and offered a one-shouldered shrug.

"I get why Yvette would hate me, but what about the rest of your pack?"

"Most of them don't know you yet. They smell your power, and some are a little afraid of you. For others, the reality of you is the end of a dream for a traditional sort of alpha," he offered.

"Your pack is afraid of me for the same reason you're attracted to me—delusions of my power," I tried to joke. "And some see me as a threat to a traditional werewolf family unit."

"Something close to that, yeah," he said.

"Well, that's comforting." I crossed my arms across my chest.

"I know that it's a lot to face, and I can't promise that things are going to change overnight. Even I don't have that sort of power. However, the more events you come to, the more you try to get to know the rest of the pack, the easier you make it for them to get to know you, and the fewer the whispers around the fire. You've already got some of the more senior pack families in your corner. You've been asked to stand when Micah and Zoe have their first pup. I know Alicia told you what that means."

"It's a lot of responsibility," I said.

"That it is, but it's also a stance from them, putting themselves in your camp. They—their parents, grandparents, and rest of their family— they would back you over Yvette any day of the week."

"Because I helped them?"

"Because you helped them. You know how I knew you were the mate—"

"Please, don't, Erik," I interjected.

"Jakob, please, listen to me—hear me out on this. I know you don't like the word, and I know that for you it isn't true—at least not yet. It's true for me, though. It's always been true for me. Please," Erik said. My head demanded I should say no. My heart, however—that part of myself that dreamed and whispered—it wasn't fighting anymore. I knew, deeper than my bones and blood, I was giving in.

I exhaled, my breath shaking. There was too much going on and only so much I was able to process, so I closed my eyes and focused. I searched for anything that would soothe me, and I remembered what I had said to Nathan the final time I had seen him. The words of Nachman of Breslov were to me now—as they had been then—a source of strength:

"A person needs to pass over a very narrow bridge and the essence is to not be afraid at all."

Here I was, on the narrow bridge. It would be easy to fall, to let my fear overtake me. I inhaled, exhaled again, and finally opened my eyes. "Go ahead," I said, my voice faint if firm. "I can get through this."

"I knew you were the mate I wanted from the moment I saw you dancing in the club. You didn't care what the world saw, and that's someone I want by my side. More than that, I remember the first time I called you after the bite. Do you remember that night?" he asked. I nodded. The first time Erik had called me had been to help a young pup who was in his first transformation. His family members and his alpha had been unable to get him to return to his human form. I had fought with myself, but I had come, and through the correct combination of herbs and chants, had brought him back to his human skin. I had been well compensated for that.

"You came. You were willing to help a family you didn't know and willing to work hard. You were there, standing for them, helping them get their son back. True, we could have found a way, but in the end, you came, you helped. You put the needs of others before your own, and you knew if you had wanted to you could have put it aside. But you didn't. You stand for others when you know it's the right thing to do. I knew then that there would be no other mate for me. You made sure to get what you needed, but you put someone else before your own desire, and that's what any good person should do and what is required of both an alpha and their mate," Erik said.

I couldn't help myself then, despite all of Cara's teasing, despite everything that might come after. I surged forward, wrapped my arms around him, and leaned up. Caught off guard as he was, he staggered back slightly, but he smiled down at me and brought his lips to mine.

Our kiss was far from elegant. It was all tongues, teeth, and misplaced lips. It was frantic, a war. When I pulled back from him, there was a smirk on his lips. His arms were on my waist, keeping me in place. "Did I say you could kiss me?" he teased.

"You finally got what you wanted, didn't you?" I asked.

He leaned down again, brought his nose along my neck, and inhaled deeply, slowly, as he pressed his lips to my throat. I shivered. We ground our hips together, quickly, harshly. I felt him through the denim—hard, aching, needing. I matched him. The months of only my own hand, nights knowing no touch save my own… they added up. Witch's fire raced under my skin, in my veins and bones. Rather than with anger, every cell of my body sang with lust. Libido, heart, desire—they all won out. I had no more fight in me, no more struggle to offer. He had won. I was giving in.

Erik kissed me again, slowly, languidly, and our tongues danced together. My eyes were closed. Sight would have been a distraction I couldn't afford. He ran his fingers up and down my spine, and I trembled against him.

"Not yet," he said. "But if things keep going like this, I think I just might." His voice was honey and dark things my body ached for. I rolled my hips again and my hardness dug into his thigh. He looked down at me, his eyes bleeding black. The wolf was closer to the surface now, and it pulled me back from the fog of lust on which I had been coasting. I stepped back and he came toward me. Then he looked down, genuine confusion on his face.

I saw Erik hunting for words. They were just out of his reach, on the tip of his tongue. As I looked at him, the witch's fire danced on my skin and in my eyes behind my glasses. It had come unbidden, and my entire frame was wreathed in eldritch light that cast flitting distorted shadows throughout my kitchen.

"What I need, Erik," I said, my voice stronger than I had thought it would be, "is to be sure of myself. You came into my home with all those beautiful words, and now I—" My eyes traveled downward and I could see his jeans doing a poor job of concealing his own excitement. My pants were likewise tented, and my blood swam. My basest instincts screamed to me, telling me to go over, unzip his fly, and swallow him home. My libido was urgent, craving, pulsing. It needed to have him, but I had been well trained. My grandmother's lessons had not gone to waste. I knew better than to make any decisions spurred by passion alone. I knew to wait.

He chuckled low and deep and his black eyes flecked with gold traveled down my slender frame. "Trust me, I know what you felt, what you're feeling. Why are you fighting this?" he asked.

"Because…." I said.

"You have to know just how much that makes you sound like a toddler," he said. I huffed out a breath but managed not to cross my arms over my chest. He wasn't all wrong. He had seen into me, through me.

"I know, but it's true."

"So, you're fighting me—this, us—because you can?" He crossed his arms over his chest and looked every inch the parent, scolding a child. It helped quench my lust ever so slightly.

"You know why I'm fighting this. I've told you," I reminded him. I was making so much progress, I didn't need to be my own worst enemy now. Was I willing to fall into a bed with him again just to understand my place in his pack?

"Jakob," Erik growled my name. "I've been trying to come correct, like you wanted. I've been trying to meet you halfway. I've been doing what I can. What else do you need from me? What else can I do to show you that I want to be yours and only yours?"

My body tensed like a string humming after being plucked. Now, especially, I needed to be sure. I pushed myself back and stretched out a palm. A salt shaker flew into it And I drew a circle and called to the heart of my house, to the bones holding my home together, and to the earth on which my home was built. The familiar kitchen, the werewolf offering himself to me, the distant breathing of the cat—everything disappeared, and I was alone, focused only on myself.

I was rooted, and magic sparked and pulsed in me, danced along my skin, in my veins, and through my bones. I listened and waited to hear the small, still voice. It would tell me, confirm what my heart knew, perhaps what it had always known. Despite not asking for Erik, despite never seeing myself as the mate of an alpha, despite not wanting the responsibility that would come from taking the role, there I was, already serving, already embracing the chaos. Humans, my babcia had told me, were unique for their ability to find patterns in chaos. It was in understanding those patterns that we could find G-d.

The total silence was broken by a whisper that ran along my spine and perched right against my ear.

"Är du min?" I asked, repeating a question he had asked me in the throes of passion. He let loose a small snort.

"Ja," he whispered. "Jag är din." It was soft, barely above a whisper, but it carried. I didn't need to know the exact translation to know what he meant. I had asked. He had answered. He was mine.

I extended my toe and broke the line of salt, and power fell away as easily as it had been gathered. This time I leaned in slowly. He mirrored me, and our lips touched. It was chaste at first, unhurried, exploratory.

This was what our first kiss should have been, I thought to myself as he wrapped his arms around me and pulled me closer. This was what I had needed, what I had craved.

After over half a year apart, it took us a while to find a rhythm, but not as long as I thought it might. Timid kisses became bold, and my fire wrapped around us, pulled us close, bound us in ways that words couldn't. I pulled at buttons and felt warm skin beneath my questing fingers. His nipples were stiff to my touch. When he tugged at the hem of my shirt, I pulled away so he could undress me all the easier. Within moments, skin was pressing skin, and I was walking us backward. I led us from the kitchen and into the bedroom. The cat, at the foot of my bed, lifted its head. It jumped down and fled to another of its private places, and I was thankful. I didn't want it as a voyeur.

Erik and I wasted no time stripping down. Much to my surprise, he pushed me onto my bed and took my weeping cockhead between his lips. He sucked with wild abandon, hollowing his cheeks and taking me to the root in a single motion. My moans seemed to spur him on. He traced a vein with the tip of his tongue and caused my toes to curl. This was better than I remembered, had dreamed of. He was totally focused on me, his lips and tongue moving. He took a long moment to tease the root of my member, humming, the sound traveling through my entire being.

There was an audible pop as he lifted his head, his eyes twinkling with mischief. He loomed over me, pressing down, and our erections ground against each other over and over as he kissed me. I ground against him like a madman—and maybe I was.

"Lube?" he asked when he broke our kiss.

"Bedside table, but I don't have any—" I stopped myself. I hadn't bought condoms in a long time—I hadn't thought that I would need them. I should have bought some earlier today; Cara had even asked me if I was on my way to get them. I hadn't, because I was too damn proud. Now here I was wishing I hadn't been my usual self.

"You do remember I'm a werewolf, right? I can't catch human diseases. I used the condom the first time because I didn't want you to think I was someone who had to go bare. Right now, Jakob, what I *need* is to feel you in me. I *need* to feel you come in me, Jakob. I'm yours, Jakob, and I'm going to prove that to you," he said, his lips ghosting my ear, my neck. I felt the desire pouring off him. I had been expecting him to top me, as he had before, but he was willing to bottom for me.

My breath shook as I exhaled. "Are you sure?" I asked. I knew what I had just heard, but I needed to confirm it, needed to know that I wasn't dreaming. Erik pressed his lips to my collarbone, then to my nipple—which he nipped—and he turned his gaze up to me.

"Jag är din," he said. Then he kissed me, took my shaft in his hand and stroked it, teasing my crown with his thumb. I squirmed against the bedsheets. This was all-consuming—overwhelming in the purest, most primal of ways. There was nothing outside except for us.

"I might not—I mean—are you really sure you want to—I mean—" My tongue tripped over itself as I struggled to form the right words.

"Jag är din," he repeated as he traced the pulsing vein along my member, teasing me. "I am yours. Fuck me, claim me, have your way with me—or if you want, make love to me." There was a moment of hesitation with the last of those words, as if he couldn't believe he had said them. "Do with me as you need, as you want. I am yours, Jakob."

"You're going to need to be patient," I said, my voice low, a little bit unsteady.

"Patience is a virtue," he said with a small smirk.

With shaking hands, I took the bottle of lube. He laid himself out, impossibly large on my bed. He looked over his shoulder at me and winked. My eyes burned as I took in the sight of him, hair cascading down his neck, hanging loosely to the right. His lips were twisted into a sinful smirk. All the muscles of his body were on display, like a model that any artist would have killed for. He arched his back, rounding out his powerful ass. Cool lubricant filled my palm and I brought my hand up.

I tried to be as gentle, as cautious with him as he had been with me. I worked with one finger first, feeling his heat, the reaction of his impossibly tight body, taking its time in opening up to me. He might have been a virgin, ready for his first time. He had never told me of his previous partners, and I had never asked. Those were stories we would tell each other later. I crooked my finger and searched for his prostate. When I found it, he released a moan that made me curl my own toes in sympathy. I moved my finger back and forth, arching it again, seeking the same spot. Some power was with me and I found it.

One finger became two, and I twisted the digits searching for new angles, trying to get him open as best I could. While I was neither as long nor as thick as he was, I was bigger than average, and on my wisp of a frame, I looked hung. Erik rocked his hips back, met my fingers, took me deeper, faster, and clenched around me. When I pulled my fingers out, I coated my leaking erection with lube. "I won't have your stamina," I warned him. "This won't last long." I was already on a knife's edge, and the lust and anticipation rolling off Erik did nothing to ease the tension.

"We can go for a second round after this one," Erik offered. "The perks of being my own boss, and I think that your business partner would be more than happy to cover for you if she knew you were getting laid." It was too easy to imagine the smug look on Cara's face, the glint in her eyes, and to hear her cackle.

"I did not need to start thinking about Cara right now," I said, my erection flagging a little. Erik's hand shot out and he grabbed the base of my cock. In less than a second I was at full mast again and he guided me to him. He hissed and I groaned as I pressed against him and then entered him. Once in, I let instinct guide me, and I slid into him with a single liquid glide. I remained motionless until he clenched around me, tightening his body deliciously, and I instinctively bucked forward with the smallest roll of my hips.

I wasn't the master he had been; I admit that. My thrusts were erratic, and I had to focus on my breathing so as not to cum four seconds after pushing into him. Erik, however, was incredibly patient. He tilted his head back and offered a deep howl of pleasure when I hit something inside him, and I aimed myself for that same spot again. I was lucky—I found it, and Erik swore. "So fucking good, Jakob," he praised as he pushed his ass to my hips.

That spurred me on like little else. My skin erupted again in emerald flame as I buried myself in him and the fire spilled off me, onto him. It illuminated him beautifully and sank slow and deep. The fire moved in time with my thrusts. He whimpered and I felt his tunnel contract around me, milking my cock for all it was worth.

We were connected, sharing everything with each other. All we had, all we could give, we shared it all willingly. I knew what it meant. This was more than having sex—this was making love. I felt it as we pressed together, my chest to his back. I leaned down and bit him in the same spot where he had marked me, and he gave a chuckle that transformed into a groan of pleasure. Then I pulled from him, and he rolled over and opened his legs for me. I slid into him and closed my eyes.

Home. I was home in him.

I was above him then, and the light from my body cascaded, illuminating the room. I leaned down and took his lips in a searing kiss, the pleasure burning in me—in us—*through* us. We rolled together, slowly, surely, and he tightened his legs around me. "Like this," he said, and I felt him leak over both of us. "Please, like this," he half pleaded, and I couldn't say no, even if I wanted to. I began to move in earnest.

As I had promised, with me on top, it didn't take long. His hand moved in time with the frantic madness of my hips and as I squeezed my cheeks together, burying myself in him, I spat an oath in Yiddish. What I said, I can't remember. All I knew was that it spoke of how right this felt, how hot he was around me, how intense it was. I slammed forward, deeply as I could, and released myself in him, green bleeding to gold at the edges of the witch's fire wreathed around both of us.

Erik followed me over the edge less than ten seconds later, as I was still quivering through the last bursts of my orgasm. His seed coated his powerful abs and chest, and some of it landed on his neck. I leaned in and kissed him deeply. He kissed me back with the raw hunger that had been building between us since I left his home that night in May, more than half a year ago. I pulled out, but he held me close, and we were tangled in each other. He brought his lips to my forehead and kissed my brow.

"Jag är din, du är min," he whispered.

"Jesteś mój, ja jestem twój," I mirrored back to him. Polish—I had reverted to Polish.

"We really need to find a language in common," he said.

"Besides English?" I asked. He gave a low growl of pleasure and kissed the top of my head again. Then he wrapped an arm around me, pulled me closer to him, and held me still. I didn't want to go anywhere anyway.

CHAPTER 17

HOPE YOU'RE ready for today, Erik's text read. Valentine's Day was upon us in all its pink-and-white horror, and Cara and I were attempting insanity. We were trying to best our record—ten cakes in a day. When I told Erik that Valentine's Day was our marathon, I wasn't exaggerating. Since the second time we'd had sex, we had actively been trying to see each other. In addition to a stolen kiss here, a rushed meal there, and entirely too few shared nights—although it had been more than three—I had placed wards around a few homes and helped a family find lost photos. Small steps, I knew, but at least steps in the right direction.

It was still very much the early stages of a relationship, and Erik and I had discussed it at great length. After a second round, we had sat at my kitchen table, sipping coffee. The cat meowed at us, urging us to move to somewhere it would be allowed to sit on Erik's lap. When I said I wanted to be more than some trophy mate, Erik snorted coffee out his nose. I couldn't prevent myself from laughing at that. "It's not funny," he had complained.

"It's a little funny." I leaned over the table, kissed him quickly, gently, just because I could. As I pulled away, I noticed the small smile on his lips.

"You won't win every argument by kissing me," he said. Then he leaned across the table and licked a stripe up my neck.

"I know, but—" He paused midlick and arched a single brow. "Kissing can lead places," I said. Even after what we had just done to each other—twice—I was still eager for more. Apparently I had the libido of a teenager again.

"Minx," he growled. Then he put down my coffee and dragged me back to the bedroom. I had known there were things we still needed to discuss. There was much we had to settle, and I knew there would be tough days ahead. It wouldn't all be sunshine, kittens, and puppies, but as his fingers breached me, made me fist my sheets and made my eyes roll back in my head, I knew we'd find a way forward. There was still a lot I needed to learn about him, and he needed to learn a lot about me. The wards of my home no longer saw him as a threat.

ERIK HADN'T been kidding when he'd said he was coming correct. It seemed as though every day I found either a thoughtful email, a silly picture, or a small gift waiting for me when I got home. I had warned Cara that Erik was going to do something on Valentine's Day, and the banshee laughed. She had been doing a lot more of that, especially when I walked in late for the first time the morning after the new moon. I didn't have time to make an excuse; Cara had just turned to me, laughed, and passed me a mug of coffee with two over-the-counter painkillers. She didn't say "I told you so," but she didn't need to—her look did it for her.

At some point Cara would have to meet Erik. When that time came, I hoped reason would prevail. We'd have to find somewhere neutral for the first meeting, somewhere public where neither of them could resort to baser instincts. I wasn't looking forward to that headache. There was only so much I could deal with at one time.

As I opened the door to the back room of Siren's, I didn't hear the death metal medley that Cara insisted was part of the tradition. More worrying than that, I didn't smell anything in the ovens. I looked down to my phone and wondered if I was late. Seeing it was over an hour before I was scheduled to start, I wondered what was going on. Then I heard it—the sad, beautiful lilting Gaelic Cara used on the phone.

The mezuzah on my neck hummed, and I grabbed a box of salt from one of the numerous spice racks. As I moved through the kitchen to Cara's office, I picked up a knife. I didn't know what was going down, but I knew it wasn't good. Shouldering the door open, two matching sets of eyes turned toward me. If the identical eyes weren't enough, their vibrant hair and mouths—twisted in perfect mirrors of each other—told me this person had to be related to Cara. Cara brushed a hand across her forehead.

"Jakob, this is my brother, Síomón." Cara's carefully cultured neutral accent was gone. She sounded like she was just off the boat from East Mayo, Ireland. "Síomón"—she motioned with her head toward the other man (who was somehow shorter than me)—"this is Jakob, the witch who works with me."

"Are ye daft, Cara?" Síomón yelled, but his voice lacked any threat of a banshee's scream. Thank heaven for the small mercies. His Irish accent was thicker than his sister's, if such a thing were possible. However there seemed to be something a little off about it. Like his sister, his movements were graceful and otherworldly, even in anger. But his build was that of a distance runner.

"Oh, I'll show ye daft," Cara spat back, beginning to open her mouth. The temperature dropped five degrees and the silver around my neck spat green flame in anticipation of what was about to happen.

"Please," I shouted. "Let's not come to blows of any sort. My ears aren't ready for it this early." Cara and Síomón narrowed their eyes as they looked in my direction, and I took a step back. I wondered what Erik would do if I texted him about his offer to be my sugar wolf—my term, not his.

"Ye brought in a witch," Síomón critiqued. "Ye knew that was asking for trouble. Mother would be ashamed."

"Mother's known longer than you—and so have Brigid, Máire, and Siobhán." Cara drilled her fingers into her desk with each sibling she named.

"And what did they have to say about ye bringin' a witch across yer threshold?"

"They were more worried that he'd have to use magic in the kitchen to keep pace with me than about anything he might do to me. Until November of last year, he hadn't even used magic in this building. He had no idea what I was."

"I'm still in the room," I interjected. They turned to me, murder in two sets of eyes. "Shutting up now," I said. They looked away from me and resumed arguing with each other in the lilting language I had heard when I entered. Neither one of them seemed to be able to finish a thought. Granted, I didn't know the first thing about Gaelic, but it felt like there were a lot of interjections. More than once, they spoke at the same time. At one point, Cara opened her mouth and let out the start of a mournful wail. I pulled back, wincing, and brought one hand to the silver around my neck. I didn't need to do it for long—it didn't become a full cry, didn't carry the despair of death.

Before her scream was fully formed, Síomón opened his mouth and the noise coming out of Cara's throat died. I couldn't help but think that he had eaten it. All that remained where the wail should have been was a deafening, echoing silence. I hadn't heard of any fae that could do that. Then again, I didn't know much about the different clans and orders of the fae. My family had done their level best to avoid them. Yet more things I would have to add to the grimoire, I thought.

"Look, when ye get over yourself, then ye can come back. If ye can't accept my friend, then I'll see ye at Máire's birthday in March," Cara stated. Síomón crossed his arms and looked as if he was going to object. Instead he turned on his heel, muttering under his breath. I swore I heard him say something about a "stubborn banshee bitch," but I wasn't going to tell Cara that. As the door swung closed behind us, Cara sat in her chair and just shrugged.

"Family can be complicated," she offered, her accent back to careful American neutrality.

"I know. What I didn't know was that banshees could have brothers," I said.

"Síomón's an *ankou*," she explained.

"An ankou?" I asked, trying to mimic her pronunciation, but failing

"I'll explain what he is and why you shouldn't think he's a complete wanker after we get some work done. This is still Valentine's Day, after all, and the rat bastard"—she yelled the insult past me, as if her brother were still in the bakery—"should have given me some warning that he was coming before showing up unannounced."

"As you said, family can be complicated," I agreed.

"That it can." Cara nodded.

"How did you go from full fresh-off-the-boat back to middle American so quickly?" This was personal curiosity, something that wouldn't end up in the grimoire.

"Years of practice, Jakob. Years of practice." She smirked. "Ready for our marathon?"

I gave her a thumbs-up. "Let's blast some death metal." A lifetime ago, my first Valentine's Day at Siren's, I had walked into the kitchen to hear what I later learned was Necrocannibal playing at a bone-shaking volume, and Cara smirking, a silent challenge on her lips. Instead of saying anything, I walked forward and rolled out fondant, focused on making flowers out of modeling chocolate. Since then, Cara and I'd had our private competition with each other—whoever came up with the best playlist would collect any leftover cookies at the end of our shift. Cara had won the last two years, but I felt strong about my choices today.

We were elbows-deep in batter with three cakes finished as Arch Enemy blasted through our speakers in the back when it was time to open the front of house. I left the kitchen, washed my hands, and removed a smudge of flour from one cheek. I must have reeked of vanilla and red dye number three. The weekend before, I had met Terence's aunt and she, over countless mugs of tea, had passed me a few techniques that had vastly improved my ability to handle the new sensory input. Erik was also very eager to help me learn, using private exercises about control even when highly stimulated.

I stopped that train of thought. I didn't need a hardon as I served customers.

There was already someone waiting on the other side of the glass door when I turned on the lights. I didn't keep him waiting long. "Are you Jakob Ku—Kura—" He struggled to pronounce my surname.

"Kuratowski," I said. "Don't worry about it. Everyone has a difficult time at first."

"Whatever," he said brusquely and proceeded to give me a vase holding some sort of stem with green leaves and pink flowers bleeding from a white core. I held it as he turned and headed back to a van with flashing hazard lights. He was on his way before I had a chance to ask him what they were. Then I felt my pocket vibrate and removed my phone. There was a simple message from Erik—*Hope the first flowers arrived.*

What are they? I replied. I waited less than ten seconds before he responded. He had apparently been anticipating this.

Google arbutus flower. There was nothing after that, and I followed his instructions. My cheeks turned the same color as the flower as I read the meaning—"Thee only do I love," according to one page about the Victorian language of flowers. I was as embarrassed as I was aroused. I knew I was nowhere near being able to say that, not yet. But knowing what Erik felt, knowing the time he had taken to find something to match the sentiment... I was blushing. I brought the stem back with me. Then I remembered what Erik's initial message to me had read.

First of the flowers? I shot back to him. I didn't have the chance to wait for the phone to vibrate as the first of a stream of customers marched in. I was busy ringing up people and filling orders for over a half hour. When there was a break in the stream, I let out a small sigh. For the amount of business that Cara and I did, we really needed someone full-time behind the counter. I would have to mention it to her, I thought to myself as I dared to sneak a peek at my phone.

Expect a florist to deliver every hour or so, as close to on the hour as possible, Erik messaged, followed by an emoji of a heart. My cheeks were now a decided shade of red, but I was able to put my embarrassment to the side as I focused on answering every possible customer complaint. I had just finished filling a rather complicated order—one that involved the last of the red velvet cookies—when the next deliverer came in. She was younger than the first. "I take it you're Jakob K?" she asked, her voice even and calm.

"I am," I answered.

"Here you go," she said, producing two red flowers with a flourish. I would have to start gardening, I thought as I placed them in the vase next to the arbutus branch. *What did you send me this time?* I messaged Erik.

Red camellias, Erik replied. I had just enough time to look at the language of flowers site again before the next wave of customers crashed into Siren's Sweets. According to the website, one meaning of red camellias was "a flame in his heart." When Erik wanted to woo, he wooed seriously. I knew we didn't have plans that evening, but when I next saw him, I would have to think of something special for Erik—I just didn't know what would match this display. I would also have to talk to him about what was and was not an appropriate gift in the workplace. As a baker, I had already made his Valentine's Day gift—a coffee cupcake with hazelnut buttercream frosting. It was in my fridge back home, waiting for the next time he came over, which was supposed to be this weekend, after the madness of the 14th had passed.

In the remaining two hours, I received three red chrysanthemums and four sprigs of lavender—"I love you" and "loyalty or devotion," according to the website. As I headed back into the kitchen with my makeshift vase, Cara looked at me, the mismatched blooms, and the stupid grin I had on my face. "Someone's getting lucky," she said in a singsong.

"I detest you," I replied.

"Doesn't change the facts," she continued, her tone of voice unchanging.

"I loathe you," I said as I adjusted my apron.

"Is that more or less intense than being detested?" She sounded honestly curious.

"More. Far more."

"What's with all the five-dollar words anyway?"

"I'm trying to be creative here," I said.

"Save that creativity for the cakes and your beau—in that order," Cara commanded and exited to the front of house. It would require only a single gesture to put a curse on her head, but I breathed through the temptation and let the strains of The HU get me into a working rhythm. My hands were a blur as I added ingredients, removed cakes and a tray of heart-shaped cinnamon cookies from the ovens. When this day was over, we'd have to talk about getting part-time counter help—maybe even a full-time person.

At the end of the marathon, I felt the exhaustion deep in my bones. Pink and red frosting was embedded beneath my nails and I had lost count of just how many hearts and cupids I had pulled out of the oven. I didn't look up when Cara entered, but I felt her exhaustion rolling off her, and it added to my own.

"Is it closing time?" I asked.

"We survived." She looked past me to a tower cake that I had constructed. "That will be picked up in thirty minutes, and then we're done for the day."

Finally, I saw a smile of victory on her face. I extended my fist to her and she bumped it against mine. There was nothing left to say. She pulled a cookie from a tray and popped it into her mouth.

"We really need to think about getting a third pair of hands in here," I said. "We've grown, and it looks like we're going to continue growing."

"What about that kid, the werewolf you helped out? Does he need a part-time gig?" Cara asked.

"Are you sure?" I asked, both of my brows dancing high above the frames of my glasses.

"Jakob, the kid likes you, and it will give me an excuse to finally meet that werewolf of yours. If we handle it right, it might be a bit awkward, but you can have hot, sweaty make-up sex after," Cara said bluntly. I must have turned beet red based on the way Cara laughed.

"What other flowers did I get?" I was trying to change the subject.

"Five calla lilies, six red tulips, seven stems of peach blossom, and eight red roses," Cara said with a wicked smile. I pulled out my phone and opened to the saved tab—calla lilies for magnificent beauty, red tulips as a declaration of love, peach blossoms to say he was captive to me, and I didn't need to use a website to know the meaning of red roses. Erik had come swinging hard. I wasn't there yet, but if he kept this up, I might see myself getting there. I heard a distinctive click and looked at Cara. She had just taken a picture of me.

"You're just begging to get cursed," I said, knowing how shallow a threat that was.

"You're besotted, smitten, head over heels. Own it, bitch," she replied.

"Speaking of owning things, you mentioned your sisters. Why didn't you ever own up to having a brother?" I asked. Cara averted her eyes.

"Síomón's a half brother. Same mother, different fathers. As I said, he's an ankou."

"And those are…?" I asked.

"Another clan of death fae. They protect graves and cemeteries. Ankou and banshees—we're two sides of the same coin. Me and my sisters warn of coming death, Síomón makes sure the dead can rest in peace. That's why he's here. He's felt the presence of the unliving, as you call them, in the greater Cleveland area."

Gooseflesh ran up my back, and my fingers automatically dug for my phone to text Erik. "That's not good," I said firmly.

Cara's eyes locked with mine, and she saw where my hand was. "No," she said. "It really isn't." She exhaled. "Text your wolf—we'll need his help."

CHAPTER 18

THE THREAT of unlife made me remember my grandmother's story—the one she had told me about my father. One of their kind was bad enough, but according to Cara, if Síomón was here, it meant there might be a colony of them. Wherever they congregated, it was a sign bad things were sure to happen. According to my great-great-uncle, it had been a colony of unlife that was responsible for the 1934 flood in Poland that killed over fifty and was responsible for more than ten million dollars in damages in today's dollars. Another of my ancestors had found evidence of a colony in Jerusalem right after the 1837 earthquake. When I mentioned this to Cara, she said that, according to her family, it had been a colony of more than twenty that had started the Great Famine in Ireland. One of Cara's aunts, according to her, claimed to have seen a ghoul in New York in the 1980s, during the height of the AIDS crisis. I texted a warning to Erik and told him to meet us at Siren's the next morning.

If there was a chance that the undead had come to Cleveland, we'd need all the help we could get. Erik said he would be at Siren's at around seven.

I sent a quick text to Erik as I left for the bakery at my usual hour, but I took the grimoire out of my home. As I entered Siren's Sweets, I saw Cara seated in the main kitchen, studying the tile floor.

"What're you thinking?" I asked as I put the book down in front of her.

"If Síomón's senses are telling him something is up, we listen to him. The last time he had a sense like this was Hurricane Maria. That was only four of the unliving. Síomón thinks there are at least ten, maybe more," Cara warned.

"That's not good." I opened the grimoire, closed my eyes, and let the magic of the book guide me to where I needed to go. I skimmed over the pages and stopped at a line of Aramaic. It was an offensive working, crude but powerful, one that could be used to fight off the unliving.

"Any word from the werewolf yet?" Cara asked.

"I haven't heard from him since yesterday, but his second is on her way," I answered. Cara nodded.

"Brigid and Siobhán are incoming. They'll be here as soon as they can. That's a witch, three banshees, one ankou, and a werewolf. Do you think any more of Erik's pack will be willing to help us?" she asked.

"Besides Alicia, I honestly don't know," I said.

"What about your kid—" She stopped herself and I smirked. T would be willing to fight, but he wasn't my kid in any sense of the word. And he hadn't finished high school yet.

"I don't want to endanger him, not if we have other options," I said. I hoped Erik would agree with me. Then I pulled my phone from my pocket only to see that he hadn't texted me back. He had confirmed that he would be here and said there was going to be one more Valentine's Day surprise, but I hadn't heard from him since and I hadn't gotten the surprise either. Neither augured well. As Cara and I went through our notes and the hour got closer, I became ever more nervous. When seven came and I hadn't heard from him, I allowed that nervousness to morph, to blossom into full-blown worry. I had been anxious about Cara and Erik meeting, and this situation wasn't improving my nerves. Even if Erik would be angry at me for not telling him I worked with a banshee, I wanted to hear something from him.

Cara could sense the worry, the fear climbing in me, moving through me, and beginning to spiral. She put her hand on mine and I felt it then, the flow of her concern, of her own fear, but more than that, her power. Unlike wolf power, it was cool—a still, deep thing. Whereas wolf power was a star, bright and burning, her power was the darkness of the night sky or of a closed place. She squeezed my hand, and I allowed myself the smallest taste of that cool, composed power. It flooded into me, causing my eyes to roll back into my head.

"Don't waste it all in one place," she said and I nodded. She had known exactly what she was doing, and she had still offered it to me. We went back to work—I flipping through the pages of the grimoire, finding what workings I could that might be helpful, she texting lightning fast, sometimes entering a light trance, as if she were communing directly with her siblings.

It was eight, and there was still no word from Erik. While I tried not to be clingy, my fear was a palpable solid thing. I reached into a small bit of Cara's calm, of her banshee stillness, and it soothed me. I felt no urge to scream. Whatever was going on with him, his life wasn't in danger. That was some small consolation.

I texted Alicia to ask if she had seen Erik. She said that he had texted the night before. She also messaged to say that she was worried that he wasn't with me because, apparently, he had been planning on surprising me on Valentine's night by coming over.

My stomach churned, and I paced as I sent yet another message to him hoping, praying that I'd see any sign of… my Erik. Nothing, not even an acknowledgment he had read the text. I told Alicia to come over as soon as possible, and she agreed to be there when she could.

Síomón stormed in shortly thereafter. "Where da fuck is the wolf?" he asked. Apparently Ankous also growled.

"I don't know," I answered honestly.

"Bloody useful you are, witch," he spat at me. Cara moved then and stormed across to her brother. They were soon arguing in the rapid-fire lilting language I presumed was Irish. I didn't try to get in the middle of their fight. It would continue, even if I tried to stop it. Whatever they yelled at each other, I had no desire to translate.

They continued as the back door opened and two women, built on the same model as Cara and Síomón, entered. They acknowledged me with polite smiles and nods but went immediately into the fray. I moved against the wall as the two sisters—I didn't know which was Brigid and which Siobhán—seamlessly added their voices to the melee. The fight was a fluid thing, alliances shifting. Sometimes, all three sisters ganged up on Síomón, and occasionally one or two of the sisters would join him. At one point, Cara shifted to stand next to her brother and went toe-to-toe against her sisters.

There I went again, being an unprepared witch. Wherever my babcia might be, I knew she was ashamed. I only nodded briefly to Alicia as she entered, using the back door. She looked from the siblings, who hadn't stopped their verbal sparring match, to me, and then back to the siblings. One of her eyebrows rose even as she wrinkled her nose slightly. I raised my hand and indicated the chair next to mine. She took it and directed a questioning glance in my direction. "Did I come to a taping of *Springer*?" she asked. "I thought he had retired."

"Family is complicated," I responded.

"They don't look like they're related to you," she offered simply.

"They aren't," I said. I pointed to Cara, who, for the moment, stood flanked by her two sisters. Of the three, Cara was the shortest, but also the thinnest. All of them had different shades of red hair. The sister to Cara's right had dark mahogany locks, brown eyes, and a narrow face countered by a fuller figure. She wore a Celtic cross on a golden chain. Cara's other sister, the tallest of the three, had milk-pale skin, freckles, hair that would have shamed Little Orphan Annie for color, and diamonds flashing in her ears as she moved suddenly from Cara's side to Síomón's. "The one who was in the center is my business partner."

"This feels off," she said simply.

"I'll explain in a bit," I offered.

"Do you have any idea what they're saying?" Alicia leaned against the wall next to me. It was a train wreck. Neither of us were able to avert our eyes, even if we had wanted to—and I didn't know if either of us truly wanted to. It reminded me of the sort of daytime trash television I was able to watch only when I had been sick as a child and both of my parents had to be away from home.

"Not a clue, but I can tell you this much, you're going to want to cover your ears," I warned.

"Why?"

"It's about to get high-pitched in here," I said as both of Cara's sisters flanked Síomón. One of the sisters opened her mouth and a "whisper" sounded. It was heart-rending—a torrent of aural pain that ripped straight through skin and muscle to nestle in the bone. Alicia didn't have time to react. The "whisper" was over in less than a quarter of a second.

"Fae," I explained. "More specifically, banshees and an ankou."

"Madre de Dios," she said under her breath. I could feel her nails growing longer and thicker, becoming the sort of things that could rend and rip. I shot her a look, and she stopped her transformation.

"The fuck is an ankou?" Alicia asked.

With one hand I made a gesture to Síomón. "He is. And if they ever stop fighting, he might explain why he's here," I offered.

"I have a feeling that might be a while."

"I haven't heard from Erik since yesterday. Have you?"

"I thought he'd already be here. He said he was going to head to your place last night, that he was bringing you a bouquet of asters and roses, and that he was hoping to spend the night." Alicia's brow was wrinkled. I smelled her fear then, pungent and sharp, and I reached out and squeezed her hand. The back door swung open again and Terence walked in to see the battle in progress. He sandwiched me between Alicia and himself. Two werewolves were trying to protect me from a group of bickering death fae. I couldn't even be mad that he had skipped school to be here. Seeing Síomón, an odd expression came over T's face. The teen was transfixed as the ankou moved, making a gesture that took in his sisters, us, the kitchen, and maybe the entire city of Cleveland. His cheeks were red in anger and whatever he was saying, he said very loudly.

The fight showed no traces of slowing down, and I honestly had no patience anymore.

"Enough," I said as firmly as I could. Three sets of eyes shot murder at me. Even Cara seemed cross that I had interrupted her family squabble. I didn't want to think about the dynamics at play for the moment. There were more important things than whatever family melodrama was at stake. Reluctantly, Cara moved to my side.

"Jakob," she introduced, "this is Siobhán"—she indicated her freckled sister, who gave a polite nod of her head, but didn't attempt to smile—"and Brigid." Cara motioned to the fuller-figured woman, who not only curtsied, but smiled as if she hadn't been in a screaming match with her family members for heaven only knew how many minutes.

"A pleasure to meet you," Brigid said. Her accent was lighter than Síomón's but still far more present than Cara's.

"Likewise," I responded. "Those are Alicia and Terence, respectively." I made a motion to the two werewolves, both now standing and looking at us with some degree of tension. I could feel Alicia's desire to shift crawling under her skin, and I smelled Terence's anticipation. It was potent, like his sweat. I wondered when he had last showered or if this was just part of being a teenage boy that I didn't remember.

"It's not bad enough that ye have a witch working here," Síomón yelled, "he had to be a werewolf's bitch."

Both Alicia and Terence growled. I didn't need to look over my shoulder to know that their eyes were bleeding black and they were ready to shed their human skins and shred Síomón. All the siblings, even Cara, moved to form a group, the three sisters opening their mouths again. I put one hand on the silver chain around my neck and the other in my pocket. I found the salt easily and pulled it out. In my palm, it was a brilliant star.

I directed my will downward and across the space of Siren's. I worked quickly. With no fae borders in place, I was able to shape walls faster than anyone else. While fae power was strong, I noticed that Cara needed time to shape her intentions in ways I did not.

"This is not the time to start infighting with each other," I announced, and for the first time I could remember in a very long time, there was authority in my voice. I could feel the transformation beginning to edge away from the two wolves at my back, and I continued to move forward. My skin, iridescent and luminous, crackled and popped with emerald light, and I felt my eyes glowing. I was thankful we were in the kitchen. This would be close to impossible to explain to anyone walking by on the street. I waited to see if anyone would do anything. Instead, every person in the bakery seemed to be staring at me. Generally speaking, I hated being the center of attention—I did everything I could to avoid it—but I was here, and there was no way of backing out now.

"Let's get everything onto the table," I said with a firm tone of voice. "While names have been exchanged, I'm going to make one thing very clear—"

"And what gives ye the authority to speak?" Síomón interjected. I shot him a look. His jaw slammed shut, he raised both of his hands, and he stepped back slightly. It was something I hadn't expected, but I would take whatever victories I could. My bones told me I wasn't going to have many wins.

"I have the authority to speak because this place is half mine. I've helped build it. More than that, I'm the only one here who can keep a complete and total brawl from unfolding. If you want to avoid that, then I would suggest that you—all of you—" I made an expansive gesture with my hand. "—keep your mouths shut until I get everything out that needs to be said."

"I always knew you had it in you, Kuratowski. Nicely done," Cara praised. I looked at her. She closed her lips and mimed turning a lock and throwing away the key. I nodded my thanks quickly and turned my focus from her. Then I inhaled and took a second to gather myself. As with most occasions in life, I knew how I said the next words would be as important as what I had to say. I released the breath I held and offered a silent prayer for comprehension if not eloquence. Perhaps it was a selfish prayer, but I was not in any place to offer psalms of praise.

"We're all not human," I stated simply. "I'm a witch. They're fae of different stripes," I said, making a gesture to Cara's siblings. "And you two are werewolves," I continued, indicating Alicia and Terence.

"While I'm the most human here…." I said. Although I was growing more comfortable with the idea of being linked to a nonhuman group, it was not yet part of my normal day. It was still something I was learning how to live with. I saw Síomón tighten his face, looking like a redheaded Alan Rickman in one of the *Harry Potter* movies. I dismissed the comparison so we could continue. "We represent three of the four major nonhuman groups. We're here because Síomón—" I paused and nodded to him. "—has sensed the presence of the fourth. They have many names. My grandmother knew them as dybbuks. Some others have called them the shadowed, and others refer to them as living damned. The term I use is unlife. Are we all good on the terminology?"

I could see Alicia growing pale, a look of horror on her face. She knew what I was speaking about, and it was clear that she was far from happy with the development. Terence looked puzzled I had to address the ghoul-shaped specter looming in the room. The fae siblings all nodded. Even Síomón was willing to accept what I had said.

"Síomón is an ankou—"

"Ye could try and pronounce it correctly," he interjected.

"Look, we are in the middle of a potential disaster here. There are more important things than pronunciation," I all but yelled. I knew he didn't like me, and I was all right with that. He didn't have to like me— or even tolerate me. I could worry about Cara's brother liking me if we survived this. For what it was worth, he looked chastened.

"Ankou are able to sense the unliving. You can do that, right?" I hoped I had understood what ankou did.

Síomón nodded. "I can. I don't see why ye brought mutts, though. Couldn't ye have found another witch?" he asked.

"They're here because they're my friends," I said. Of all the ways I could have explained Terence and Alicia, it was one of the truest. "And because we have infestation. It won't be witches, or the fae, or shifters who are going to have to deal with the unliving. The entire city might go under, and all of us need to put our egos aside to deal with the problem."

"I'm on the same page as the witch," Brigid said, moving to a middle ground between her siblings and the werewolves. "If there are more than three of *them* here, then there's going to be a big problem. I don't feel like screaming nonstop for the next three years, and I think Síobhán and Cara both agree with me on that."

Her sisters just nodded, and Síomón rolled his eyes but seemed at least willing to accept that his siblings were able to put fae pride aside. "As the Yank—"

"Oh, stop talking like you're fresh off the boat, Síomón," Síobhán interjected. "You were only three when we moved over, and you're only doing that shtick so people don't recognize you for the Southie piece of garbage you are."

"I ain't Southie!" Síomón countered and then brought both of his hands up to cover his mouth. The Irish accent he had apparently been affecting was dropped for the distinctive tones of New England—more specifically Boston. Anyone hearing it would never be able to say anything otherwise. There was a flush on his cheeks, and Síobhán looked entirely too smug. All of his sisters did, and I wondered just how long he had gone about trying to pretend his ties to his home country were stronger than they actually were. If it had been any other circumstance, I might have allowed myself to be amused. However, this was neither the time nor place.

"As the witch—" Síomón began again.

"Jakob, or Kuratowski, if you must. He's more than just a witch," Cara shot in this time. There was a silent war between brother and sister. Cara rested her hand on me, and some of her warmth, her strength flowed into me. For the second time that day, I was filled with cool fae magic and I relaxed slightly.

"Fine, as *Kuratowski*," Síomón spat, snarling my surname like it was the worst profanity he could think of, "was explaining, I'm an ankou. We're tied to places of the dead, and we can feel when something is disturbing them, violating them. About three weeks ago, I first felt a small stirring, but with the raw numbers of grave desecrations that happen per year, I thought it was just that. But the gnawing feeling has been growing. It was just before Valentine's Day when I knew for certain. Revenants are here. At least ten, probably upwards of a dozen."

"What does —" Terence said. He didn't have a chance to continue as I fell to my knees. Blinding, obsidian-sharp pain sparked from the place where Erik had bitten me and fired along each of my bones, through all of my veins. I screamed, and while it was a pale imitation of a banshee's full-throated cry, my throat was raw in less than a second from the force of the scream. I don't know how long I cried, but it felt endless.

"The hell?" Siobhán asked.

"I didn't feed him that much power," Cara thought aloud.

"The unliving," I panted. "They're trying to eat Erik."

CHAPTER 19

"WELL, WE'RE royally fucked, and not in the good sense," Brigid swore.

"You don't need to say that twice," Alicia said. Síomón was looking at me with something other than anger or hatred on his face. For a second, I didn't recognize him. Without his trademark scowl, someone might have thought him handsome—but only for a few fractions of a second. Síomón's scowl returned with a vengeance in a matter of moments.

"We don't have much time," Síomón said. "I haven't had a chance to pull up every mausoleum, cemetery, and columbarium in the greater metro area, and in a city this size, there are going to be a few. As this city doesn't have a necropolis, they could be almost anywhere," Síomón said, more under his breath than to the room at large. Still, I heard him. Pain was no longer mastering me, no longer running wildly and harshly through me. I looked up and saw the fear, the anger, the pain on Terence's face. He wore his emotions much more visibly than Alicia. He was a seventeen-year-old kid, and his alpha, his first serious crush, was in danger. For what was about to happen, I had only sympathy.

Whatever mercy might be in the universe, we would all need it, but perhaps Terence most of all, I thought to myself. This was going to be hell. No one walked into Gehenna unscathed, and I just hoped the boy made it through the night with his body and soul intact. I looked to Alicia, who looked back at me.

"We're with you, Jakob," Alicia said. "You're more than a friend, you're pack, and pack protects its own. Is this what Terence had to give his word about?" she asked.

"Terence came in here when he had an issue with his wolf," Cara said, while my head was still spinning. "Jakob helped, and Terence didn't react well to being in the presence of a banshee. I had to scream a little."

Alicia growled but didn't do anything else. It was clear she was less than comfortable being in the same space as so much fae power, but we could work through all of this another time. Right now, we had other things to worry about. Cara was going to give in to a full banshee wail sometime soon, and that wasn't the sort of thing that any sane person was supposed to hear. The two werewolves looked at each other. "Who else can we call?" Terence asked.

"We're it, T," Alicia said. "I think this is going to be the group. If Jakob is feeling the fucking undead devouring our alpha, we're going to have to act quickly. Shit's about to go down in a big way, and you've heard a scream...."

"She claimed it was a whisper," Terence interrupted, and both of Alicia's eyebrows shot up.

"You don't have to stay—you can contact the pack, tell them to spread out and start hunting—but I have a feeling it's going to come down to us," Alicia warned. "You don't have to be around for this if you don't want to, T."

Terence, trying to be a man, standing taller and straighter, locked his gaze with Alicia's. My ears rang as the fae siblings debated locations. Síomón said something about using me to trace where Erik was, but I was more focused on what was happening between Terence and Alicia. He inhaled, held his breath for one second, then two. He let it out slowly. "I've already heard a banshee scream, Alicia. I can take this. Jakob's going to need all the help he can get if we're going to save our alpha."

I sighed. "You don't know what you're signing up for, T, but if this is what you really want, then I won't stand in your way." A part of me felt like I had just signed his death warrant, but there was precious little I could do. Death was abroad tonight. It loomed around us, darker than onyx, darker than night. Death was abroad, and I wondered just which of the banshee sisters would be the first to let out their signature cry.

A hand rested on my shoulder and I turned from the wolves. Brigid's smile was soft but didn't reach her dark emerald eyes. I tried to smile back, but my lips refused to move. Like her siblings, and despite her build, she moved with the same ethereal grace all fae seemed to carry themselves with. Someone—I hadn't seen who—had produced a map of the city. I looked down at it, then up to the fae siblings. "You have a connection to the werewolf," Síomón said bluntly, any pretense at being anything other than a Bostonian gone. "I'll loan you some of my senses, for a short time. You'll feel like shit afterward, but it's the fastest way of finding him. We have to stop this before it turns into a full-on shitstorm."

My hand went to the clasp of the silver chain around my neck. I undid it quickly and held it over the map. My mezuzah swung, making an uneven elliptic at first, but becoming a true circle within three rotations. "Alicia, I'm going to need your help also. You've known him longer than I have, and while I might be connected to him, his ties to you are older, and that's something that matters in magic," I said.

She approached and laid a hand on me. Síomón moved beside her, and while he wasn't thrilled to be standing next to a shifter, he placed his hand less than an inch from hers. I felt the heat of Alicia and the cool stillness of Síomón. They blended in me, and the sensation was far from pleasant. Uttering a short prayer, I closed my eyes and began to actively channel their combined power.

First came the pull of moon, of forest, of hunt, of the joy of running in silver shafts of night, of chase, of shedding human skin to walk on four legs. I knew Alicia's energy in an instant. Then came something different. Like Cara, Síomón's power was old. It was harder to grasp at first, dancing at the edges of my awareness, a fragment flickering just beyond my reach. I didn't chase it; I had to let it come to me. When Síomón's power deigned to touch me, I shuddered. I knew why he scowled now. It was the chill of the grave, the quiet of an abandoned churchyard, the silence hanging between memorials. His was hard clay, a potter's field, the inferno, a temperature hot enough to reduce a body to ash. His was the finality of a coffin lid shutting.

Moonlight and darkness met and mingled. I didn't have much time to shape them, direct them through me. My fingers twitched as power ran down my chain and into the charm hanging above the map—a crude pendulum. I didn't see where it flicked; I was more focused on channeling the currents of magic. The less I saw, the more I could trust to magic. Fae, werewolf, and witch's power bounded through me. I focused on Erik's face, on his cocksure grin, on his surety, and on his warmth. On his need to protect his pack. I focused on my memories of him—of the way his palm, strong and smooth, had felt holding mine, on the heat of his breath dancing along my neck. I focused on what it had been to have him on me and inside me. I remembered how he had pulled me close and deep into him, on his tightness as I had claimed him the way he had me. I admitted what he was then silently, and power surged.

The charm came to a sudden halt and held still above the map. I opened my eyes. Despite my many years in Cleveland, it was in a neighborhood that I didn't recognize. Síomón studied it and his fingers broke contact with my neck. I shuddered, feeling fae power empty from me. It was not a shudder of loss, but rather relief. To walk with the dead as he did… no wonder he didn't feel like smiling and was prone to anger. At least Cara and her sisters had brief moments of rest. They were not always screaming. For Síomón, a banshee's wail would be ever in him, always echoing, never relenting. He and Death would walk hand in hand, and he knew with certainty where he would die. I hadn't been able to see it, but I knew it. Knowing the exact time and place of your death—that wouldn't be easy for anyone.

"Lake View Cemetery," Síomón said, his voice confident. His eyes were closed. "A family mausoleum."

"There are several there—which one?" Cara asked.

"At least a hundred years of dead. It would be the largest one in the cemetery," Síomón said.

"The Chisholm's?" Cara asked. Síomón listened to something in the stillness of the room before he nodded.

"We know where to go, then." Cara turned to me. "Grab the wolves and as much as you all can carry from the kitchen. We're going to War." I heard the capital letter, and I moved quickly. I slid the mezuzah back around my neck and grabbed one of the larger knives. Bakers might not be butchers, but we could get the big knives if we needed them.

When I was a child, my maternal grandfather had told me what it was to go through Terezín. He had been freed by the Soviet Army and had left what would become the Czech Republic shortly thereafter. Even though he had been a boy at the time, his memories of World War II were incredibly vivid. For him, war hadn't ever been romantic. He had spoken to all his grandchildren about the realities of war, its horrors and its devastation. There were things he hadn't told us, didn't want us to know, but they were things that haunted him. His stories had made me want to avoid any sort of war if at all possible.

Now I had no choice but to go to War to save my Erik.

Alicia looked at the knife as I went through the spices we had at our disposal. It was one of the few times I was sad I hadn't gone into another field of cooking. Most of the time, I was very happy in the world of pastry, but right then, I would have killed for amaranth, barley, garlic, dill, or basil. Not that we didn't have heavy hitters. I reached for rosemary and then headed to the fridge to grab some fresh blackberries. "What's the knife for, brujo?" Alicia asked as I hunted for a human-shaped ginger root. We didn't have one. I bit the inside of my lip to keep a curse from flying free.

"I don't intend to stab any of the unliving, if that's what you were thinking—at least, not physically," I said. I had moved over to the cutlery by then, knowing we had a sterling silver spoon somewhere. The more silver, the better.

"They're not literally eating him, are they?" Terence asked. I looked up as I pulled out the spoon. My grandmother would be proud. I was a prepared witch at last.

"Not yet at least," I tried to reassure Terence. "Unlife has a single desire—they're driven only by their hunger. They're corrupt. They're trying to take Erik's power, his life force. Once they drain that, he'll be of no more use to them." I didn't want to think about what they would do once they finished.

"Unlife—" The teenage werewolf said, taking a moment to weigh the word on his tongue. "What will happen if they get Erik's power?"

I sighed and looked to Alicia. She looked at me, and I hated what I was about to say. However, I knew I had to say it. This was what pack witch did. Granted, it wouldn't be my only duty, but right then, it was what I needed to do. I looked back to Terence, saw his growing discomfort. I would give the boy credit. His instincts were strong.

"Wherever unlife goes, misery follows," I said. "The more power they have, the bigger the trouble. They're tied to plagues, famine, and death."

"If we don't take care of this now, we may as well head to Detroit," Alicia said. T shuddered, and I couldn't stop myself from laughing, just a little. I was still hunting in the kitchen when I found something I hadn't expected. There was a cast-iron skillet buried deep in one of the cabinets. I didn't question why she would have one. I would take anything I could. As I dug it out, I had no doubt that it was the genuine article. I had no illusions of looking like the hero of Disney's *Tangled*, but the piece of cast iron in my hands did make me feel rather badass. I passed the skillet to Alicia, who looked puzzled but accepted it.

"You do know I'm going to go all claw and fang with any of those bastards we find, right?" she asked.

"It's not a weapon for you. It's one for me," I said as we moved to the small space at the back of the kitchen near the back door.

"You're going to brain the undead with a skillet?" she asked.

"It's cast iron," Siobhán explained. "In his hands, if he's as powerful as Cara says, it'll be better than a gun."

Alicia looked at me, then down to the skillet again. There was a sort of respect on her features I hadn't expected. Cara saw the chef's knife in my hand.

"If you lose that, you're buying me a replacement," Cara said.

"Fair enough—if we survive this. Who's driving?"

"You're not. I'm shocked your sedan is still on the road. The state should impound it," Alicia chimed in.

"I know. Did your alpha tell you that he had to come rescue this one during the first snow of the season, back in October?" Cara teased.

"Yes. Said the witch kicked him out of the house like a puppy. I would have paid good money to see it."

"Me too, " Cara said. This was my worst fear come to life—Cara and Alicia were seemingly getting along. If I survived, I would never be able to live down the constant teasing. I cleared my throat and tried to resume an aura of authority.

"If you two can please stop talking about Prudence…." I trailed off, a blush rising to my face.

"You named your car Prudence?" Síomón asked. Despite his nature as an ankou, despite the fact we were about to drive out and deal with one of the most serious threats I could imagine, despite everything, he was smiling. I was tempted to curse then, but I didn't want it looming over our heads as we drove out to Lake View Cemetery.

"Seriously, why Prudence?" Terence asked.

"Now is so not the time to talk about what I named my car. She—it—doesn't have the space anyway."

"Well, neither of us came in a minivan," Siobhán offered. Brigid just nodded.

"All right, then, two carloads," I said. It was the first thing I had said that no one argued with. I wasn't sure if I should be panicked or relieved, so I went with relieved. Panic would arrive soon enough.

"I'll be one of the drivers," Alicia volunteered. "I can take five comfortably, maybe all of us if we put one of the seats in the back of my SUV."

"That won't work for me, sadly," Brigid chimed in. "I'd get motion sick." This was surreal. We were facing down the possibility of unlife draining an alpha werewolf of his power, and we were discussing travel arrangements as if we were driving down to an Ohio State game rather than fighting for the future of the city. Eventually, we were able to settle that Terence, Síomón, and I would travel with Alicia. The banshees would take their own car. As much as Síomón might have disliked me in general and werewolves on le, we needed to be in the same vehicle, as our combined senses might be able to root out any unlife not already in the mausoleum.

It was a practical solution for a worst-case scenario.

CHAPTER 20

ALICIA APPARENTLY needed no GPS guidance as we tore through an unusually still February morning. She drove over the speed limit, but not fast enough or recklessly enough to attract the attention of Cleveland's finest. That would have been just another layer of icing on the cake. I groaned internally at the fact I had just made a bad pun. The car was silent, no one speaking.

Around the halfway point of the drive, another burst of pain shot through me. As it radiated black and twisting from the site of Erik's mark on my body, I gave a pathetic imitation of a banshee's wail. I had hoped all of the power had burned out by now, but I was wrong. Even as my hands fisted on my thighs and my eyes rolled back, Alicia kept her eyes on the road ahead, but put her foot down more firmly and picked up speed. Tears streamed down my cheeks as I rocked, trying to drive the pain out of my body. It was building, growing, the only thing I could focus on.

To my shock, Síomón touched my shoulder. The pain ebbed, and I could breathe. With each breath, the pain became as distant as the memory of a dream upon waking. Síomón's usual scowl was missing.

"It's an ankou trait, one to help our sisters," he said.

"Easing of pain?" I asked.

"When a banshee screams, she feels the pain, the horror, the agony of death. Granted, not all deaths are painful, but it is the pain of the family, of those left behind. It's a kindness, a sympathy, that developed with us. No one should have to feel what my sisters do—and as an ankou, I can get flickers of it. There's only stillness, and darkness," Síomón said.

"That's all kinds of messed up, dude," Terence offered. Síomón turned to him, and I was ready to break up the coming brawl, even with the ache still fresh and most of the pain still sitting heavily in my blood. But his face showed only resignation, fatigue, which was somehow worse.

"If you think that's bad, you should try living with my nightmares," Síomón said simply. Alicia, Terence, and I all shivered. The ankou clearly needed a holiday, but because of what he was, because of his nature, his only relaxation would come after he died. In the moment of power that he shared with me, I had learned something—even death wouldn't offer any relief to the ankou; his would be an endless watch, as the ankou who followed would draw upon his strength, even in his grave.

Alicia barely paused at any of the stop signs and I didn't blame her. Panic was contagious, and I was near that point. Out of all of us, Síomón was the calmest person in the car. I opened the grimoire, thumbed through it, and found one formula. But when the time came, I would be casting with my instincts. I hoped they wouldn't abandon me and leave me for dead.

We stopped on a residential street, and the car with the sisters stopped a moment later. All of us stood without speaking for the longest time. We all knew that this might be the last thing any of us did.

We must have looked quite the ragtag bunch—three sisters with flaming red hair, all wearing thick jackets; Síomón in his peacoat and, of all things, ear muffs (though with his sisters, it made some sense); a teenager with mild acne scaring, dressed in a lightweight windbreaker and blue jeans; Alicia, who looked like she could have come out of a North Face catalog; and myself, wearing my old jacket, holding the cast-iron skillet in one hand and the knife in the other. If I was a betting man, I would have put money on the unliving.

Síomón led the way, turning into a small cul-de-sac. Right beyond it was the fence of the graveyard. Síomón held up his hand and silently commanded us to stop. We circled around him, and he scanned all our faces, his mouth was a hard line, his eyes were narrowed. "This," he said, keeping his voice low, "isn't going to be pretty. Brigid, Siobhán, Cara— if you want to run, now's the time."

"You're crazy if you think any of us are going to run, Síomón," Siobhán said. Brigid and Cara nodded. I had seen Cara totally focused before, but those moments paled in comparison to the look on her face now. She was every inch a warrior. She was ready, she was certain, and I wished, not for the first time, that I had half her confidence.

"All right, then, let's talk tactics," Síomón said. "Kuratowski, I want you in the back. You're strong, but we're going to need you working to keep us on our feet and to handle any revenants I'm unable to catch.

Cara, Siobhán, Brigid, you're on point. Keep your mouths away from the werewolves. If you need to scream, aim it directly at any fucking unlife we come across. We're going to need to hit them with everything we have. While they might not suffer as much as the living, they're not ankou—your cries will slow them down. Werewolves, I know this is your alpha, and that you're worried about him. However, please do what you can to keep Kuratowski safe. He and I are the best chances we have at dealing with anything. Anyone have any issues with all of this?"

"I'd suggest that I'm one of the points," Alicia said, holding up her hand. "Yes, I know that I might be in the line of fire for a banshee scream, but just in case these things aren't where we think they are, we're going to need my nose to find Erik."

Síomón thought about the suggestion for a long moment and then gave the briefest of nods. "All right, Cara, stay on Kuratowski. You know what you need to do?"

"I'll scream long, loud, and directly at one of those motherfuckers," Cara said. Síomón grinned as he nodded and turned. He held both of his hands in front of his face, and I felt the stirrings of power, rushing, racing, vying to reach him. A faint gust of wind ran over the pavement and stirred the loose snow. Then he turned up a path that hadn't been there a moment earlier, a gap between the homes that was as solid, as real as the road beneath us. Siobhán, Brigid, and Alicia led the way, and the rest of us followed less than a second later. As soon as we were all on the grass of the cemetery, there was a second gust of wind and the path was no longer there. Where we had entered was barred by a solid fence. I looked to Síomón, who just raised a shoulder as if he had done nothing special. For him this was likely a daily thing.

As we entered the cemetery, I had the distinct sensation of being in one of the better George A. Romero movies. We moved over the grass as silently as we could. Síomón paused now and then, and the three women leading the way didn't need to look back to know when to stop. Row after row of markers told their silent stories, and we proceeded as best we could between them, trying not to disturb the snow.

From the corner of my eye, I saw a darker shape weaving through the graves. I turned; so did the rest of the group. A raccoon stared back at us. I would have laughed if I hadn't felt cold rush down my spine, far too intense even for February in Ohio. Then I spun and saw my first unlife. The descriptions of my ancestors, the story my babcia had told me on her deathbed, did not do it justice. Impossibly tall, it had sunken features, skin that had no shade whatsoever, and fingers that were too long and bent toward the sky. Somehow I managed not to scream. Instead, with my hand on the cast iron, jade flame erupted. *"You're an ugly-ass motherfucker,"* I cursed. The iron sparked and hissed, and a hole erupted in the shambling thing's left shoulder, exposing yellowed bones and black ichor.

Síomón was next to me in a moment. He held out his hand. There was a shimmer in the air, and the unlife tilted its narrow face first one way, and then the other. Then its lower jaw flew to the side as something heavy and invisible collided with it. Ichor pooled as the creature fell and evaporated into the air. One down.

"So that's why you don't swear. I understand. You don't want to be ripping holes into every rude customer you come across," Cara said, her Yiddish crisp, clean, and perfectly understandable. I turned to face her, my jaw wide open.

"You can speak Yiddish?" I asked.

"Of course," she said with a shrug. She had the smuggest of all possible grins. How long had she been waiting to do this? I was about to ask another question when Siobhán shot a look over her shoulder. It was clear who had taught Cara that skill.

"Blow his mind later, Cara. We have more important things to do," Siobhán answered, her Yiddish as good as Cara's.

"What are you all saying to each other?" Terence asked.

"She"—I made a quick motion with my head toward Cara as we began to march again—"has been holding out on me. Apparently, she can speak Yiddish."

"Oh." Terence didn't say anything else. All of us were focused on the headstones around us, on the faint hints of wind moving over the gravestones, on the stirrings of snow and how light and shadow played with each other. We were all a little jumpy. This was a more recent addition to the cemetery. Here the stones still had shine. These were graves still visited. Wreaths and frosted flowers attested to the care, devotion, and love of living hands. The mausoleum we were going to might be a tourist attraction, but it wouldn't have this sort of cleanliness. It would be polished for visitors, but it would lack real affection.

We moved slowly as we stepped from the snow to the pavement. My grip on the skillet was white-knuckle tight. Síomón paused, and from behind me I heard a mouthless scream. I spun on my heel. Not having time to find words, I brought the skillet up in an arching motion. It connected with a torso covered in woven skins. There was a satisfying thrum that traveled down my arm, but it lashed out at me with a tail. I dropped the skillet as I danced out of its way. It kicked it to the side and hissed. Before it could bring its dripping fangs into my arm, Síomón stepped forward and an invisible wave of power ripped through it, forcing it to stagger back. This was followed by a deafening, heart-rending scream that caused it to fall back and slithered on its tail.

"You worthless shit stain!" I yelled, the Yiddish echoing among the stones, the blackberries in my hand glowing. Its twisted back split with green fire, and in less than a second it too was ash.

When we regrouped, we were all much more cautious. At one point Síomón fell to one knee and buried his fingers in the snow at the side of the plowed pavement. His eyes were closed. The skin on the back of my neck rose, prickling at the cold and in anticipation. Alicia and Terence let loose low, deep growls, and I spun to where they were looking. Cara and Siobhán moved quickly and fanned out ahead of the werewolves. I took the salt from my pocket and made a quick, crude circle around myself and Síomón, hoping my magic wouldn't affect his working too much. Invisible walls slammed into place at the same time that Cara and her sisters opened their mouths.

If the cry of one banshee is a soul-rending sort of experience, there are no words for a trio screaming in sync with each other. No poets, musicians, singers, painters, sculptors, or any other artists who have attempted to channel despair in its most primal state have been able to express what I heard then. It was as if a hook—old and made of wrought iron—had found its way to my heart and was trying to pull it from my chest—and that was with magical protections in place. I didn't even want to know what Alicia and Terence might be feeling. Call me selfish, but there were certain things in life that I was happier not knowing.

The cries of the banshees died down as two wolves—Alicia's dark gray and Terence's a smaller white—leapt forward. Only then did I see it. It was impossibly tall, skin the color of ash, with three arms (the usual two, and one sprouting from the center of its chest), and all of its palms were twisted skyward. Unlike the other revenant, this one only had a slash across its egg of a face. The slash opened, exposing rows of rotting, dripping teeth. A tubular snake of a tongue shot out and crashed into

Terence hard enough to send him sprawling back and slam him into a headstone. The creature's hand caught Alicia on her right haunch and flung her frame over rows of markers. I grabbed the silver charm around my neck and witch's fire erupted around Síomón and me—eldritch emerald a brilliant beacon in the gray stillness as I narrowed my eyes.

"Back the fuck off, you shit-for-dick piece of filth," I spat. A tendril of green flame erupted on the creature's central arm and it unleashed a deep hiss, its thrashing tongue aimed heavenward. Keeping one hand on my necklace, I clutched the salt tighter. I focused on it and connected to the circle surrounding Síomón and me. Lowering itself to its spiderlike limbs, it let loose a silent roar and charged directly at us. I noticed it had yet another set of arms sprouting from its back, ending in sharp talons. It was seriously angry.

A blur of ivory slammed into its side, and I heard a low, harsh growl. The thing shrieked as it slammed into grave markers, ashen skin ripping open, obsidian ichor dripping, coating the snow. Turning its large head, a forked tongue rocketed out and rushed toward Terence.

"Piece of shit fire," I yelled. Less than a second before it would have collided with Terence again, its tongue split from its body, fell to the ground, and evaporated instantly into the winter air. A silent howl of pain erupted from the creature as it turned its eyeless face toward me. It rocked back as another trio of banshee wails crashed into it full force, deepening the holes from its stumble over gravestones. Onyx liquid poured from gaping wounds, but the creature had only one thing on its mind—its hunger. It was being denied a meal, and it would take whatever and wherever it could. We were in its way, but between banshee screams, a wolf's jaws, and being hit by my curses, it wasn't looking too keen. Before it could let loose another of its mute screams, a gray shadow ran from between the gravestones and clamped razor-sharp fangs into its throat. Alicia was as determined as the unlife, and I would have placed my money on a pissed-off beta werewolf any day of the week.

With a sudden motion of her head, she ripped a large gash near the base of its throat. Raven ichor cascaded from the wound, and it fell to the ground. Like its companion before, it disintegrated instantly, body melting before our eyes in less than three seconds. Not a trace of its passage remained. Even the black blood on the wolves' muzzles vanished. Síomón stood then and nodded to me. I moved a toe and broke the circle, and jade fire vanished into the air around us.

"Remind me not to tell Máire about this one." Siobhán tilted her head in my direction. There was a wicked grin on her face.

"Why?" I asked.

"Máire works in Los Angeles. She'd abuse cursing powers to shorten her morning commute," Síomón said. Eyes closed, he shook his head from side to side.

"Lots of help you were," Alicia sniped at Síomón. She had resumed her human form and stood stark naked, not bothering to dress again.

"I had to keep focus to make sure it was visible. It had been tracking us ever since we took the first two down," Síomón offered with a shrug. Three down, and if Síomón was right, there were at least seven more to go.

"How many more are there?" Terence asked. He was in his human skin again and was as naked as Alicia. He had a hand on his ribs, clearly still sore from being slammed by the tongue of an unliving being. None of the fae seemed affected by the nudity. Considering what we were up against, I wasn't any too bothered myself. I could worry about modesty later, if I lived through this.

"Five," he said and I stared at him. He shrugged. "I estimated, and this is a best guess. It's not an exact thing, my ability to sense them. They're harder to pin down than I'd like to admit. We still have the heavy hitters ahead."

"This is so not the time to talk about baseball," said Brigid.

"If you can't talk about baseball at the beginning of a possible disaster, when can you talk about baseball?" Síomón asked.

"You," Alicia interjected, "are all crazy. If we make it through this, remind me to get you a beer."

"Only if you join me in a vodka shot," Brigid responded quickly.

"Make it tequila, and you have a deal," Alicia said. I didn't need to look at her to know she was smiling. The madness was spreading, apparently. None of my ancestors had ever described a state of battle frenzy, but this might have been close to it. Here we were, having dispatched two revenants, about to face at least five more, wandering in a snow-covered cemetery in the middle of winter in Ohio. Battle frenzy must be catching. If I couldn't slap them back into sanity—and I didn't relish the thought of trying that—then I might as well go on the journey with them.

We continued along the cement road that wound through the cemetery. There were a few smaller mausoleums, different names etched into the stone. None of them caught Síomón's attention, so I decided to follow his lead. This was his area of expertise. As we made our way, we listened to the wind move between markers, and I thought of the last time I had visited my grandmother's grave. I had left a pebble on her grave marker—white and flecked with bits of quartz. She had collected such stones when she was alive. I remembered tracing the Hebrew letters of her real name with my index finger and how the faint warmth rushed up my arm and around my heart. She had been with me then.

She was with me now as my finger, responding to nothing I could see, erupted suddenly in witch's fire. A shadow from a nearby tomb hissed, pulled itself away, and tried to run. Síomón's hand shot forward, and there was another shimmer in the air. Whatever it was, whatever it had been, erupted into a rain of black ichor, which evaporated before it hit the ground. "Half-formed," Síomón said. "Something that might have become unlife if we had let it." Terence and Alicia snarled at where the potential unlife had been, but we kept on moving.

Buried partially in a hillside, the Chisholm Mausoleum bled darkness. A shudder ran through me when I saw it, and I grabbed for the thyme and muttered a quick prayer. The leaves bled white flame for a fraction of a second before whatever guarded the door rushed forward, slammed against me, and sent me flat on my rear and about four feet back. I was winded, I was in pain, but most importantly, I was angry, and it was the right type of angry. I was on my feet before Cara or Alicia could reach me. Terence had white fur erupting from his body, his jaws getting longer and narrower as I marched past him. Siobhán and Brigid let loose ear-piercing wails before a tentacle of shadow shot out, wrapped around Siobhán's throat, and lifted her from the ground. Brigid managed to dodge a second tentacle, even as she turned her mouth to it.

I pulled the knife from where I had stashed it and held it for a moment as all became still. Now was the time—I knew it deep in my bones. I pierced my fingertip, blood and steel joined together, and the blade slashed through the air. No command, no words needed. There was a flash as the tentacle strangling Siobhán evaporated. I saw Síomón, his fingers spasming as he wrestled with invisible power, and looked past him, at the door blocking my way. It was darker than dark, and malice poured from it—a wave of it rolled out, trying to push us back. I held the knife straight out toward it and was forced back a quarter of a step, but it was me alone this time. I was its focus.

I closed my eyes as my power gathered behind me, in me, around me. I hadn't made a circle; I had no formal prayer. But I knew in my bones this would be the great working of my life. I could feel the tendrils of power from Alicia and Cara, from Síomón as he continued to battle something I couldn't see, even from Terence in his lupine form.

Síomón wanted to be in the mausoleum, so I would help him get there. Looking at the abyss where the gate should have been, with my grip tight on the knife, I made a swift motion across the back of my hand, and more of my blood spilled on the snow. "You will let me see my mate," I commanded, my voice low, deep, biblical Hebrew echoing in the night air. The wall of shadow before me quavered as I twisted the knife. Blood, metal, and will. I knew witch's fire was covering my skin, was on the knife, was in my eyes. My glasses melted away beneath the inferno. I repeated the command, and tongues of peridot flame leapt from my mouth into the air.

I repeated the command a third time, and there was a cry that Cara or her sisters might have claimed as one of their own as the darkness ripped and ichor spilled out, a burst dam of malevolent force. This was no place for subtlety and no time for finesse. I ran forward, not caring about the formation we had agreed on. I ran forward, and two wolves and an ankou rushed after me. I ran forward to Erik, who was sprawled on the ground, blood dripping from his side and shoulder. One of the unliving was perched over him, its mouth a vertical slit of an opening, showing two tongues. Two more were behind it. I slashed with the knife, and an arc of witch's fire rushed forward, burning their chests. They pulled back, and the one looming over Erik lowered its head. It bellowed and rushed toward me, but I thrust the knife at it, and a spear of fire erupted in the center of its chest as I yelled, "Stay off my mate, you damned worthless dickless motherfucker!" The Yiddish was crude, but it served its purpose as the thing erupted in fire.

I was oblivious to the fighting, the screaming, the battle around me as I fell against Erik, wreathing both of us in witch's fire. I kissed him, breathing my power into him. I whispered one word against Erik's mouth—"Mate." My surrender, my acknowledgment, and my final acceptance in a single word.

"Mate," he said back, faintly, gently, barely above a whisper. Outside the corona of green flame that was leaping, lighting, warding off any unlife who dared approach, none would have been able to hear him. That was fine by me. Erik Lindstrom was alive. He was mine, and I was his.

He was my mate.

EPILOGUE

THE INVITATION was unexpected and made what was going to be a difficult day more complicated than it should have been, but Erik had reassured me he would be with me through all of it. Thus, on one of the few pleasant April Saturdays Cleveland got, I adjusted my tie as I stepped into a redbrick church and made my way to a back pew. I sat there quietly, ignoring the swarms of people milling about and the conversations that bounced between Korean, English, a Chinese dialect I couldn't identify, and a handful of other languages. Cara wasn't here and thus wasn't able to translate. When I had told the bride I was bringing a plus-one, she likely assumed it was my business partner. I had clarified it was my boyfriend. Erik growled at my use of the word—half pleasure, half desire. The bride was surprised and there was a long moment of silence. She had said as long as we kept out of the way, and I made sure the cupcakes were set up, I was welcome to. I knew what she had been hoping. But even if I had still been interested in Nathan, I was too professional to steal some wedding thunder.

"I don't see why you couldn't have foisted this on Cara," Erik murmured in my ear as he sat next to me in a slate-gray suit that clung to him like sin on a holiday. I was grateful that I was already seated. I didn't need to be making a spectacle by sporting a raging erection at a client's wedding.

"It's what the bride asked for. There's one rule in my industry—"

"Is it like your babcia's one rule?" Erik teased, a broad grin on his face. He had been practicing. While he would never be mistaken for a native Polish speaker, his accent was getting at least passible— or so my uncle Noah had said when we had traveled to Pittsburgh for his birthday last month. Introducing a boyfriend to my family had been a nerve-wracking experience. But Erik had put up with my extended family better than I could have hoped, suffering through my numerous aunts and uncles poking and prodding him, including my aunt Charlotte, who had said that he could use a little more meat on his bones. He had given a low huff at that, and I had laughed. Then he had narrowed his eyes at me—a silent promise of a punishment later. It had been one I had deeply enjoyed.

"Something like that. The rule in the wedding industry is, never mess with what a bride wants on her big day. That's how fights start," I said. Erik nodded in agreement.

"Have you seen many?" he asked.

Before I could answer, Pachelbel's Canon boomed and echoed around us. Erik and I stood and turned. Bridesmaids and groomsmen walked toward the altar. I saw Nathan, a fake smile on his face, walking arm-in-arm with a pretty bridesmaid who wore a rosy pink dress, the cut of which was more modern than I would have expected. If he saw me, he gave no indication. As he walked past, Erik growled subsonically. Humans might have felt something, but they wouldn't have been able to hear anything. For me it was bell clear. Even with two full moons as the pack's witch, I was still adjusting to the heightened senses. I extended my hand to Erik's and squeezed it firmly, tightly, to let him know where I stood. He squeezed back, just as firmly, just as possessive.

Then Nicole stood at the door. She was a vision in white. The smile on her face was the opposite of her brother's. She was clearly excited for this day and for what it represented. She walked down the aisle with regal poise and grace. Her steps were carefully measured, and it was clear she was used to having the eyes of everyone in the room on her. She was everything a bride aspired to be.

When she made it to the altar, Erik's hand was still in mine. He leaned over to me and pressed his lips to my ear. "So, when do you think we'll make it to a *chuppah*?"

"Someday," I said.

"My stubborn mate still," Erik whispered. He squeezed my hand and I squeezed back as hard as I could. I wasn't shocked to hear he was thinking of a wedding day, and I was only a little surprised to hear his correct usage of Hebrew. Since rescuing him from unlife, there hadn't been a single Friday when he hadn't shared my *Shabbat* table. Paying like for like, I had come to as many pack events as my schedule allowed, even if Cara was giving me the stink eye for leaving work early. There was still some resistance to me in the pack, but we were making our way forward. He hadn't promised me an easy road, but he was there, standing with me, fighting with me, and that made it worth the while.

He had been pushing hard for us to cohabitate, to share everything, to live truly as mates ought to, in his opinion. I was reluctant to give up my space and wanted some more time dating him, getting to know him, before I would consent to a wedding. Although I would admit sometimes my mind wandered, and I wondered if there were ways to combine my Judaism and the rites of his pack. He was apparently ahead of me on that. I wasn't there yet, but I knew it wouldn't be as long as he feared it would. Soon, we would have a space to call ours.

From the altar, I felt Nathan's eyes search the crowd, scanning for me. I could feel Erik begin to tense up, and I turned my mouth to his ear. "Jag är din, du är min," I breathed to him. I could feel him relax.

Turning his mouth to my ear he breathed, "Jesteś mój, ja jestem twój." That was enough, and I squeezed my mate's hand. He squeezed right back.

THE END

Keep Reading for an Excerpt from
Shortbread and Shadows
by Amy Lane

HEART OF LIVING WOOD

"MORTY?" LACHLAN stage-whispered. "Are you sure you put him in the right place?"

Morty Chambers, Lachlan's second cousin, looked up from his computer at the registration desk of the Sacramento Convention Center and rolled his eyes. "You say that like we haven't done this dance for over a year and a half," Morty said dryly. "Yes—see? Here's the floor plan."

"But he's not here yet!" Lachlan was starting to get worried. Everybody else on the vendors' floor was already set up.

"Look, Lock—same as I always do, at your request. His booth is right next to you, where he will continue to ignore you because he isn't that excited about you, no matter what you think."

Lachlan let out a grunt. "No, no, that's not it."

"Face it, Lachlan. He's just not that into you or he would have said more than boo to a mouse over the last two years!"

Lachlan let out a *sigh* of frustration. Morty did have a point, but then, Morty wasn't on the receiving end of a big pair of gray eyes and a mouth full enough to promise all the delights of Sodom.

Or maybe shortbread, since that was the guy's specialty.

"No," Lachlan said, confidence in his voice that he was far from feeling. "I really don't think that's it." Lachlan didn't elicit that response from people, dammit. He… he was cute! He knew it! He was smart, he was funny—he'd worked hard at that! Taken improv classes, taken drama, done college standup. He'd been shy as a kid. Who wasn't? But people *liked* Lachlan. He could usually walk into a place and gauge which girl or guy, as in this case, would be his for the taking.

He'd *gotten* that vibe from Bartholomew Baker; dammit, he *knew* he had. But a year and a half of dedicated pursuit, and nada.

"Then what?" Morty demanded. "This kid—I've seen him. You talk to him, and he gets all cow-eyed and quiet. You think that means he *likes* you?"

"Well, yeah," Lachlan said. "He's shy." It had been a while, but Lachlan recognized the signs. Bartholomew Baker, who didn't even laugh at the pun that was his last name, was perhaps the quietest man Lachlan had ever met. But Lachlan, who actually worked on his funny stories with his sister at home, had seen Bartholomew cast sly glances and small smiles his way when Lachlan had been engaged with his own customers, and whenever they were both quiet, he'd seen, and appreciated, Bartholomew's wide-eyed silences as Lachlan tried to entertain him.

He'd also seen Bartholomew get into the conversation, grow somewhat animated, and then stop himself, as though hearing an unkind voice.

Those were the times he bolted for the bathroom, leaving Lachlan in charge of his bakery booth, as Lachlan was obviously not to be trusted with his words.

Whatever voice Bartholomew heard that made him do that weird bathroom thing, Lachlan would like to give it a good talking-to. For a while he'd been able to do his own thing, date around, sleep with the occasional offer, but rarely twice. Lately, though, there'd been nobody. Lately, he'd been dreaming about that kid—big gray eyes, sand-colored eyebrows arching expressively. At first glance Bartholomew appeared pale with just the slightest tan on his face and wrists, with perfect skin.

A little closer and Lachlan could make out freckles on his nose and a teeny brown mole in the corner of his mouth.

And his smile was crooked—almost physically so, because he bit his lower lip on the right side every time he let his lips quirk up too far.

Lachlan pulled his attention back to Morty with an *actual groan* of frustration. "Morty, I swear by all that's holy and unholy, Bartholomew Baker is crushing on me as bad as I'm crushing on him. He's just too shy to so much as have a conversation."

Morty scraped back his thinning hair from his shiny scalp and blinked at Lachlan through little teeny rodent eyes. Lachlan wasn't sure which branch of the family Morty was really from, but his mother had always told Lachlan to be nice to Cousin Morty because he was blood.

Lachlan had sometimes suspected she meant "He *gave* blood," but that was immaterial.

"Well, that's a laugh riot in a relationship," Morty muttered. "The actual hell, Lock! How are you supposed to have a good time with someone who looks panicked and bolts every time you say 'Good morning'!"

Breathe. In through the nose, out through the mouth. Meditation. And Morty might live to set Lachlan's schedule for yet another week.

"Haven't you ever looked out across a calm lake? It's beautiful at first. Everything's reflected in the surface—the sky, the mountains, the trees." *Like Bartholomew's eyes*, he mooned, but he wasn't going to say that to Morty. "But underneath that pretty surface, there are some *really* awesome things going on. Fish are fighting the good fight, downed airplanes, hidden treasures, and the pureness of water itself. Don't you want to dive right in?"

"To where some mutant fish just swam out of a skeleton to nibble on my toes? No!"

"Oh my God, you're missing the point!" No wonder the guy had two ex-wives.

"Yeah, probably," Morty admitted, rolling his eyes. "But that doesn't change the fact that the floor is open in fifteen minutes, and you need to finish setting up, and Mr. Wonderful still isn't here!"

Lachlan had to check the vendors' floor again to be sure, because Bartholomew was always at least half an hour early. He *had* to be. He had too much to do, including set up luscious draperies in teal green and turquoise blue with his logo in the center that he used as tablecloths, and a wooden rack that was somewhat substandard in workmanship but very clever in design in that it showcased row upon row of tidy loaves of different kinds of sweet bread without ever once allowing the soft little bricks to squash each other. He also had a rack—again, the workmanship was substandard, but the purpose was perfect—for row upon row of large wrapped cookies and blocks of shortbread, all with a sticker showcasing his business logo and a website and phone number for *Shortbread and Shadows* baked goods and catering.

And that alone would be a complex setup, but Bartholomew wasn't a one-man show.

He had a smaller rack that advertised soaps and essential oils that his friends made—*Jordan's Oils* and *Kate's Boudoir*—and another rack that sold bright pot holders and hanging kitchen towels made by another friend—*Pincushion Products*. And of course, he needed to bring in his back stock, because nobody could bake like Bartholomew, and it didn't matter how shy he was, those tiny loaves sold big.

In one of his rare moments of volubility, Bartholomew had professed that he'd thought of selling those giant jelly jars with the dry ingredients of a recipe mixed inside and the list of wet ingredients that needed to be added on the lid.

"Why don't you?" Lachlan had asked, enchanted. When he *did* speak, Bartholomew's gray eyes grew wide and luminous, and his cheeks got this excited little crescent of pink along the cheekbone.

And his voice was so much deeper than anyone expected, every single time he talked.

"Because I don't know if it will turn out the same," he confessed, his face going blotchy and scarlet. "When I bake, it feels like magic, right? And sometimes I throw in ingredients that I never would have thought of and call it my Magic Cookie or Magic Loaf for the day, and make that part of my recipe. I wouldn't really have a chance to… you know, touch my work, if I didn't see it through to the end."

"It's a calling," Lachlan replied, looking at his own shelves full of cunningly made little toys, plant racks, walking sticks, bookends, and wall plaques. "It's like, when you're doing your thing, that craft understands you. Your fingers, your hands, your heart—they all take you to the right place."

"Yeah," Bartholomew had said, and Lachlan realized they were gazing stupidly into each other's eyes. At that exact moment he'd thought, *Yes! Bartholomew is going to kiss me! Or ask me out! Or say "Marry me and let's adopt!"* and Bartholomew had leaned forward on his little stool and his eyes had fluttered, and Lachlan had leaned forward in return and….

Bartholomew zoomed up from his chair and bolted for the booth's exit in the back, calling, "'Scuse me, I've gotta pee!"

Lachlan had almost cried.

And he didn't feel so great right now, looking at the empty booth where Bartholomew was supposed to be.

Fretting, he started to put the finishing touches on his own booth, with his bold, plain logo in black and white. Since it was an alternative-universe fiction con of some sort, he made sure his wooden swords with the intricately carved handles as well as the magic wands with *their* intricately carved handles were all prominently on display. He also made sure his cashbox and Square were exactly where they were supposed to be, and his business cards—designed by his sister, so they looked better than his tablecloth—were easy to spot.

He saw the first few customers wander onto the floor and had a shock. What convention was this again? He pulled out his program and raised his eyebrows.

Para-Fantasma-Con.

Oh. So paranormal, science fiction, urban fantasy, and probably epic fantasy as well. That would explain what the cosplayers in *Lord of the Rings* regalia were doing side by side with the entire complement of *Voltron.*

And trailing behind them was practically all of Hogwarts.

Wow. Just… wow.

That was some eclectic fanbase. He summoned a grin, because he really did love seeing everybody all dressed up and in character, and then his eyes drifted to Bartholomew's booth and the grin fell away a little.

He should have been there by now.

All of a sudden there was a kerfuffle by the entrance, and Lachlan looked up in time to see Bartholomew and four other people Lachlan vaguely recognized, loaded with boxes and hauling ass through the beginning throngs.

"Bartholomew?" Lachlan asked, surprised.

"Sorry," Bartholomew muttered, dodging around half of Hogwarts. "So sorry." He smiled greenly at Lance from *Voltron,* his gaze so faraway he didn't even notice the guy was decked, hot, and appreciative of Bartholomew's gray-eyed beauty. "So sorry." He hustled to the booth and looked around with a little moan.

"Oh, guys. I… I'm seriously… I don't know where to…."

"Here," said the wide-shouldered, no-necked guy that Lachlan recognized as Josh Hernandez. "Kate'll stay here and help you set up, and we'll go get the rest of your stock, deal?"

Bartholomew nodded, eyes losing some of their glaze. "Yeah. Thanks, Josh. Guys. I don't even know…."

Alex Kennedy was a compact person with rusty hair and the scalpel-sharp gaze of an analyst. Any kind of analyst—Lachlan wasn't picky.

And today he looked like he got dressed in a hurricane.

"None of us could have anticipated…." Alex threw his hands in the air.

"God," Kate said. "Seriously. None of us." She was a voluptuous girl with brown-blond hair, green eyes, and the most adorably pointed chin Lachlan had ever seen.

But she wasn't looking adorable now—she was looking scared, as all of Bartholomew's friends shuddered at Alex's words, including Jordan Bryne, who even Lachlan had to admit was the most beautiful man he'd ever seen. Taller than the others, with striking cheekbones and shock-blond hair, he looked like Alexander Skarsgård's younger brother.

"One thing at a time," Jordan said. "We'll go back and get the rest of the stock. Barty, you and Kate start setting up. Kate, maybe make sure you use the smoky quartz, brown jasper, and amethyst weights to hold down the drape. You brought them, right?"

"*So* on it," Kate said, nodding. "And I've got the sage and lavender in the diffuser." She grimaced. "You, uh, wouldn't want to run a protection circle, would you?"

Jordan shook his head. "All I brought were the gold and orange for success. I didn't bring black, brown, or white. Sorry."

Kate shrugged. "No, no. We were all…." They shared a look and let out a breath.

"Okay. Let's get moving."

Jordan, Josh, and Alex took off, and Bartholomew and Kate started the sort of ritual dance they'd practiced often to set up. Bartholomew's friends didn't always stay for the whole event, but Lachlan had to admit they were great at setup and takedown.

Except in this case they both kept stopping and looking around, seeming to breathe a sigh of relief whenever things appeared perfectly normal.

"Can I help?" Lachlan asked after a moment when their shaky hands were making him twitchy.

"Sure," Kate said at the same time Bartholomew said, "That's kind, but we've got it."

Kate leveled a killing look at Bartholomew. "Isn't that how we all ended up in this mess in the first place?" she demanded.

Bartholomew looked at her unhappily and swallowed, then looked at Lachlan and smiled shyly. "I'm sorry," he said. "Thank you, Lachlan. That would be nice."

Lachlan had to refrain from holding his hand up to his heart, because it fluttered badly. "What do you need me to do?"

"If you could shake the tablecloth out and set up the racks," Kate said quickly. "I'll set the stones up in formation." She sighed. "I wish we had some damned thread."

"I can get you some yarn," Lachlan offered. "Here, let me set up the racks and I'll go ask Ellen. She does spinning and weaving demonstrations. I'm sure I can get the colors you need."

He took the tablecloth from the plastic bin Bartholomew kept for setup without needing to be shown. He'd watched Bartholomew countless times, Bartholomew so completely immersed in his task, sticking his tongue out of the corner of his mouth while muttering to himself, that Lachlan could have set the booth up in his sleep.

Which reminded him…. "You guys know, I've seen your booth setup a thousand times. I've never seen the stones *or* the string. What are you using them for?" Particularly when everybody seemed so stressed and out of time.

"Nothing," Bartholomew said at the same time Kate said, "Protection."

Lachlan's hands stilled as he settled the tablecloth, the pentagram with the cookie in the center logo facing out toward the gathering crowd.

"Protection?" he asked. "From what?"

Bartholomew licked his lips and gave Kate a pleading look. "Kate, do we really have to—"

"Barty, there was a flock of starlings. And I know the damned things are always spinning around in the fall, but they were flying *upside down*."

Bartholomew's face—already sort of pale and hard to tan—went downright mashed-potato pasty. "But here… there's no magic here," he practically wailed. And then his eyes, gray and shiny and luminous, met Lachlan's. "Almost no magic here," he whispered apologetically.

Lachlan grinned, both trying to get him to snap out of whatever funk he seemed to be spiraling into and charmed.

Almost no magic. Like Lachlan *was* magic. Lachlan's instincts had been right on point. Bartholomew *was* that into him!

"We don't know that for certain," Kate snapped. "And after those starlings…."

They both shuddered, and even Lachlan, who knew nothing about magic or omens, could tell that a giant flock of birds flying upside down was bad on both points.

"What makes you think it's you guys?" he asked.

"We cast a spell," Bartholomew said, surprising him. In spite of the rather whimsical name of the booth, *Shortbread and Shadows*, Lachlan never would have expected someone as... well, grounded, to be mixed up in something like witchcraft. Dress up for the conventions, yes. Bartholomew had a rather handsome set of bardic leathers, done in green, that he wore sometimes when he knew for certain the theme was Renaissance or sword and sorcery. But actually casting a spell?

Lachlan shifted uneasily. "Who's you?"

"Never mind," Bartholomew whispered. "Here, give me the racks—"

"No, no. I'll set up the racks. You stock them."

Lachlan got to work on the wooden racks, attempting to find some purchase. "I just never knew real witches before," he said, smiling like it wasn't a bad thing. "My grandmother used to leave out beer for brownies, though."

Bartholomew and Kate met eyes. "I'll tell Jordan," she said, like they'd actually said something. "He'll probably try it."

"Try what?" Lachlan worked very hard not to break the wooden rack he was fiddling with. "And please don't take this the wrong way, but this thing is a cheap piece of shit, and I'd love to make you another one that might actually set up without threatening to snap into kindling."

"I...." Bartholomew cleared his throat. "Your work's too good," he said. "I'm afraid to even price them out with someone who knows what he's doing."

"Our friend Dante made these," Kate said. "During his woodworking phase. He, uh, didn't stick with it long."

"For you, I'd do it at cost," Lachlan said, only because "free" would sound too much like a come-on, and for heaven's sake, he had Bartholomew talking! The surest way to shut him up would be to make him feel like there was something more at stake than shelves.

Bartholomew looked at the shelves and then looked at Lachlan. "Oh, I couldn't—"

"Sure you could," Lachlan said, deciding that wasn't a no. "I'll bring you the first one next week. There's nothing wrong with the design here. It's just the craftsmanship is a little—" He searched for a word. "—inexperienced." To his amusement, Bartholomew's cheeks went bright red.

"Not everyone is… uh… experienced," he said weakly, and a thick silence fell, interrupted only by the clicking sounds of the shelving.

"There," Lachlan said, organizing the shelves where they usually went, in an even, three-point presentation across the table, with a gap on either side for taking money. "Kate, is this fine for where you want your stones?"

"Yes," she said. "Thank you." She shot a glare at Bartholomew. "Barty, do you want to help him round up the yarn? I'll set up the stock."

Bartholomew sent Lachlan a hunted look. "Sure," he said. Then he seemed to pull fortitude from his feet. "Lachlan, I can go talk to Ellen. You have your own booth to look to."

Lachlan looked behind him and almost groaned. A troop of four high-school-aged attendees were gathered around the wands, each one of them wearing a scarf of one of the four schools of Hogwarts that had obviously been knitted by hand—possibly by one of the wearers.

"I'll be right back," he said. "Bartholomew, you keep stocking. I want to talk to you."

He wasn't sure if he imagined Bartholomew's "meep" or if he'd actually made the sound, but either way, he appreciated the sentiment. Lachlan finally had an excuse to butt into Bartholomew Baker's life, and he wasn't going to waste a second of it.

D. E. PAULSON has done a number of things before trying his hand at writing romance novels. While *Sugar, Spice, and Spellcraft* is his first novel, he has been a lifelong storyteller. In addition to writing, he has taught English as a Foreign Language and has worked/is working in museums and libraries. He has lived in quite a few places including New England, California, the Pacific Northwest, the Midwest, the Kingdom of Denmark, and the People's Republic of China. Currently he lives somewhere west of the Mississippi with a furry little terrorist (otherwise known as a cat). If you want to know what he's working on next, you can find Paulson on Twitter at https://twitter.com/author_paulson or on Instagram at Paulson_author.